BURNER

A NOVEL BY
ROBERT FORD

This book is dedicated to Tod Clark.

May the Long Pig Saloon never run dry.

PREFACE

The topic matter of this novel is the most terrifying thing I've considered in my life—as a husband, a father, a friend, and a man.

No writer wants to cause true emotional trauma to a reader, but the terrible truth is life doesn't provide trigger warnings. The evening news and social media don't come with them either. Real life hits you with a sledgehammer when you least expect it.

But unlike those examples, the novel you hold in your hands is not a surprise. It's a known thing, at least to me, and any opportunity to avoid additional mental pain should be taken—and more importantly, offered.

This book deals with brutal material. It is violent. There are drug and rape references. This was not an easy book to research, because, the more facts I uncovered, the more difficult it became to accept this is an actual reality in the world.

You can choose to avoid these kinds of things—in both fiction and the daily news—but to ignore them, to turn away and pretend they don't exist in the world we live in, is akin to sticking your head in the sand.

Whether we decide to look or not, these things still exist, even if only in the shadows.

This novel has to do with guilt. With redemption. With how pain and experience change you. It has to do with action as well as inaction. Because seeing something wrong and doing nothing— nothing at all—is the worst kind of evil there is.

Evil is unspectacular and always human,
and shares our bed and eats at our own table.
—W.H. Auden

You can choose to look the other way,
but you can never again say that you did not know.
—William Wilberforce

CHAPTER ONE
IRIS: now

"This is *not* an interrogation."

"I know, Doc." The detective put his hands on his hips, pushing his suit jacket back to expose the badge clipped to his belt. "The District Attorney wants me here to make sure all the I's are dotted and the T's are all crossed."

"You're here for observation only." The man flipped through a thick stack of papers in a manila folder, pausing to scan details. He spoke without looking up. "*I* run the room. If I feel you're a distraction to a proper evaluation—"

"I *said*, I know." There was an edge to the detective's voice— the tone of someone familiar with power. "Look, I get you wantin' to be all professional about this for the courts, okay? I *get* it, but come on, Doc. Even *you* have to admit this is some pretty fucked up shit."

It wasn't the first time the doctor had been called in to do a psychiatric evaluation for the Harrisburg Bureau of Police, but it was the first time he had been called in on anything like *this*. He closed the folder and hefted it out in front of him. "This everything?"

"Including her report cards from grade school." A prideful smirk decorated the detective's expression. He turned away to look at the two-way mirror set into the wall before them. "Some twisted shit, Doc. Some really twisted…"

The doctor sighed, and matched the detective's gaze. Behind the mirror, a woman sat at a metal table in a small room. She wore a short sleeve, orange jumpsuit with Dauphin County Prison stenciled across the back, and a gray long-sleeved thermal shirt beneath it. Her straight, light-brown hair was limp and her bangs hung down over the right side of her face to reach her shoulders. She sat, unmoving, with both feet on the floor and her arms crossed in front of her.

Taking a deep breath, the doctor exhaled slowly, and then opened the door. The detective followed, closing the door behind them.

The room was simple and functional. The walls were painted eggshell white, with no artwork to convey a comfortable setting. A water cooler in the corner, a table with two chairs, and a cheap, wheeled office chair by the doorway were the grand sum of the room's contents.

"My name is Dr. Walker." The doctor pulled the empty chair away from the metal table on the opposite side of the woman. He put the manila folder down, sat, and scooted the chair farther away to give him room.

The woman glanced at him, but didn't speak.

Dr. Walker shifted the folder to reveal a cloth case beneath it. He unsnapped a catch and exposed an iPad, and then crossed his legs, propping the device against his knee. He woke the device from sleep and maneuvered through the icons on the screen.

"Mind if I smoke?" A crinkled pack of Winstons lay on the table in front of her.

The man continued on his tablet without looking up. "I'd prefer you didn't, but—"

The woman cut off the rest of his reply with the sound of a lighter being flicked and a sharp inhale.

Dr. Walker turned to the man sitting in the wheeled chair he had moved to the corner of the room. The detective stood and walked toward the water cooler, retrieved a metallic silver ashtray resting on top, and then set the ashtray on the table.

"Miss Sanders, do you know why we're here?"

The woman snickered, making the hair covering the right side of her face ripple with motion. "Because of what I did."

The doctor adjusted himself straighter in his chair. "Yes, of course, but we're here to do a psychiatric evaluation to determine—"

"What's that?" The woman took another drag from her cigarette.

Dr. Walker nodded understandingly, a slight smile on his face. "Sometimes a psychiatric evaluation is done when—"

"I received a medical degree from the University of Maryland and graduated fourth in my class." The woman glared with her one visible eye. "I know what the fuck a psych eval is, *Doctor*."

Dr. Walker cleared his throat and reached for the manila

folder again. He flipped through the paperwork, pausing on several sheets. "Yes." He closed it again and put the file back on the table. "Yes, I suppose you would."

The detective snorted from his chair in the corner. Barely above a whisper, he shook his head and spoke to himself. "Ted Bundy was smart, too."

The doctor turned back to his iPad and jotted notes with a stylus. His gaze remained focused on the screen as he casually spoke. "Please leave the room, Detective."

The man exhaled sharply and stiffened in the chair.

"I'm sure you have other I's to dot and T's to cross somewhere else." Dr. Walker lifted his head and looked at the other man.

The Detective's face flushed. He nodded and made a frustrated grunt as he sucked against his teeth, but he stood from the chair and walked from the room.

The woman reached forward to flick ash from her cigarette into the tray. The long sleeve shirt pulled from her left wrist and the motion caught Dr. Walker's attention. The flesh of the woman's entire hand was covered in burn scars, but a deep, healed, furrow was along the outer ridge, leading from her wrist to the first knuckle of her little finger—a different kind of wound.

Sliding the ashtray closer, she pulled the fabric of her sleeve down further. Her gaze remained locked on his eyes.

"Let me save you some time and trouble, Doctor. Yes, I am mentally competent. I am *very* mentally competent." She glanced at his tablet and motioned to it with her hand holding the cigarette. "I'm sure you're recording all of this, so *yes,* I did it. Yes, I planned it, and yes, I'm guilty." The woman took a hard drag off the Winston. "I'm fully aware of what I did and I'd fucking do it again."

The woman looked down at her lap and then her focus returned to the doctor's face. "The only thing I feel remorse for is not having the discipline to make it last longer."

CHAPTER TWO
IRIS: then

"Honey? What time do we have to be there again?"

"Not until seven." Iris stopped in the hallway and craned her head around the doorframe of the bathroom. Behind the frosted glass of the shower, she could see Nathan's naked silhouette. She raised an eyebrow and smiled to herself. For a moment, Iris considered shedding her own clothes and joining him. Between final exams for both of them, and her interviews for fall residencies, it had left little time for having a life, let alone making love. She missed him.

Iris pulled herself away from staring at the glass shower door and shook her head, even though the smile remained on her face. Time enough for that later. Nathan had finished his exams and it was two days until her graduation ceremony. Tonight, they were going out to celebrate with friends and maybe continue the party back here.

She put her hands on her hips and looked around the living room. The TV screen was dusty from not being used. Nathan's clean laundry from several days ago sat, untouched, in a basket on the coffee table, and a stack of week-old mail rested on a pizza box beside it. The vacuum cleaner sat next to the couch with the best intentions of getting used, but Iris couldn't recall the last time it had been run—not that they had been at home often enough to get the carpet dirty.

No one was invited over with the place looking like this.

Iris sighed. Hectic schedules don't make for tidy apartments. She lifted the basket of Nathan's clothes and headed toward the bedroom. He could handle vacuuming and taking out the trash when he was done in the shower.

The bedroom had hampers of dirty clothes for both of them, but for the most part, it wasn't a complete mess. She put the basket down and started folding Nathan's t-shirts and tucking them into place in his dresser. She tossed a pair of his jeans onto the bed and started pairing his socks together.

Iris pulled Nathan's sock drawer open and froze. Among the mix of business and plain white cotton socks, a square velvet box was nestled in the upper right corner. Her stomach flipped. Iris swallowed hard as she reached for the box and paused. She leaned toward the door to the hallway and listened to the shower still running.

She opened the lid and felt the tight, unused hinge of a new jewelry box, and bit her lip. Resting in a slot of padded velvet, sat a white gold engagement ring. The tooling along the sides appeared antique, the engraving delicate, and the diamond a beautiful round cut. It was simple and elegant without being gaudy.

So beautiful.

Tears sprung to her eyes and Iris snapped the box shut, putting it back in place among the socks. Her stomach flipped again and she felt a shiver go through her body. She wanted to scream. She wanted to jump up and down and wave her hands and let happy tears fall down her cheeks.

Instead, Iris stepped back, sat on the bed, and took a deep breath. She laughed and smiled to herself as she wiped her eyes. Her phone buzzed in the pocket of her jeans and Iris pulled it free, smiling harder at the name on the screen before she answered the call.

"Hey, Mom!"

"Hi hon. Getting excited yet?"

She wanted to whisper to her mother, to blurt out what she had just discovered, but Iris bit her lip and stretched back on the bed, keeping the secret tight. *"Ohhh* yeah and so is Nathan. He's so glad to be done with this year."

"I bet he is. One more left for him, well, one more until he's a doctor, you know what I mean. Nathan's a good man. It'll all pay off for you two."

"He *is* a good man." Iris glanced at the hall and smiled.

"Your dad and I are heading down about ten o'clock Saturday morning."

"Mom, the ceremony isn't until one in the afternoon."

"You know your father. He hates to be late, plus, he'll need to stop and pee at least three times on the drive down."

Iris shook her head. "He really needs to get that checked. He has a bladder of a Chihuahua."

"His doctor says he's in good health. Nothing wrong but growing older. Hey, I saw the pictures you posted online. You like your new haircut?"

Iris ran a hand over the back of her head and down to her neck. A pixie-cut, the hairdresser had called it. It felt strange and light, especially considering she had hair mid-way down her back only a week ago.

"I'm getting there. It's easy to style, I'll say that. Five minutes in the morning and I'm out the door." Iris laughed and heard the shower turn off. She thought of the ring and bit her lip as she rolled over onto her stomach and propped herself on one elbow. "Mom?"

"Yeah, honey?"

"I just..." Iris felt her eyes get glassy. "Thank you and Dad. Really. For everything. You two—"

"Honey." There was a pause on the other end of the line, and a sigh. "It's what parents are supposed to do. We've been happy to help you however we can, and your dad and I are so proud of you."

"I know, Mom, but you and Dad worked so hard to get me through college and... I'll pay you back. I will! I'm—"

"It's never been about the money, sweetie. You don't have to—"

"Then you and Dad come live with me and Nathan when you get older, okay? I'll take care of you both."

There was soft laughter on the phone. "Okay. You've got a deal."

Iris smiled at the concession and her voice softened. "It's really all coming together, isn't it?"

"Your dad and I told you it would. Remember in your first year when you called us crying? We told you how hard it would be, but it would all be worth it."

"What was it Dad said? Sometimes happy tears come with a little blood? Something like that? I don't remember exactly but it was one of his cryptic sayings."

"I don't know. He's a crazy ol' man."

Iris smiled. "Yeah, he is. But he was right. Both of you were."

"Mmmhmmm. Sometimes, parents are." More soft laughter from her mother and the familiar sound of coffee being pouring into a mug.

Iris could picture her mother's face as she spoke. Her kind eyes wrinkled at the corners as she smiled.

"I love you, Mom."

"I love you."

"Can't wait to see you both. Tell Dad I love him, too, okay?"

"I'll tell him. Oh, and let Nathan know that Dad has a tee-time set up for them in two weeks. I forget the course, but I'm sure it's somewhere snooty."

Iris sat up on the bed as she realized the shower had stopped, and imagined Nathan toweling off in the bathroom. "I'll let him know. I'm sure they'll have a great time. They always do."

"That's because your father sneaks a pint of liquor onto the course. He thinks he's being slick, but he can't get it by me. He's such a lush when he plays golf."

Iris laughed and smiled at her mother's tone of voice, the mischief there, the love. She could almost see the twinkle in her mother's eyes.

"It's good for the two of them. Makes me happy they get along so well."

"Me too, honey. Well, I've got to run. I've got lasagna in the oven for dinner and your dad likes it crispy but not burnt. We'll see you Saturday."

"Bye, Mom."

"Bye, honey."

Iris tossed her phone to the bed and heard the bathroom fan stop running. Her gaze turned to the laundry basket and her stomach dropped, eyes going wide. She leaped toward the dresser and slid the sock drawer closed as Nathan came walking into the bedroom.

He held a towel closed around his waist, and stopped to stare at Iris, turned toward the basket of laundry, and then gave a quick glance at his side of the dresser. He had the slightly scared expression of a child getting busted for being in the cookie jar. "I uh... I can put—"

"You can put your *own* laundry away. I'm going to vacuum and take the trash out." Iris skated past him into the hallway, biting her lip again to keep from laughing.

Yes, everything really *was* coming together.

CHAPTER THREE
IRIS: then

Iris slipped on her high heels and gave herself a once over in the bedroom mirror. Red dress. Red heels. Red lipstick. If *this* wasn't a celebration get-up, then she didn't know what was.

Dammmmmmn. I look hot!

She grinned at herself and walked down the hallway into the living room. Nathan was sitting on the couch, scrolling on his phone.

He looked up at her and his eyes went wide. "What... who are you? You've got to get out of here. My girlfriend is going to be home any second and—"

"She the jealous type?" Iris sat on the edge of the couch and reached out to trail her index finger from Nathan's neck down to his chest. "Tell me about her."

"She's got beautiful eyes. Incredibly sexy, but..." Nathan smiled and shook his head. "She's a college nerd. Studies all the damned time and—"

Iris leaned down and kissed him slowly, passionately. She felt one of Nathan's hands slide along her waist and tighten. Iris pulled away and stood.

"You look..." Nathan sighed. "*Soooo* hot."

"Yeah?" Iris's gaze ran over Nathan's black suit and opened collar white shirt beneath. "You're lookin' pretty damned fine yourself."

"I'm still not used to your new haircut though. It's sexy, *it really is,* but you don't look old enough to drive yet."

"You don't think it makes me look like a boy?"

Nathan leaned back, and Iris watched his eyes go from top to bottom and back again. The tone of his voice was low, his sensual voice. "*Ohhh* no. More like a young Demi Moore."

Iris smiled and raised an eyebrow. "Is there a thing there?"

"You kidding? You have no idea how jealous of Ashton Kutcher I was. When I was a teenager, and my dad died, I swear my mom must have watched the movie *Ghost* about a million times. I wanted Demi Moore to teach me all sorts of things."

"You realize you're a couple decades younger, right?"

Nathan shrugged and shook his head. *"Annnnd?"*

"You're a cougar hunter."

Nathan waved a hand at her verbal jab. "Yeah, yeah, whatever. Point is, you're going to get carded until you're forty with that haircut."

Nathan rose from the couch and Iris stepped closer, lightly tugging the lapels of his suit jacket. She smirked. "I'll be getting carded at forty while you're going gray, bald, or both."

He cocked his head to the side, smiling. "Oh, is *that* what you think? Well, I'll be the hottest balding gray-haired man you've ever seen."

Iris scrunched her face up at him. "George Clooney. Jeffrey Dean Morgan. Brad Pitt. Those? *Those* are hot older men. But you?" She took a breath and exhaled, feigning consideration. "You'll be more like a… Steve Buscemi."

Nathan grabbed her waist and pulled her close as she burst into laughter. "Oh, what the hell, Iri—"

Iris kissed him to cut off his words, and could feel his smile beneath her lips.

CHAPTER FOUR
AUDREY: now

"Sign here, here, *annnnnd* here." The man pointed to several blank lines on a sheet of paper, and slid it across the desk, along with a pen. His face was somber, but the expression appeared comfortable and at home.

The woman on the other side of the desk was attractive, though her eyes were cradled by dark circles. Her face was absent of makeup, and reddened, as if she had recently been crying. Her dark hair was straggly and unattended to. She set a crumpled tissue on the desk, and then used the pen to sign the bottom of the paper.

The small office was quiet enough to hear the ticking of the wall clock. A cheap bookshelf to the right of the desk was lined with important looking binders and books, and the top shelf held a row of framed photographs including the man, a smiling woman, and a handsome, clean-cut boy in his early teens.

Reaching forward, the man used his fingertips to move the signed paperwork back in his direction. "I'm sorry." His expression was pained, but the deep lines on his face proved he wore this expression often. "I'm so very sorry for what you've been through."

The woman nodded wordlessly. Her eyes were lifeless. Dim. She sighed and shifted in the chair, and then stood.

"Mrs. Dugan?"

She turned to see a tall man in a gray suit standing at the office doorway.

The woman nodded at the man behind the desk, reached forward to take the crumpled tissue, and mumbled a *thank you*. Her voice was strained and weak. She walked toward the gray-suited man and he stepped aside to give her room, and then stepped into the polished tiled hallway.

"Mrs. Dugan, I'm Detective Blevins." The man in the suit spoke in a low voice. "I can't imagine what you're going through right now, but I'd like to talk with you. There's some questions about—"

"Why?" Her eyes brimmed and tears spilled down her cheeks.

She paused, her head down, and sighed. "Does it even matter now?"

The man hesitated and then pressed on. "It's best if we do it now. Please. Just to... clear some things up."

Her shoulders slumped but she nodded. Audrey raised the tissue and wiped at her cheeks. "How did..." She cleared her throat as they began walking down the hallway toward the glowing red EXIT sign. "Can you tell me how exactly was she found?"

"Video cameras. Big Brother is everywhere these days and we got her on some grocery store footage after an employee thought she was shoplifting. One thing led to another and... old fashioned detective work made up the rest."

"Too little, too late, though."

"Unfortunately, yes. I'm sorry."

The woman chewed on her bottom lip and released a heavy sigh. "Okay, then. Might as well do it now."

When they reached the end of the hall, the detective pushed the exit door open and the two of them left the deathly loud silence of the building behind them.

CHAPTER FIVE
AUDREY: then

"It's important to understand the potential outcomes, good and bad."

Audrey Dugan exhaled slowly and nodded. Doctor Scavone was in her mid-fifties, at most, and had stopped by three times this afternoon. The woman spoke slowly but efficiently. There was empathy in her voice, mingled with the practicality of someone familiar with the nature of human health and the raw and brutal cruelty it often held.

"This is a critical period of time for people who have suffered a stroke. The blood flow to the brain gets interrupted, and that deprives the brain of oxygen."

Audrey nodded and chewed on her bottom lip as she listened to the woman's explanation. She was trying to focus on the doctor's words, even though it was difficult with the sound of the heart monitor's rhythm punctuating every other syllable.

"Some patients come out of it and have minor complications afterward. Balance problems, partial paralysis, things like that. But rehabilitation can help improve recovery."

"How bad was it? Paul's stroke? How... serious?" Audrey fought the urge, but she glanced at her husband lying in the hospital bed.

The left side of his mouth was distorted, his lips drooped in a mockery of a sad-faced theatre mask. She had never seen him look so weak. Paul was a big man, tall and muscled even in middle age, but he appeared frail and thin and small in the hospital gown. It fit loosely around his neck and Audrey could see the burn scars on his right collarbone curling from beneath the fabric. She knew the flesh beneath it, had memorized every freckle and mole.

How many nights have I fallen asleep with my hand against those scars? Those along his collarbone and the ones farther down, along his side? How many nights listening to his breathing as we both drift off?

"Mrs. Dugan?"

Audrey turned to the doctor, marginally aware the woman had been answering her question. "I'm sorry."

"It's okay. This is a rough thing to go through." The doctor sat down in the chair beside Audrey. She took a deep breath and exhaled. "Paul's stroke was very serious. He received medical attention pretty quickly after it happened, and that's a very good thing. We're giving him medication to help break up any clots that could possibly cause another stroke, but again, this is a very critical time. There are no guarantees."

Audrey nodded and ran a hand over her face. She almost felt out of body, as if this was happening to someone else and she was watching it all play out. She and Paul shouldn't be here. This was all a stage play. An afternoon soap opera.

"I have to go make my rounds, but I'll be back to check on you, okay?" The doctor stood from the chair, placed a hand on Audrey's shoulder and gave it a gentle squeeze before she walked from the room.

The heart monitor chirped Paul's pulse, and Audrey leaned her head down. Tears threatened and she bit them back.

Not now.

She sniffled, clenched her teeth, and then shook her head and stared at Paul again. His eyes were closed and his breathing was steady. Audrey wanted to put her hand against his face, feel his warmth and knead his flesh, smooth it with her intent alone until it looked normal again. She leaned back and crossed her arms.

It was a waiting game. Her phone buzzed in her purse and Audrey pulled it free. A text from Sarah showed on the screen.

> See you in two weeks, Mom! Love and miss you
> and Dad! Ireland is AMAZING, but I'm ready to
> be back home! Gloria says hi!

She felt the strange, chilling swirl of detachment along her spine, and a dreamlike out-of-body sensation filled her. Since the hospital had called, Audrey had been considering whether or not to tell Sarah, and had decided against it. There was nothing she could do anyway, and Sarah only had two weeks remaining in her study-abroad semester in Ireland. Being so far away had been tough at first for her, but Sarah and her roommate had become best friends. That eased the homesickness and let her focus on enjoying the experience.

Sarah's such a great kid. She deserves to have a great time. Upsetting her will achieve absolutely nothing at all.

Audrey slid open the text message and replied.

> Love you, too! Can't wait to see you! You and Gloria enjoy it while you can!

Audrey slid her phone into her purse and thought back to when Paul had gotten deployed for Afghanistan. Sarah had barely been three years old at the time. Deployment had always been a shadow hovering over their military household during the first few years of marriage. A lot of *what if* questions hung like cobwebs in dark corners, recognizable but ignored.

And then it finally happened, and Paul had been called to active duty. A tour.

Lots of video calls and juggling time zones, but somehow, they had made it work.

Audrey lived on base, kept her budget lean, and took care of Sarah the best she could. A military spouse's time was hard when their other half was away on tour, but Audrey had known from the start it would be—maybe not everything, but enough.

Talking with other wives had helped some. Sharing the loneliness and struggles of being a single parent. It was always worse at night. The cold bed felt empty.

Some women strayed when their husbands were overseas. They filled the void in temporary fashion with men who were merely placeholders.

But Audrey never had. There had been opportunities aplenty from men on base, seeking prey just as lonely and hungry as the military wives their soldier husbands had left behind. But Audrey had ignored their advances each and every time.

It was a waiting game.

When Audrey had first gotten the call that Paul's convoy

had been hit in the field, it scared her so badly she had crumpled to the kitchen floor, expecting the clipped military voice on the phone to tell her Paul had been killed in action. The pain and misery hit her so hard and so fast she barely heard the Sergeant explain Paul was alive but had been badly injured. An IED had exploded beneath their Humvee, and even though the vehicle had been armored, it had been bad enough to shred the side of Paul's body with shrapnel.

After his medical discharge, when he got home, Paul was the same in many ways, but a changed man. There were never any serious symptoms of PTSD. He didn't start living in a bottle of alcohol. Didn't argue with her or get abusive. No, Paul internalized the things he had seen and done. Sometimes, he would stare off in the distance with a hollow look in his eyes. Audrey couldn't imagine what the man must have seen. She never wanted to try, either.

Paul had nightmares for a while when he got home. Audrey had taken to either holding him tightly like a child and soothing him back to sleep, or making sure he was fully awake, free from the clutches of his dreams, and then she would make love with him. It was always slow and quiet, extra gentle and tender with him. Sometimes it was two, three o' clock in the morning, but she did it to calm him down. To relax him. He'd had enough pain overseas, and she only wanted to take it away.

Eventually, the nightmares seemed to fade away.

When Sarah was nine, they took a family vacation to the Outer Banks, and spent three weeks on the beach and kayaking in the rivers and playing UNO until they all got tired.

Audrey smiled at the memories.

Paul is a good man. Brave. A great husband. Amazing father. He didn't deserve—

A flicker of movement caught Audrey's attention and she snapped her gaze up to the shape of Paul's body, beneath the blankets. His left foot twitched. Audrey stood up and went to his bedside, staring down at his pale face. "Honey?"

His eyes moved behind their lids and he shook his head slightly side to side.

Audrey gently put a hand against the crown of his head and brushed his hair as she used to do when he woke up with bad dreams. "*Shhhhh,* Honey, it's okay."

Paul's eyes fluttered, as if he was fighting to pull free of slumber and open them to see the source of her voice. His gaze was wild and roaming, but then his focus settled on Audrey's face. The slightest uplift at the corner of his mouth, and then his expression darkened. He opened his mouth to speak and closed it again.

"*Shhhhh.* Baby, it's okay. You're going to be all right."

Audrey had never seen her husband cry, not once, in the time she had known him, but looking at her, his eyes turned red and glassy. He raised his right hand from the bed and made a motion with his hand, pantomiming writing.

"It's okay, honey. *Shhhh.*"

Paul's forehead wrinkled and he made the motion for writing again, but more forceful this time. She nodded and went to her purse, pulling out a pen and a folded hospital brochure on the facts of having a stroke. Audrey brought it back and sat down on the edge of the bed beside him.

Paul took the brochure and laid it on his stomach, and then used the pen.

The stroke had done some damage, but hopefully Doctor Scavone was right and rehabilitation would help. Audrey watched as her husband wrote in the messy scrawl of a child's handwriting. He let the pen drop to the blanket and nudged the brochure in Audrey's direction.

She picked it up and looked at what Paul had written in the margins of the brochure.

I'M SORRY.

Audrey shook her head at the man she had married. Her tears could no longer be contained, and she put a hand against his cheek. "Baby, there's nothing to apologize for." She kissed her index and middle finger and moved them to touch his lips. Audrey smiled. "I love you. You're going to be okay."

The side of Paul's unaffected mouth lifted slightly, and

his pupils rolled back to show the whites of his eyes as they fluttered like scared moths.

Paul began to shake on the bed.

CHAPTER SIX
AUDREY: then

Audrey sat down on the lounge chair and uncapped the bottle of Grey Goose vodka she had brought with her from the kitchen. Normally, the blue lights on the interior of the pool gave it an otherworldly glow, but now they made everything seem as if it was carved of ice.

Tilting the bottle at her lips, Audrey took a swallow, and then grimaced as the liquid hit her throat. She had never been a heavy drinker, and rarely hard liquor. Originally, Audrey had picked up a bottle of white wine from the rack in the kitchen, but pulled the vodka from the freezer instead. After today, she wanted to feel numb.

No, that wasn't entirely true. She *already* felt numb. Audrey wanted to slip into oblivion.

A secondary, massive stroke.

Dr. Scavone had sat and told her how sorry she was, even reached out to hold her hand, but none of it mattered. Even modern medicine had its limits.

There had been a *Life Transition Consultant* at the hospital who had talked with Audrey. The man had given her one brochure about grief counseling and another listing helpful things to focus on after a spouse's death. The man had looked at her with an expression of empathy, but Audrey could tell it was only part of his job persona. He pressed on, asking her questions she thought she would never have to answer this early in life.

Did your husband have wishes for after his passing?

Is there a funeral home you and your husband are associated with?

Audrey heard the man's voice from a far distance, like the incessant buzzing of an insect vying for attention. She couldn't remember how she had responded.

They had given her a white plastic bag of Paul's belongings— the clothes he was wearing, his watch and wedding ring, his wallet, keys and phone. Audrey had taken the bag and floated from the building into the parking lot to her car. She set the bag on the passenger seat and almost reached over to buckle the thing in place.

She didn't even remember the drive home.

Audrey drank from the vodka bottle again.

She had picked up her phone several times at the hospital, but couldn't bring herself to call Sarah. Couldn't figure out how to even *begin* telling her that her father had died.

There is no one else to call.

Audrey's own parents had died years ago in a car accident, both of them taken by a drunk driver. Paul's father had passed away long before the two of them had gotten married, and his mother a few years back from cancer. Except for the occasional business party, they had kept to themselves in life and enjoyed it that way.

Not a single other person to call.

A shiver went through Audrey's body as the alcohol settled in place. She shook her head at the sensation, and raised the vodka for another drink, taking a long, three-count swallow.

After Paul had gotten home from Afghanistan, he had been adamant about never having a funeral. No gravestone. No memorial. She had argued about the process of it all, about giving closure for the living, but he wouldn't have it.

Cremate my remains, he had said. *Everything else is wasted effort.*

Paul had been a man of efficiency. I'll give him that, Audrey thought. *The man of the house.*

The thought had occurred to her that she didn't even know if Paul had life insurance. She supposed so. It was something Paul would do. He handled all the financials for the house, paying the bills, setting up retirement accounts, and everything else so she wouldn't have to bother. Audrey never even saw bank statements, content to use the debit cards when she needed, confident the funds would be there.

They had come a long way from the days of living on base and scraping to get by. After Afghanistan, they had lived off military benefits alone for almost a year before Paul found work as a security consultant.

After that, money was never an issue again. Big house, nice cars, Sarah's college paid off before she even began, and four weeks of vacation every year, wherever they wanted to go.

Audrey closed her eyes. Tears scalded her cheeks.

I'm going to have to take over everything. And I know nothing.

Audrey swigged from the bottle again, spilling some over her chin. She raised an arm and angrily wiped her mouth.

What do I do, now? There's no funeral to plan. No wake.

One day, Paul is here and now he's not. Do I keep getting up for my morning swim? Doesn't that seem, somehow... cold-hearted? My husband just died and I'm still working on my backstroke as if nothing happened?

I have to start cooking dinner so it's a meal for only me.

What do I do with his goddamn clothes?

Hot saliva flooded Audrey's mouth and her stomach rebelled, suddenly and violently. She snapped upright from the lounge chair and turned to throw up on the cement.

Her hair fell around her face and Audrey sat the bottle of vodka down, reaching behind her head to gather her hair as she heaved again. The smell of vodka, mixed with stomach bile, assaulted her as tears fell from her eyes and her nose ran. Audrey coughed and cleared her burning throat, and then lay back down on the lounge chair.

She closed her eyes and found the oblivion she sought.

CHAPTER SEVEN
IRIS: now

"This isn't a confession, Iris. It's only a discussion to—"

"I know what it is, Doctor Walker. I only wanted to set things straight from the start." Iris stubbed out the end of a cigarette and reached for the pack of Winstons, shaking loose a fresh one.

"Both of your parents… they passed away?"

"They're dead, yes." Iris gave a humorless laugh and nodded as she lit her cigarette and took a drag. "Mom died in her sleep from a heart attack. My father committed suicide."

Doctor Walker leaned back in his chair, adjusting the iPad against his knee. "Depression run in your family?"

"Wasn't mental illness, Doc, but nice try. He killed himself because of… everything."

"Everything? What does that mean?"

Iris took a breath and flicked her cigarette into the ashtray. She snorted and shook her head. "Now I remember why I hated psychology."

"You minored in child psychology at the University." Doctor Walker leaned forward and set the iPad on the table beside the manila folder.

"Mmmhmm." Iris nodded. "Most people treat kids like they're stupid, you know? But they're not. Kids aren't stupid at all." She took a puff from the Winston and flicked into the ashtray again. "They're young, inexperienced people. Everything is new to them and they're trying to cope with it all, to understand all these unfamiliar things. At times, life can be overwhelming to an adult, so for a child…" She shrugged and let her words trail off.

"What led you to choose that as a minor?"

"I wanted to know how their mind works. What really makes them tick, you know? Not candy or toys, but what truly motivates them. I wanted to know how to make them feel better about themselves." Iris adjusted the pack of cigarettes and put the lighter on top of the box. "It's hard to be different when you're a kid. Children have such a wolf pack mentality. They can be cruel and unforgiving to those who stand out. They do bad things because some other kid is doing it, and as a group, those bad things become somehow acceptable."

"Do you think what you did is acceptable?"

A slow smile crept onto her face. She rocked back and forth slightly in her chair but didn't answer.

The doctor set his stylus down beside the iPad. "Did *you* stand out as a child? Were you different?"

"Christ, Doc." Iris cleared her throat and scooted her chair closer to the table. "Did you read my files at *all* or are you just phoning this one in today? Billing by the hour?" She shook her head, took another drag, and exhaled smoke from her nose. "Yeah, I was different as a kid."

"Childhood was difficult?"

"Seriously? Christ, Doc." Holding her cigarette out to her side, she stared at him. "I was always smarter than most kids. And some teachers." She shrugged and brought the cigarette to her lips for a puff, continuing to speak as smoke leaked from her mouth. "But a difficult childhood has nothing to do with..." Iris waved her hand around. "This."

She propped her elbows on the surface of the table, and there was clear amusement in the eye not covered by her hair. "Besides your house and car, what's the most beautiful thing you own? No, no... not *beautiful*... what's the most *expensive* thing you own?"

Iris rested her chin on the palm of her hand holding the cigarette, and looked like a bored student waiting for an answer from the teacher.

Doctor Walker pursed his lips and stared at the ceiling. "I suppose it would be a painting from..." He shook his head. "No, it's a first edition of a book."

"What book?"

"Treasure Island."

"Good book." Nodding, Iris straightened up, and puffed on her Winston. "How much did you pay for it?"

The doctor shifted in place. "I'd rather not say."

"Come on, Doc. What was it, a grand? Two?" She waved her

hand and shook her head. "Doesn't really matter. No pun intended, but do you treasure it?"

"Yes."

Iris sniffed and leaned forward. "How much would you pay for a person, Doc?"

Doctor Walker tilted his head. "Most people would say you can't place a price on human life."

"That's not what I asked you." She shook her head. "I didn't say human life. I asked *how much… would you pay… for a person?"*

Iris smiled at the man's silence, watching his expression. "To *own* one, Doc. To have them as your toy to do with whatever you wanted. How much is that worth? More than your first edition? Less?"

CHAPTER EIGHT
IRIS: then

Downtown was bustling with people heading to dinner and the string of outdoor bars. Besides the occasional car horn, live music drifted from multiple sources in what the locals referred to as *Restaurant Row.*

"You going to be okay having drinks tonight?" Iris held Nathan's hand as they crossed the street.

Nathan nodded. "I have some nicotine gum if I need it, but I haven't even had a piece of that in a few days."

"I'm proud of you for quitting." Iris smiled at him. "I can't believe you were a smoker, though. As a doctor, you—"

"Yeah, I know." Nathan took her hand in his as they stepped onto the sidewalk. "I *know*, okay? It's bad for me, blah blah blah."

"Gina's going to be there tonight. I'm trying to get her to quit smoking, too. She's going to be a *pediatrician,* for God sakes!"

Nathan turned to Iris. "Gina's going to be here? Maybe she and I can step outside later and I can take a little puff? *Ohhhh*, it would taste *sooo* good! Just one little—"

"Nooooo!" Iris stopped walking and stiffened her grip on his hand.

"Kidding!" Nathan grinned at her. "I'm kidding!"

"What in the *hell* am I going to do with you?" Iris shifted to him, face to face.

"Hopefully, lots of really dirty, filthy—"

"Shut up." Iris laughed and they continued walking to the entrance of the Harp and Fiddle restaurant.

The place had been renovated a year ago, and had been a hot spot in town ever since. Antique copper tiles decorated the ceiling, and the floor plan was divided into a dining room on one half and an ample sized bar on the other. The polished mahogany bar top was accented with a refrigerated steel rail set into the wood to rest your beer glasses and keep them chilled. The local elite came to slake their thirst on expensive bourbons and rare whiskeys, while the hipsters sipped on cucumber mojitos and smoky mezcal drinks.

During happy hour, it was almost impossible to get a seat at the bar, and the restaurant's website *strongly encouraged* reservations.

Nathan spoke with the hostess and told her he had booked a table for five. She smiled and turned to lead them through the crowd to the dining area, seating them at a table at the rear of the room.

Iris glanced up to see Gina strolling from the bar to their table. She had her hair up and was wearing a black sequin dress. Gina maneuvered her way between the tables, holding up a pint glass of something pink at the top and orange at the bottom. The girl grinned as she approached. "Well, *helloooooo*, Doctor!"

Iris returned her smile and stood to give her a hug. "Hey, Doctor!"

"Yeah, this won't get old at all." Nathan mumbled as he stood, and gave Gina a hug and kissed her cheek.

The girl laughed as she pulled a chair from the table and sat down next to Iris. "Don't be jealous, big boy. This time, next year, you'll be in the doctor's club, too."

"Are Shelley and James here?" Iris sat down and scooted her chair closer to the table.

Gina shook her head and took a sip from her drink. "Should be any second, though. Shelley texted me a few minutes ago and said they were parking right around the corner."

"James is a good guy. Always did like him." Nathan pulled his napkin down to his lap. "His girlfriend is high maintenance, though."

Iris swatted his shoulder. "Leave Shelley alone. She grew up that way, she can't help it if her parents are wealthy."

"Doctor!"

Iris looked up to see James walking toward the table. He stuck his hand out to Gina and she shook it with a dramatic, exaggerated pump, laughing, as she pulled him in for a hug. "Doctor." James turned to shake Iris's hand as a blonde woman in a silver dress closed in behind him.

"Doctor!" Shelley hugged Gina and turned to face Iris. "Hello Doctor!"

"Oh God." Nathan raised his hand to get a girl's attention. "Waitress? Whiskey! Just bring the whole damned bottle."

The group broke into laughter before settling into their seats.

They ordered dinner, and the drinks kept flowing, making them reminisce their time since first arriving at med school. Iris kept thinking to herself how quickly the time had gone. It hadn't—*not really*—not during the all night study sessions and exams. But in many ways, it felt like she had only stepped foot onto campus a few months ago. And now here they were, two days before graduation. Iris knew she still needed more education to get where she really wanted to be, but the first chunk of hard work was done. It brought such a deep satisfaction of accomplishment, and Iris realized how proud of herself she was. She quietly scanned the people at the table and smiled.

How proud of all of us, I am.

"So, what now? You two still moving to Wisconsin?" Nathan leaned on the table and asked James.

"Sticking to the plan. Two weeks from now."

"Too damned cold up there for me." Nathan sipped from a glass tumbler.

James shook his head. "It's not for everyone, I'll give you that, but it has a summer. About five or six days of it."

"I love the cold." Shelley piped in.

Nathan grinned. "Of course, you do."

Iris gave him a gentle kick beneath the table and caught his amused expression.

"I'm headed to Virginia." Gina sucked the last of her drink through the yellow straw in her glass and caught the waitress's attention for a refill. She turned back to Iris. "And I guess you're staying here 'til our baby boy finishes next year?"

"Absolutely. That, and..." Iris squeezed Nathan's arm and leaned onto the table. She glanced shyly at the table and continued in a lowered voice. "I have an interview next week at McKinley and Associates."

"Get the hell out of here." Gina's expression was sincere surprise. "I mean, with your transcripts, I get it, but McKinley and

Associates? Who's the interview with?"

Iris smiled sheepishly at Gina, whose expression only deepened.

James leaned forward. "Not Tod Clark?"

Iris nodded and her smile grew wide. She hadn't told the news to anyone but Nathan.

"*Hooooolllly* shit." James reached for his glass. "Clark's a *god*."

"Yep, he is. And Dr. Wonders put in a good word for me."

"Professor Wonders always did like you." Gina smirked as she spoke, directly to Iris.

"True, he might have, but Wonders is a hell of a doctor. The man's probably forgotten more about medicine than most of us will ever know." For the last week Iris had been buzzing with excitement over the interview and now the news was out. She smiled and sighed.

Shelley gave an appreciative nod. "With your transcripts, and a recommendation from Wonders, that position is yours. Clark is the best reconstructive surgeon on the East Coast."

"Damn right, he is. For *now*." James lifted his glass toward Iris. "You're really on your way, hon. I love you and I'm proud of you."

Grabbing her glass, but rolling her eyes, Shelley joined in and smiled as she raised her glass to join James in his toast.

"Don't forget the rest of us when you're vacationing in Cabo." Gina smirked.

"I don't know about Cabo. Italy, maybe. But that's not all I have planned." Iris heard her own words before she could stop them.

"Oh, do tell." Shelley drank from her glass of Chardonnay, her face that of a suburban housewife hungry for some juicy gossip.

"Yes." Nathan leaned forward, an eyebrow raised in surprise. "Do tell."

Iris glanced at him and cleared her throat. "Okay... yeah, there might be some great vacations." She turned to Gina and smiled. "But I want to split my time."

"Doing?"

"What I really want to do is work in the States for, I don't know, seven or eight months out of the year, and then go to places where parents can't afford to pay for their children to get reconstructive surgery. I'll do it pro-bono if I have to, college loans be damned, but there are so many people way less privileged than us. I want to do what I can to help pay it forward."

Nathan's attention drifted from her, and he sipped from his bourbon, focusing his gaze on the table.

"Are you for real?" Gina asked.

"One hundred percent. I want to help them. I want to give back."

"Wow. That's…" Shelley looked at her glass of wine and then back to Iris. "That is truly admirable."

"You're a saint, you know that, Iris?" James gave her a nod and lifted his drink again. "Here's to one hell of a future… for all of us." The group joined him, clinking glasses in a toast.

They stayed to finish their drinks, and then James and Shelley were the first to stand from the table. As it often does, it became a domino effect for the rest of the table, and not long after, the three of them stood to leave the Harp and Fiddle.

"Next time we see each other, we'll be wearing graduation gowns." Gina grinned.

Iris, unexpectedly, felt her eyes get glassy, but it wasn't sadness. It was pride. "We did it."

She sighed, shook away the threat of tears, and gave Gina a hug. "We really did it."

CHAPTER NINE
IRIS: then

"When were you going to tell me this plan of yours?"

There it was.

Iris scolded herself internally. She had known the impulse conversation was going to come back to bite her as soon as the words she had spoken at dinner tumbled out of her mouth. She noticed Nathan had both of his hands in his pants pockets, hiding from view, so she couldn't reach out and hold one. He only did that when he was upset.

"Honey, we've been so busy with finals and interviews and everything, there never seemed—"

"*Nooo*, no." Nathan shook his head. "Iris..." He stared skyward and then sat down on a bench by the entrance to the Harp and Fiddle. There was an ashtray filled with sand and an assortment of cigarette butts. Nathan stared longingly at the collection of them for a moment. "We've been together for almost two years, now. Living together for close to a year. This isn't some... *college relationship* for me." He leaned forward and rested his elbows on his knees.

Iris sat beside him. The slight buzz of the evening's drinks fading with the jolt of serious talk. "It's not like that for me, either, honey. I *love* you. I do. More than anything. I just—"

He snapped his head up. "Do you trust me?"

"Of course, I do."

"Then you need to trust me enough to talk about things like this. I don't want to be the guy who hears it for the first time like everyone else at a dinner with friends." Nathan looked away from her and sighed. "If we're going to be together, this affects *our* life, you know? This isn't like *Honey, I want to live in the Hamptons.* This is *Honey, I'm going to be away in another country three or four months out of the year.*"

Iris put a hand against Nathan's back and rubbed softly. He was right and she knew it. It was one of those things she always meant to bring up but hadn't. It was something she had wanted to do since she was a senior in high school but had never told anyone. She always expected eye rolls and placating nods from people who wouldn't understand, so she had kept the entire idea to herself.

"You're right." She leaned against his shoulder. "You're absolutely right and I'm sorry."

"I love you, Iris." He straightened, pulled away, and turned to face her. "Before you, I don't think I ever truly realized what that meant, but with you... Look, I'll support you in whatever it is you want to do. But you have to trust me enough to let me do it."

Nathan's expression was serious, but it was more than that. Iris could see the hurt in his eyes and she felt it well up inside herself. She nodded at him and whispered.

"I'm sorry. It's just..." Tears sprang to her eyes and she sighed. "Why do you want to become a pediatric heart surgeon? Is it the money?"

His expression turned agitated, defensive. "Of course, not. You know the reason why. My cousin Arnie died when he was eight because—"

"Yes, I *do* know. And you don't want to do this because pediatric heart surgeons make almost three-quarters of a million a year?"

Nathan shook his head dismissively. "There's a lot of money in it, but that's not the reason why, no. I want to do it to help kids."

"To help kids." Iris nodded. "But what about the kids with no insurance? The kids who are orphans from war or whose parents live in villages too far away from real medical treatment?" She leaned against his shoulder and rubbed his back again. Her voice softened. "We're doing what we're doing to *help* people."

He stared at the sidewalk for a moment and when he spoke again, it was without looking at her. His voice was calmer, missing the rough-cut edge of hurt feelings. "So, where would these countries be? The places you want to go?"

Iris shrugged. "Africa. Parts of the Mid-East. South Amer—"

"*Everywhere*. You can just say everywhere."

She chewed on her lower lip. *Ohhhh, Iris.*

In the long silence, she continued to lean against Nathan and eventually heard him clear his throat. "These places... you think maybe there'll be a need for a pediatric heart surgeon?"

Iris smiled and raised her head to look at him. She felt her heart swell and that familiar ache there at how much she loved the man in front of her. "I think there's a pretty good chance of it, yeah." She lifted up to kiss him and it was tender and soft. The tension of the conversation eased. Iris pulled back slightly, looking into Nathan's eyes. "We both have a lot of education left, but after that... you wanna have an adventure with me?"

He smiled, gave a sharp laugh and shook his head, but it was an action filled with amusement. "You really want to make the world a better place, don't you?"

"If we can, shouldn't we try?"

They hugged each other as they sat on the bench, and Iris breathed in his cologne. She kissed his neck and pulled away.

Nathan smiled. "I can see it now. You and me on a talk show. The foundation of Doctors Nathan and Iris Noble have saved close to—"

"*Yeahhhh*, about that. *Ummmm...*"

Grinning, Nathan stood and took her hand. "Okay, okay, your name can go first, whatever, I'm—"

She rose from the bench and kissed him, cutting him off mid-sentence, and then pulled back. "Besides, you're not exactly a doctor yet, *soooo...*"

Nathan's mouth widened and he shook his head. "That's a low blow, Iris Sanders. Unnecessary roughness."

She laughed out loud and gave him that full-of-mischief smile of hers he was so familiar with.

"Come on. Let's walk over by Lakewood." Nathan grinned at her.

"Really? It's getting late and—" Iris pulled back as her mind trip-fired and she bit off her protesting words. Lakewood had a grander name than it should. The main focus of the park was really more of a pond than a lake, roughly the size of two football fields side by side, but it was beautiful. She and Nathan had spent more than a few afternoons there, sharing a bottle or two of wine and a picnic lunch. On their very first date, they ended up there, sitting and talking and feeding the geese.

It was the perfect spot for a man to get on one knee.

CHAPTER TEN
AUDREY: now

"Are you telling me, after everything, she could *walk* on this?"

"Mrs. Dugan, it—"

"Oh *pleeease,* call me Audrey. I insist people call me by my first name when they're feeding me bullshit." The exhausted tone of her voice didn't match the frustration of her words.

"Mrs... Audrey, I'm not saying that at all, but contrary to popular belief and what Hollywood has taught us, things aren't that cut and dry." Detective Blevins leaned back in his chair. "There was a psychiatric evaluation, and the District Attorney reviewed the transcripts. As far as *walking,* no. Considering the..." He paused, appearing to search for the right word. "...extreme nature of things, I expect insanity to be part of the defense strategy."

"Have you read the transcripts?"

The detective nodded. "I have."

Audrey glanced down at her purse in her lap. Her gaze rested there a moment and then she focused on him. "And what do you think about an insanity plea?"

The man was quiet for a moment, and then he licked his lips to moisten them. He cleared his throat. "I don't think it'll hold up in court."

"Why not?"

Detective Blevins stared at her for a moment, reached into his inner suit jacket, and withdrew a silver rectangular box. He set it on the table and turned to her. "Mrs. Dugan, would you mind if I recorded this conversation? I can't take notes very quickly and I..." He shrugged. "My short-term memory is shot to hell."

Audrey stared for a moment and then shrugged. "Sure, it's fine. I don't care."

Nodding, the detective pushed a button on the recorder, and leaned forward on the desk. "Audrey, what can you tell us about the barn on your property?"

The woman blinked at him. Her gaze flitted across her lap and then circled back to him. "It's... a barn. I mean, it's not used much anymore except for storage. Summer things, lawn furniture, and stuff for the pool. Things like that."

"And was it always used for that?"

"Yes. I mean, since Paul, my husband, passed away."

"And before then? Before your husband died?"

Audrey gave another soft shrug and shook her head. "Back then, it was Paul's. Sarah and I weren't allowed out there. Man cave, you know?"

"An off-limits, man cave?"

"Mmmmhmm." Audrey nodded. "It was Paul's barn. No one else was allowed out there."

"Until Paul died?"

Audrey leaned back and folded her arms across her chest. "Detective, what… I don't understand what any of this has to—"

"Mrs. Dugan, I'm going to ask you a very important question." He steepled his hands together as he looked at her. "It's very important, so I want you to take some time and think on how you should best answer."

The detective sighed and took a slow deep breath. "Mrs. Dugan, did you know her?"

Audrey held the man's gaze for a moment and then her attention fell to her purse and remained there.

"Mrs. Dugan?"

Audrey stayed quiet and still in her chair. An injured bird in tall grass, trying to decide on having the will to go on or not.

Detective Blevins leaned forward on the desk. "Mrs. Dugan?"

Audrey lifted her head and put her hand to her throat. "Do you… do you have any water?"

He nodded and pushed away from his desk. "Water or coffee?"

"Water, please."

Detective Blevins took several steps to a small fridge along the right wall of the office. He withdrew two bottles of water from inside, went back to the desk and handed one over as set the other beside his desk lamp.

Audrey twisted the cap and took a long drink. She pulled the bottle away, and then took a shorter sip before she capped the bottle and set it on the desk. "Detective, are you married?"

"At one time, I was. Two years together, but it didn't take."

"Did you love her?"

"We were *married*."

Audrey nodded at him, and a soft, humorless smile appeared on her face. "That doesn't mean anything. Married doesn't necessarily mean love. Some are for convenience. Others, sure, they're real love, but some marriages are just to stop people from being lonely."

"Valid points." The detective nodded. "Mine was a little bit of both, but yes, I loved her. What kind of marriage was yours?"

Audrey's eyes got glassy. "The real 'til death do us part kind. It was love." She reached for the bottle, reopened it to take a drink, and then set the bottle on the desk with the cap beside it. "You get to know a person in a marriage. How they like their coffee. Whether they like scrambled or runny eggs. Whether they lean toward being a giver or a taker or a good balance. You find out little things, big things too, but you get to *know* them. The facets. The layers to a person."

She shifted in her chair. "But there are always secrets. Every man is an island and all that."

"I suppose so, yeah. You can know someone without really *knowing* them. We see it all the time during investigations."

Audrey nodded and pulled a tissue from the pocket of her jogging jacket. She uncrumpled it, crumpled it again, and then repeated the process.

"Mrs. Dugan…" Blevins reached for a foam cup of coffee on his desk. "Tell me what happened after your husband died."

Audrey closed her eyes, took another deep breath, and let it out slowly.

CHAPTER ELEVEN
AUDREY: then

Audrey woke up in the lounge chair a little after four in the morning. For a few moments, she remained still, her eyes opened slightly as she listened to the chirp of the crickets, and farther off, the cheerful, high-pitched chorus of spring frogs.

Sitting up slowly, Audrey braced for the slam of a hangover, but there wasn't any.

Throwing up is probably what saved me.

Audrey sighed and looked at the glowing blue water in the pool.

Why not?

She stood and took her clothes off, piece by piece, and dropped them onto the lounge chair. Naked in the darkness, Audrey felt the soft wind against her skin, took three steps, and dove into the pool.

The cool water skated over her bare flesh and Audrey remained under, opening her eyes and swimming until she reached the pool wall. She came to the surface, shook her head and blinked.

She remembered the first time she had gone swimming nude in the pool, not long after they moved in. Sarah had been in school, and Paul had texted he would be coming home early to work there for the afternoon.

Audrey figured she would give him a thrill at seeing her swimming naked when he got home and walked out to say hello, so she had tiptoed outside with a towel wrapped around her. They only had one neighbor, and they weren't even close, but still.

When Paul got home, she was in the pool, water up to her neck, smiling at him as he opened the sliding glass doors. He walked to the edge of the pool, began speaking with her, and froze mid-sentence.

Audrey had grinned at him then, watching the lightbulb go off in his head, realizing his very naked wife was in the pool in front of him.

Paul grinned and held Audrey's hand as she stepped from the pool, and when she reached for her towel, he grabbed it and laughed. They ran inside, giggling, and went straight to the bedroom like horny teenagers left alone at the house.

That had been the first time, but not the last. When Sarah was old enough to start doing sleepovers at houses of her friends, Audrey and Paul had started to swim naked together at night when she was away. After Sarah left for college, sometimes Paul pretended to be surprised at catching her swimming in the nude, and they made love in broad daylight.

No, Audrey corrected herself, *it would be much more accurate to call that fucking.*

Outside, in the middle of the afternoon. Sometimes on the concrete surrounding the pool, and other times on one of the lounge chairs.

Audrey glanced in the direction of the neighbor's house.

Their house was close enough to have seen them having sex in the back yard, but somehow, the chance of being seen had made things even hotter. Some nights, they had made love again, soft, and slow, and tender.

But outside like that... that had been pure sex. Hungry, hard, and fast, filled with passion and raw desire.

Audrey swam toward the steps, grabbed the railing, and walked from the pool. She gathered her clothes from the lounge chair, and went inside the house. Damp footprints in her wake, Audrey walked through the living room and down the carpeted hallway to her bedroom. She put the small bundle of her clothes on the bed, and went to dry off in the master bathroom. When she walked back out, Audrey paused at the end of the bed, and stared. Nothing in the room had changed, at least not visually, yet it seemed empty, strained of life.

I'll be sleeping alone.

Audrey turned to her dresser, withdrew a pair of panties, and pulled them on. Moving to the other side of the room, Audrey knelt and slid open a drawer from Paul's chest of drawers. She withdrew a faded green sweatshirt, and pushed the drawer shut.

Audrey wriggled the shirt over her head as she walked to the living room.

I simply can't handle sleeping in bed by myself. Not right now. Not yet.

She grabbed the quilt from the back of the couch, and stretched out on the cushions, smoothing the blanket over her body. The remote was on the coffee table in front of the couch, and Audrey picked it up and turned the television on. She flicked through the channels, shut it off again, and turned into the couch, toward the spot where Paul used to sit.

The faintest scent of his cologne was still there.

It had been a long day, and a long night. Even though she had thrown it up, Audrey had to admit the short-lived numbness from the vodka had been pleasant.

But now, alone in the empty quiet, Audrey felt herself crumble.

CHAPTER TWELVE
AUDREY: then

Audrey watched the coffee pot reach its 12-cup line as it brewed. Sleep had been fitful, and her eyes felt raw, as if she had been crying in her dreams. She opened the cabinet and pulled two mugs out, stopped and stared at them for a moment. With a shaking hand, Audrey returned one mug back to the shelf.

After pouring herself a cup of coffee, Audrey headed back toward the living room where she glanced at the white bag on the kitchen counter. Audrey had noticed it earlier when she woke up, but couldn't remember bringing it into the house.

She sat on the couch and flicked the television on, immediately changing the channel to the news. They had usually watched the morning news together, enough to at least catch the headlines of what was happening in the world. Paul would usually have an opinion to voice out loud before he left for the day. Politics. Sports. Wars around the world. Paul was well versed in all of the major news topics.

Audrey turned the television off.

The bag, on the kitchen counter behind her, issued a series of muffled vibrating sounds and went quiet again. Audrey set her mug on the coffee table and walked to the counter. She peeled the plastic open and saw the fabric of Paul's suit folded up neatly at the bottom. Resting on top in a separate, smaller, plastic bag were his wallet, car keys, and his iPhone. Audrey lifted the phone and touched the screen to bring it to life.

A missed video call from Sarah, and a text:

Miss you, Daddy! See you in two weeks!

Audrey closed her eyes and released a breath. She checked the time and saw it was barely past eight o'clock. Ireland was five hours ahead.

Not yet. I'll wait and call Sarah later, after her day is done.

She set Paul's iPhone on the counter. Audrey had no idea how to even start the conversation with Sarah. She glanced at the phone again.

His office. I have to call and tell Paul's office. At least that'll be a start. A practice?

Audrey pulled Paul's wallet and car keys from the bag, and lifted his suit jacket free of the plastic. She felt around the inside jacket pockets and withdrew three business cards. They were simple linen paper stock, thick and a creamy off-white color.

In the middle of the card was:

Paul Dugan

Custom Components

A phone number and three diamonds were printed in red ink at the bottom of the card—nothing else. No logo or address or website or even an email. The business cards were as unfamiliar to Audrey as the phone number.

Audrey moved to the living room couch and picked her phone up from the coffee table. She took a deep breath and dialed the number on Paul's business card.

She heard the ringing sound once, and then there was a change in the humming tone on the other end of the line. It rang once more, and then there was nothing but silence—not even a recorded message for voicemail. Audrey ended the call, and compared the number on the business card to the one on her phone's recent calls list to make sure she had dialed it correctly. The numbers matched, and she hit the call button again with the same results.

She checked the suit pockets of Paul's jacket once more, and withdrew a red plastic pen from an inner pocket.

COVENANT SECURITY

She rolled it over in her fingers and saw a phone number on one side with VENDOR SAMPLE stamped beside it. Audrey smiled at the pen. Paul's name and information had popped up on some mailing list a few years ago and at least once a month, he received some sort of vendor sample from what he used to call *trash and trinket* companies trying to wrangle business out of him. They never did, but they kept trying.

There was a collection of miscellaneous items in the kitchen, grouped together into that all too familiar junk drawer every household owns. Customized pens and notepads, lanyards, and colored stress balls—all of them vendor samples sent to Paul. Every few months, Audrey would sort through the cheap plastic goods and toss certain items in the garbage.

Audrey stared at the phone number on the pen. It was different than what was on the business card. She picked her phone up and dialed the number on the pen. Someone answered on the first ring.

"Covenant Security, how may I direct your call?"

The woman's voice was pleasant and upbeat, and it caught Audrey off guard. "I uh... yes, could you connect me to Human Resources, please?"

"Absolutely. I'll transfer you to Cathy Gonzalez, our head of Human Resources. One moment, please."

Easy listening music kicked in and Audrey listened to Don Henley as she waited. It stopped abruptly, and another woman's voice spoke in her ear, delivering a voicemail recording. Then a beep.

"Hello, um... my name is Audrey Dugan and I'm calling because..." She let out a breath. It would be the first time she had spoken the reality out loud. "My husband works for your company and he... he passed away yesterday. I wanted—"

There was a click on the other end of the call and then a woman's voice. "Hello?"

"Yes, hello?"

Audrey heard the woman sigh. "Mrs. Dugan, I'm so sorry. I heard you begin to leave a message. I'm so sorry to hear about your husband."

"I... thank you." Audrey cleared her throat and shook her head.

There was the sound of fingers typing on a computer keyboard. "What was your husband's name, Mrs. Dugan?"

"Paul." Audrey heard herself speak, but her voice sounded small.

"Okay." The sound of the keyboard working again. "Paul Dugan? D-U-G-A-N?"

"Yes."

"Hmm." The tiny, sharp double-click sound of a computer mouse. "I don't have any record of a Paul Dugan."

"You're based in Harrisburg, right?"

"That's right, Harrisburg, Pennsylvania."

Audrey sat up on the couch. "Is there another division my husband could be based out of for some reason? Another location?"

"Was your husband in marketing?"

"No."

The sound of a chair creaked on the other end of the call. "Covenant Security has two locations. Harrisburg, Pennsylvania and Tampa, Florida. The Tampa office is marketing staff only."

Audrey swallowed hard. "Could you please check again?"

"Mrs. Dugan—"

Audrey squeezed the phone and felt heat rush through her body. "For the last seven goddamn years, my husband has been leaving the house every morning and telling me he goes to work at your office. For *seven* years." Audrey's face was burning. Her throat was dry. She lowered her voice, but inside she felt ready to shatter onto the floor like so many glass beads in a jar. "Could you *please* fucking check again?"

The woman on the end of the call sighed heavily, but Audrey heard the creak of the chair and the clicking sound of the keyboard resume.

When the woman spoke again, her voice was softer. "Mrs. Dugan, I'm sorry, but... there's no record of your husband, *at all,* on our payroll system, not even on our list of independent contractors."

Audrey slid from the couch to her knees and let the phone fall to the floor.

Oh Paul... what have you been doing?

CHAPTER THIRTEEN
IRIS: now

"There's this thing they teach women in self-defense classes. Don't scream rape if you're in trouble or no one will come. They teach them to yell fire instead. Everyone comes running for that."

Iris stubbed a cigarette out in the ashtray, adding to the two butts already there. "You believe it?"

The doctor shrugged and nodded slightly. "I've heard it often enough. I think there's probably a kernel of truth in there somewhere."

"Why do you think that is?"

The doctor adjusted his position in the chair and crossed his ankles beneath the seat. "Why do *you* think that is?"

"I think…" Iris snorted and shook her head. The hair falling across the right side of her face swung out of the way for an instant, revealing more branches of scars on her neck, along her jaw, and extending up her cheek. "I think most people, *most…* innately want to help others. I believe that. But it's very difficult to be the first one to take a step. It's much easier to walk by and ignore it, pretend you don't see the reality in front of you. No one wants to get involved with a rape. That's… messy."

"And fire? Why do you think people come running to a fire?"

"People love watching a fire." The woman's gaze rose to meet the doctor. "It's beautiful and destructive at the same time. It's dramatic. People love drama."

"Exciting?"

Iris pulled a fresh cigarette from her pack and lit it. She took a long drag, with her eyes leveled at the doctor, and smiled as she exhaled. "Very."

CHAPTER FOURTEEN
IRIS: then

"Do you remember that cheap wine we bought on that one picnic?"

Iris laughed and squeezed Nathan's hand. "That strawberry stuff?"

"Not even strawberry, but yeah, *that* shit! What the hell was it? Boone's Farm… Mountain Berry, I think." Nathan winced at the memory.

"Yes, Mountain Berry!" Iris laughed. "Because we argued about what a mountain berry was and finally agreed it had to be deer shit."

"That wine tasted like ass in a glass."

Nathan's comment broke her and Iris laughed even harder, her eyes leaking at the corners. She stopped along the walkway, turned against Nathan and hugged him tightly. They held each other as their laughter died down, and Iris sighed the satisfied breath that happens after a release of true laughter.

The water of Lakewood was calm enough that the reflection of the half-moon overhead was perfectly still. The scene was so beautiful and serene, it could have been on a Hallmark calendar. Lights were spaced out along the asphalt path winding around the pond.

"Come on." Nathan took her hand and led her farther down the path to the edge of the water. Silhouettes moved soundlessly in the middle of the pond, gliding over the moon's reflection—ducks going for a nighttime swim.

Iris felt her heart beat faster.

Beautiful setting. Romantic.

She bit her lip.

He put his arm around her waist as they stood still and looked out over the pond. The ridge of trees and shrubbery shielded the pond from the streetlights. It was a tiny, dark, oasis in the middle of the city. It was perfect.

"So… *Saint* Iris."

"Shut up." She nudged him and he laughed.

"This changing the world thing." Nathan gently squeezed

her waist. "My dad still knows a lot of venture capitalists, angel investors, you know? I was thinking maybe at some point we could reach out—"

"I don't want to turn it into some moneymaking thing."

"Shhhh." Nathan turned and kissed her. "You have to let me finish."

"Okay. Sorry." Iris put her hands up in surrender.

"We could talk to them and pitch our idea. They're a bunch of sharks, yeah, but they also donate a ton of money to philanthropic causes. Giving our time and skill is one thing, but we're going to need supplies and airfare costs and hotels or whatever. I really think they could help with this. Maybe it starts with the two of us, and when word spreads, other doctors will join in."

"Oh, yeah?" Iris tilted her head and smiled at him. "Starts with the two of us?"

"Yeah." He took a step away and took both of her hands in his. "This is important to you, so it's important to me. If you truly want to make a change in the world, then let's *really* change it."

Iris squeezed his hands in hers. Her heart felt ready to burst free of her chest. Her mother's words came to her then—*Nathan's a good man*—and Iris realized how foolish she had been to keep her dreams secret from him. He *was* a good man, and she loved him so deeply, it hurt.

Nathan smiled and stared into her eyes, and then eased from her grip.

"Speaking of... changes." Nathan moved his hand toward the pocket of his suit jacket and his smile deepened. He didn't look nervous at all about this. He looked confident and sure.

Oh my God. OhMyGod. OhMyGodOhMyGodOhMyGod. This is happening!

Heat coursed through her body, and Iris felt her heart pounding.

"I love you, Iris." Nathan took a half step backwards. His gentle gaze was focused on her face. "And I—"

She saw Nathan's focus shift from her eyes to over her shoulder, behind her, and then they widened in surprise.

When things happened, they happened quickly.

A figure lunged from the shadows, and Iris had time to see the bright glint of sharpened steel sink into Nathan's side, through his suit jacket. Nathan's body contracted and his mouth opened in a wide *O* of pain. His face contorted, and the knife blade flashed again, the steel bloody now, plunging into his upper chest, his white dress shirt painted red.

Iris opened her mouth to scream and felt a brutal crack against the back of her head. Her legs turned to jelly. She began to fall, but darkness took her more efficiently than gravity, and Iris never felt herself hit the ground.

CHAPTER FIFTEEN
IRIS: then

The world was a river of onyx.

Sensations and images came to Iris in razor sharp flashes, like a camera taking photos in a pitch-black room. She felt an occasional constriction of something around her left bicep and the pinprick of a needle at the crook of her elbow, along with a warm, cotton-candy rush through her veins.

Thick bristles of rope bit into the skin around both of her wrists. The cord was taut, pulling her arms out to her sides like an offering strung up and awaiting old gods. Beneath her body, the fabric of the sunken mattress was gritty, stinking of sweat and filth.

She saw a short window, roughly a yard wide, high up and close to the ceiling. It let a single beam of daylight bleed through the shadows of the room, and dust motes floated in the air. Iris stared at them as she drifted on gossamer clouds, detached from her body and what was happening to it.

Bare, sweaty flesh, and heavy weight pressed down on her over and over again.

Iris was an entire universe away from their urgent thrusts, lust rolling off of them in billowing red clouds. She watched, floating from up above, as they finished with their toy, leaving their warm, sticky violence on her, *inside* her, leaving it to dry and crust like the old memory of something bad.

Tattoos and bald heads. Others with long greasy hair. Some faces had beards, and others were almost clean-shaven. Those with a short crop of whiskers ground against her skin like wire brushes. The smell of liquor and tobacco was thick and heavy on their breath like syrup. Some wore thick silver rings or necklaces. Others did not.

Hard, calloused hands squeezed her skin. Pinched. Gripped. Caressed. Slapped.

Laughter from throats lined with gravel.

The smell of her own urine and the warm flooding release of it, soaked the mattress around her waist. The stink of her body, used and unwashed. The sounds coming from her mouth were no longer words, but whimpers. Primal, animalistic cries.

Sometimes she heard them speak to each other, curse-lined conversations about meaningless things. Iris heard someone ask what happened to her body. The laughing response; *Does it matter?*

Iris drifted in the onyx river.

CHAPTER SIXTEEN
AUDREY: now

"I wasn't a kept woman, Detective."

The man gave a slight shake of his head. "Even if you were, not my place to judge."

Audrey brought the tissue up to wipe at her right eye first, and then her left. "There's a pool and a nice house and cars and things, but I wasn't one of those women who gets their nails done every week and heads off to yoga class every morning or..." She stopped and daubed at her eyes again. Her hands waved away her thoughts and drifted down to her lap like frightened birds settling to roost.

"I didn't know half of what Paul took care of. When he died, everything he took responsibility for became mine in a flash. The house, the money, our daughter. I was responsible for everything." Audrey sighed. "Everything."

Blevins nodded and stayed quiet.

The door of the office swung open. "Good afternoon, Detective." A man in a dark blue suit hurriedly walked into the room, and stood in front of the desk. "I'm guessing I don't need an introduction, so I'll skip to the part where I tell you my client and I will be leaving. *Now.*"

Audrey turned to see the man's face, and her expression was one of both recognition and fear, of old memories resurfacing after being put to rest.

"Abner Stone, as I live and breathe." Blevins said. "Now what brings you down here at this time of day, counselor? Shouldn't you be drinking eighty-dollar glasses of bourbon, right now?"

"Detective." The man in the expensive suit gave a reproachful shake of his head. "You know better than to interrogate someone without offering them legal representation. And is that..." Abner cocked his head toward the silver device on the desk. "Are you *recording* this conversation? You're fucking kidding me, right? None of that is admissible and I don't give you permission to record *me*, so you can turn that off right now."

"Admissible? Who said anything about a trial? Mrs. Dugan and I were just talking."

"Uh huh. Well, I hope you enjoyed your conversation, because it's over." He put his hand against Audrey's back. "Mrs. Dugan, come with me."

Audrey sat in place, her steadfast attention on her lap. "No."

Moving to her side, Abner offered his hand to help her from the chair. He lowered his voice. "Mrs. Dugan, you should really come with me."

"No." Audrey shook her head.

The attorney crouched beside Audrey's chair, becoming eye-level with her. His face was blotched and strained, as if his necktie was too tight. "Right now, Mrs. Dugan, I *truly* think it's in your best interest—"

"You're not my attorney. But even if you were..." Audrey turned to face the man. "You're released from your duties."

Abner blinked at her. Patches of high color in his cheeks deepened and he turned away from her. "Detective, may I have... a moment alone with my client?"

"I think you mean *previous* client." Blevins smirked and leaned forward. "In fact, since you don't represent her, you're a common citizen now, counselor. You really shouldn't even be in here. Official police work going on."

The attorney's entire face flushed red and he turned, with gritted teeth, toward Audrey. He glared at her, inches away. "Maybe you've forgotten the agreement you have with my... associates."

"It was never an agreement. It was a demand." Audrey took a deep breath. "And your *associates* have nothing to leverage. Not anymore."

The muscles in Abner's jaw pulsed. He rose to his feet and stared at her, speaking through his teeth in a harsh whisper. "You fucking cunt. You have no idea—"

"That's enough!" Detective Blevins pushed his chair back, stood from his desk, and walked around to the other side. He stepped close to the attorney and spoke in a thin even tone. "I don't give a goddamn what kind of rock star lawyer you are. Get the hell out of my office."

Abner tilted his head slightly to the left, and then to the right. His glare remained on Audrey for a moment longer before he turned to the other man. "Have a great evening, Detective."

Audrey let out a deep sigh as the attorney left the room. Blevins walked over and closed the door, and paused, his hand still on the doorknob. "Mrs. Dugan?" He sighed, returned to his desk, and sat down. The detective loosened his tie.

"Sorry for being so blunt, but can you tell me what the hell that was all about? Abner's *always* been an asshole, but not once, not *ever*, have I seen him get worked up like that."

Audrey's face was void of expression, a blank slate considering the man's question. "Did you stop the recorder or did you get all of that?"

Detective Blevins glanced at the silver box and then back to her. "It's still recording."

Audrey nodded. "Good." She reached for the bottle of water, took a drink, and then set it back on the desk. "Abner was never my attorney, nor Paul's."

"Then why would he barge in here like—"

"Paul knew him. I'm certain he did. I... I knew him by face only." She closed her eyes tightly and inhaled sharply through her nose. "The day after Paul died is when things... that's when everything started."

CHAPTER SEVENTEEN
AUDREY: then

None of it made any sense.

Audrey ran through the conversation she had with the woman in human resources. Almost every day, for the past seven years, Paul had gotten up, dressed in a suit, and left for work just after eight o' clock in the morning. In the evenings, he would talk about security projects he was working on for various clients. He would discuss how things went over budget on this or that. He spoke of people in the office. Once every two months or so, he would go away on a business trip for two or three days at the most. Always checked in with Audrey when his flight landed and he got to the hotel. Always called to say goodnight to her and Sarah.

For the past seven years.

I don't have any record of a Paul Dugan.

Audrey shook her head.

Then how were the goddamned bills getting paid? Where was the money coming from?

She reached for her phone and scrolled through her contact list until she saw the listing for her bank and pressed the call button.

Less than an hour later, after answering security questions and replying to a verification email, Audrey had set up online access to the joint account she and Paul shared. It had been years since she had even *seen* a bank statement, let alone bother with direct access to the account. She had never needed to. Paul took care of it all. She had the debit card for the joint account and used it whenever she felt like it. There was never a question of whether there was enough money, and it simply wasn't something she and Paul talked about. She felt stupid now, but the topic simply never came up.

Audrey logged into her account using her laptop. The account balance was listed at the top left of the website and Audrey felt a gut punch as breath left her. She stared at the amount and read her and Paul's name at the top of the screen, double-checking it really was *their* account and not some complete and utter mistake on the bank's part.

There was close to nine hundred thousand dollars in their account.

Audrey's hands shook as she clicked on the transactions tab. A full accounting of the current month to date appeared on screen. Most of the lines were red for purchases and payment of bills, but one deposit line stood out in green. It was two weeks ago, in the amount of exactly thirty-five thousand dollars.

Audrey clicked for the transaction record of the previous month and saw a similar report. Most of the line items were red with two large deposits—one for thirty grand and another for forty-five thousand.

She clicked on the deposit line and it led her to another screen. The deposit had come from *The Hawkins Group*. Audrey scrolled through the other deposit and found they all came from the same source.

Each month was close to the same balance of transactions— only the deposit amounts changed. Some were as low as fifteen grand, and others as high as seventy thousand dollars. There were payments made to various sources, as high as thirty thousand dollars. All of the payouts were to vague acronyms.

Audrey pushed her laptop away from her and stood up.

She paced the living room and forced herself to slowly breathe in and out. Audrey stopped and crossed her arms, stared past the boundary of the living room to the closed wooden pocket doors leading to Paul's home office.

Like the barn, Paul's office had been off limits to her and Sarah. When he worked from home, the doors were closed and it was an unspoken rule to leave him alone until he emerged. Besides the first week they had moved into the house, Audrey didn't think she had ever set foot in the room, not even to dust or clean.

Marching to the office doors, Audrey reached out toward the handles and paused.

Paul is dead. Nothing is off limits anymore, and it's time for some answers.

Audrey slid them wide open, slamming them back in their frames.

The room smelled of him. The scent of Paul's cologne and the strong masculine smoke of the occasional cigar lingered in here. Stepping inside, Audrey crossed the room to Paul's desk, and sat down behind it in his cushioned leather chair. There was a gentle creaking sound beneath the seat as she turned in it. Audrey moved the mouse attached to the desktop computer, and the monitor brightened as it woke from sleep. A window pop-up asked for a password.

"Fuck." Audrey whispered to herself as she stared at the empty spot on the screen and leaned back in the chair.

The password could be anything.

She turned her attention from the computer screen and pulled open a side drawer of Paul's desk to see a row of hanging file folders with tabs in his handwriting: IRAs, MUTUAL FUNDS, COLLEGE, TAXES, LIFE INSURANCE.

Audrey pulled the folder for life insurance from the drawer and set it on the desk.

Guess I'll be needing that information, won't I?

The thought tumbled loose in her mind and she felt her breath hitch in her chest. The sheer enormity of how much she had been in the dark about, and how Paul had taken care of everything hit her. She wanted to ball up her fists and slam them against the top of the desk, but she stopped herself. Audrey shoved the file drawer closed, reached below the desk to the stationery drawer, and yanked. It jostled in place but didn't open.

Audrey's insides boiled as she marched back to the bag of Paul's belongings on the kitchen counter.

His office was off limits and there was still a locked desk drawer anyway?

She swiped his keys out of the plastic bag and flipped through the key ring.

That one's house. Car.

A third full-size key.

Barn maybe?

Everything on the key ring was full-sized and not small enough to be a key to unlock a desk drawer.

She bit her lip and closed her eyes as her insides trembled with emotion.

Fuck it!

Tossing the keys on top of the counter, Audrey spun around and headed toward the pantry. On the floor below the racks of boxed pasta and canned goods, rested a gray plastic toolbox. Audrey crouched and popped the latch on the case. On top of the inner tray was a small hammer. Grabbing it and a flathead screwdriver, she marched back toward Paul's office.

Audrey didn't hesitate as she hammered the screwdriver into the seam between the bottom of the desktop and the drawer and leveraged it downward like a crowbar. There was the sound of something straining and then a brittle popping noise as the drawer hardware gave way and separated from the thick slab of wood.

Setting the tools aside, Audrey jerked the drawer open. There was a black plastic tray liner, which held normal desk items—paperclips, a small box of staples, a pair of scissors. Beyond that, in the main section of the drawer, Audrey shifted over business cards for the pool cleaner and lawncare company they used, several pieces of paper with phone numbers on them and nothing else. She flipped the cover on a green spiral bound notebook and saw the first page had numbers and dates scrawled on it like an accounting sheet. The numbers were large figures— all of them over ten thousand. The rest of the pages were blank and unused.

She moved the notebook aside and stopped at what she saw toward the front of the drawer. Her shoulders sank and the back of Audrey's throat felt bitter and acidic. For a moment, she only stared, accepting it was one of those crossroads in life where either choice happens to be a wicked one, but then Audrey reached out to pick up the flip-phone. It was matte black and compact. She turned it over, set it down on top of Paul's desk and stared at it.

Less than a month ago, she had read part of an article in a magazine at the gynecologist's waiting room, *Cosmopolitan* or *Vanity Fair* or something of the like. The headline had been *What to do when you find out your significant other has a secret phone.*

A *burner phone*, the article had called it. A cheap, throw-away phone often used by drug dealers and criminals because, if the phone and phone minutes were paid for in cash, it was untraceable and cheap to replace. Before she had gotten called in to see the doctor, Audrey had taken one thing away from what she had read—the phones were never used for anything good.

They were used for things best kept secret.

CHAPTER EIGHTEEN
AUDREY: then

Maybe he found the goddamn thing on his lunch hour or something.
Maybe it's a work phone, for business only.

Audrey stared at the flip-phone like it was a dead animal. A
rotting mouse Paul had left behind.

I'm sorry.

Sorry for what, Paul?

What work? What business? There's no fucking record of him!

Paul's office felt too confining. It was hard to breathe with
the scent of his cologne in the air. Audrey grabbed the phone in a
clenched fist and almost broke into a run. She had to get out of the
house, away from his presence.

Audrey walked outside to the lounge chair she had napped in the
night before, and picked up the uncapped bottle of vodka, still sitting
where she'd left it. She tilted it to her lips and took a sip. It burned
against her throat and for a second, her stomach clenched and almost
revolted at the revisited taste. Audrey shook her head and took a larger
swallow before she sat down at the table and chairs.

She turned the phone over in her hand, thumbing it open and
then snapping it shut again.

Open. Close. Open. Close. Open.

The dark screen was slightly smudged, though the edges of
the phone were still clean and in good shape. It was fairly new.
Audrey looked at the small keyboard of buttons and bit her lip. She
snapped it shut again.

Part of her wanted to throw the thing right into the deep end of
the pool and watch it sink. Let the chlorinated water destroy all the
tiny circuits and chips hidden behind the matte black plastic. She
gritted her teeth and gripped the phone tightly until she heard its
case groan from the stress.

Audrey wanted to scream. She didn't want to do this. Whatever
secrets Paul had, she wanted to let them die along with him.

What good would this do? What would it do at all, except
taint my good memories of him and our marriage? Had Paul

been having a goddamned affair?

Audrey brought her trembling hand and the phone to her lap, flipped the phone open and used her thumb to press and hold the power button. A second later, it vibrated in her hand and she watched as the screen flickered to life.

A series of tones released from its small speaker and the screen showed a WELCOME TO NETWORK graphic before it changed to a main screen showing several rows of icons.

A pop-up appeared on-screen:

(2) VOICEMAIL MESSAGES

Audrey read the phone number after the message. *Her* phone number.

She closed her eyes, put her head down, and let out a heavy exhale. She had called the number on his business card earlier. It was *only* a business phone. That's all it was. The number on Paul's card had only been a forwarded business line.

But what business? Covenant Security didn't even know he existed!

Audrey opened her eyes and scrolled through the icons on the phone. Except for her two calls, there was no other call history. She thumbed to the contacts. Empty. Text messages were clear.

She released another heavy sigh, shaking her head with relief as she closed the phone. Audrey set it down on the table, and felt tears run down her cheeks. Her chest felt tight and she suddenly gulped a deep breath, almost as if she'd broken the surface of the pool water after a dive. Audrey lifted the bottle of vodka, took a swallow, and winced.

Okay, so it's a phone he used, for whatever reason, but through his business card. But what does that even mean? That lady in human resources has to be wrong. She has to be.

The phone vibrated against the glass table and Audrey flinched at the sudden outburst. She grabbed it and flipped the top open to see a notification of a text message. Audrey selected it to read.

New product of possible interest.
Unique condition. Premium segment.
Auction Estimate: $25–$40k
Broker: $15k
Complete profile available. Reply YES for current
product photos.

Audrey read the message, and read it again. She selected the reply button, typed out YES, hit send, and waited.

Nothing.

She took a breath and folded the phone shut. She glanced at the bottle of vodka, realized she could feel the mild burning buzz on her empty stomach, and turned her attention to the water of the pool instead.

The phone buzzed in her hands and she flipped the cover back immediately.

TEXT MESSAGE (3) PHOTOS

Audrey selected the text message and the screen switched to show a spinning hourglass icon over an image as it loaded. The photograph was blurry at first, and then it became clearer in stages.

The air escaped from Audrey's lungs in a hard rush.

The photo was of a girl—couldn't be older than eleven or twelve—clothed in a clean white tank top and loose fitting, pink panties. Her red hair was pulled back in a frayed ponytail and her expression was blank. Her brown eyes were devoid of emotion. Freckles dotted her ivory skin in a soft spray, covering her cheeks and shoulders. The speckles should have continued to the skin of her upper chest but the flesh there had been interrupted, *altered,* into parallel lines of dark pink.

Scars.

Audrey's hands shook. She flicked her tongue to moisten her dry lips. She felt a pressure behind her eyes, but also a release, as if she wasn't quite still encased in her own body. She pressed the down arrow button on the phone to get to the next photograph.

This was the same girl but a different angle—a photo from behind her. The scars continued on the girl's shoulder blades. She was thin, barely into puberty, and the shining pink flesh were slices of her innocence on display.

The third photo was split—front and rear angles—revealing the girl without any clothing, showing the full range of scar tissue swirling from her thighs up over her bird-like ribs to her neck. Her arms were at her sides, no attempt at all to cover herself.

Audrey felt sick to her stomach. She slammed the phone shut and reared back to throw it toward the pool water, stopping at the last moment before letting go. Her eyes blurred with tears.

No. Absolutely not.

Not Paul. This is some fucked up prank of—

Audrey flipped the phone open again and replied to the text message:

> You sick, twisted FUCK! Never contact this number again!

She closed the phone and threw it on the table, watching it skid across the glass surface to stop at the other edge. She wanted to throw up.

There are truly some sick goddamned people in this world.

But not Paul. No way he was connected to… whatever the fuck this is.

Audrey breathed through her mouth slowly, trying to calm her heart. She reached for the vodka and took another drink, buzz be damned. Her body was shaking.

No way.

Audrey looked at the phone, silent and waiting on the table.

But where did the money come from?

CHAPTER NINETEEN
IRIS: now

"I was insignificant. A *thing* as unimportant as an ashtray or a pack of matches. Something to be used however they wanted, and forgotten and ignored when not."

The doctor stared at the woman silently. He blinked several times, cleared his throat, and averted his eyes. He leaned forward, resting his elbows on the table. His eyes met hers again and he spoke softly. "Iris, why... when you came back, why didn't you tell anyone about—"

"If the detectives had done their job, then none of this," she leaned forward on the table as well, and took a drag from her Winston. "*None* of this would have happened."

"And what you're saying is true?"

"Why would I make it up?"

The doctor shrugged. "Considering the... situation, it's not uncommon for someone to create fabrications of—"

"You think I'm lying?" Iris shifted her arms out, palms up. "You fucking think I'm *lying?*" She pulled back the cuffs of her long sleeve shirt to reveal a thick quilt of burn scars on her wrists and forearms, and then reached up with the hand holding a cigarette to rake her bangs away from her face. Iris held her hair at the side of her head, and glared at the man on the other side of the table.

Raised welts arced and curved over her entire right side, twisting from her neck and the line of her jaw, up over her cheekbones and forehead. Her eye on that side was clouded, the blue-white, almost translucent, color of skim milk. She was breathing heavily, her nostrils flaring. "Does this look *fabricated*, Doctor Walker?"

The man swallowed hard and shook his head. He looked away. "No, it doesn't."

Iris held her hair back for a few moments longer, even though the doctor's focus wasn't in her direction. She let her hair drop back down, covering the side of her face again, and pulled her sleeves back down to her wrists. She leaned back in her chair, away from the table.

The doctor looked at the two-way mirror and Iris caught his action. She turned with him to study the reflection.

"They're watching?" She raised her hand holding the cigarette, flipped her middle finger, and spoke directly to the glass. "*Of course,* they're watching. If only they had done their fucking job back then as well as they are right now."

Iris sniffed and took an angry, fast puff from her cigarette and stared at the table as she exhaled. She stretched her hand forward and flicked ash into the tray. "My life was... *dismantled.*"

The doctor didn't reply.

Iris slowly lifted the cigarette to her lips. Her breathing had calmed. She took a long, casual drag, exhaled a controlled breath, and then spoke. "Everything I cared about was taken away from me."

CHAPTER TWENTY
IRIS: then

Iris had moments of consciousness, of being aware of her surroundings and what was happening around her. There were times she could feel cigarettes being snubbed out on her thighs, collarbones, the base of her neck and shoulders. She had flashes of clarity when she could smell cigar smoke and feel embers being scrubbed out along the base of her spine as someone or *something* continued to thrust inside her. Iris began to recognize the sizzle of her skin and the syrupy smell of her own burning flesh.

Bare flesh all felt the same, instruments of pain, but the objects they used on her varied—beer bottles, an axe handle, the barrel of a pistol, other things. Iris heard them turn her into a betting game.

How many strokes until she bleeds?

She glimpsed money change hands as the room swirled around her.

The pain was pristine, almost elegant in its purity. If she was still fully tethered to her body, the sensations would have taken her breath away and made her throw up from the trauma. Iris's legs and hips were patterned with black and purple bruises from their hands.

She wore a costume of violence.

Laughter and yelling tried to break through to Iris, to punch a hole in the heroin womb protecting her from the world happening beyond. She succeeded in pushing the noise away unless she was shaking, sweating and sick, from not having felt a needle against her skin in a while. Then, in those moments, her entire body was a live wire of nausea until the sweet pinch of a syringe would visit her arm once again, making everything float away on spider silk strings.

She registered being fed sometimes, and liquid poured into her mouth. Hotdogs. Junk food. Beer or whiskey. The sweet taste of a soft drink. But that wasn't often. Iris didn't care.

Drifting.

Sometimes, Iris would wake in the middle of their violent thrusts and primal grunts, smelling their alcohol stink. In these moments, she disgusted herself—how her sex reacted to the sensations and she became aroused. It made her want to vomit from her own body's betrayal. She cried sometimes, but her tears brought anger, and anger brought their open-handed slaps or fists to quell it down inside her again.

In the periods of time she was left alone, Iris stayed quiet and pushed her head against the pillow, breathing in the stench of sweat and pain. She wasn't here. She couldn't be. This was happening to someone else.

Golden flecks floated in the sunbeam from the window, and Iris stared at them. Her stomach clenched and she felt sick. Snot ran from her nose, and a headache throbbed inside her skull. Her body was slimy with her own sweat and that of her abusers. Iris closed her eyes and nausea swirled in her guts.

She heard the sound of shuffling feet beyond the closed door of the room, but kept her eyes closed and concentrated on the low voices.

"Get the fuck outta here. I thought she was fuckin' fourteen, fifteen at the most!"

"Well, she's not. It's been on the goddamn news. Med student in college."

A man laughed. "Holy shit. Ain't never fucked a doctor before."

"Well, I hope you enjoyed it because she ain't stayin' here."

Iris heard the sound of a lighter being flicked and someone taking a harsh drag on a cigarette.

"Fuck're you talkin' about?"

"Exactly what I said. She ain't stayin' here. She's too hot and we're too close. Get her the fuck out of here."

"To where? You want me to dump her?"

Iris heard the sound of feet scuffing against a floor and the pop-top of a can being opened.

"Give Dalton a call."

"Delaware Dalton?"

"You know any other Daltons?"

"No."

"Then call the one you fuckin' know. He won't pay much, but he'll pay somethin' so it's better than nothin'. Drive her over there in person if you have to, but she's gone."

Iris heard someone drawing on a cigarette and then a forceful exhale.

"C'mon, man. The news will die down. It's not like—"

"What the fuck did I say? I want her out of here. Clean her up and get her the fuck out. *Today.* I'm serious as a heart attack on this."

"Okay! *Fuck!* I'll fuckin' call Dalton, then."

The doorknob rattled and Iris heard the door swing open. Footsteps came close to the bed and stopped. The person crouched down beside the mattress and she could hear them breathing. Iris kept her eyes closed.

Fingertips ran down the side of her face and then a hand cupped her left breast briefly, before it continued to trail down her stomach.

"Mmmm. Damned shame. The boys and I was just gettin' to know you."

Iris felt calloused hands on her left arm, lifting it and wrapping a rubber tube around her bicep. There were several soft noises, unrecognizable, and her left arm was pulled straight. The puncture of the needle sliding into her arm came next, and Iris let herself get swallowed up.

CHAPTER TWENTY-ONE
IRIS: then

In her dream, Iris could smell Nathan's skin, kissed by the sun, of the hot boardwalk along the beach, gray wooden planks, worn and smoothed by millions of footsteps. Her dream smelled of happiness. Nathan, swimming in the ocean, his strong arms waving at his sides, guiding him through the waves.

Iris smiled in her darkness.

She heard a loud whine of metal against metal. Her eyes flashed open and squinted reflexively at the light. The sky overhead was bright and fierce. Rough hands lifted her free from the trunk of a car, straightening her up so her feet landed on the ground. She tried to stand but her knees wouldn't lock and Iris felt a thick arm around her, keeping her vertical. The man holding her wore a jean jacket with the sleeves cut off. Bald with a goatee. Tattoos across his skull. An eagle with its wings spread. Three number sevens.

She stumbled and he held her up. Her feet moved on their own accord and Iris smiled at the sight of them, amused at watching one bare foot move in front of the other. Someone had dressed her in stained sweatpants and a too-large sweatshirt. The air felt cool as it curled beneath the loose-fitting fabric.

Iris could barely feel the soft scuff of the pads of her feet against the cement. She wanted to be in the dream again with the smell of salt water and the feel of sand beneath her feet. She wanted to laugh at Nathan's easy smile and how the sun shone against his tan skin. Iris closed her eyes and leaned against the man holding her.

The world tumbled as the man released her and Iris's eyes flashed open to see a green canvas cot before she fell hard, face down, onto its stiff cloth surface.

"Jesus fucking Christ! Cletus, it can't even stand up on its own?" A man's gruff voice—one she hadn't heard before.

Iris heard metal clanging against metal but her eyes were so heavy she kept them closed.

"Kind of a hard sell when they *can't fucking stand up* on their own." The same man's voice, angry, and then Iris heard the sound of shoes scuffing on cement. "It's damaged all to hell."

"I'm sorry, all right, man? Wasn't supposed to be a trade, originally. We were gonna keep it."

"So why the change of heart? Clearly, it was being *enjoyed*. Looks like a fuckin' ashtray at a poker game."

There was a moment of quiet and Iris heard someone hawk up phlegm and spit. She fought to keep listening.

"Turn on the news lately?"

"Are you fuckin' kidding me?" The voice gave a harsh exhale. "It's a hot product? I cannot *fuckin'* believe you brought me—" The voice released a slow controlled sigh.

"Deke told me to bring her here. He said you're the man to take care of things."

The man sniffled and cleared his throat. "Deke said that?" His voice was less excited now, calmer.

"He did."

"Look... I'll give you two grand. If it's too hot for Deke to hang onto, then it must be pretty goddamned hot and the profit margin is tighter."

"I can get more 'n two grand taking it to Essex and pimping it for a night on the streets."

"Then go fuckin' do it. It's going to take me at least two fuckin' weeks to get it off the smack you guys jacked it up on. That's half a fuckin' month. Here. At *my* place, for a hot product. Two fuckin' weeks wondering if the new mailman or the guy who reads my gas meter is a Federal Agent, waiting to call the dogs on my place. So *yeah, Cletus...* it's two grand. Two fuckin' grand. Take it or leave it."

Iris heard the pause in conversation. She straightened her bare legs and arched her back. She could feel every woven thread in the canvas cot against her bruised and wounded face. Her lips tasted like butcher paper. The joints of her body ground like rusted machinery.

"Fine. It is what it is."

"Uh huh, that's what I thought. And tell Deke the next time he sends a product attached to headline news without giving me a heads up, it'll be the last goddamned time we do business. You dig?"

"Yeah, man, I dig."

Iris heard the sound of paper sliding against paper, the rhythmic sound of someone whispering as they counted.

"See ya, Dalton."

Footsteps faded. The metal against metal whine broke the silence again, and Iris heard, as much as felt, a single person's footsteps approach the side of the cot and the sound of chair legs sliding across cement, closer to her.

"All right, then. Let's have a look."

Iris felt her shoulder being raised, and her body followed, turning her onto her back. Her arms were lengths of unbaked bread dough, and she felt hands sliding up the sleeves of her sweatshirt, inspecting her arms. The sweatpants were pulled from her hips and then taken off completely before her legs were inspected as well, fingers gently pressing against her bruised thighs.

"Jesus Christ, what did they do?"

Her legs were spread, and she felt fingertips pressing the tender flesh around her vagina—but not sexually, more like a medical exam. The man's voice was an angry whisper to himself. "Fucking hell. Those motherfuckers. Those tweeker, white power, Nazi motherfuckers."

Iris heard the man sigh and the sound of his knees popping as he stood up. His footsteps retreating from her. She let herself slip into sleep.

The sensation of slippery warmth gliding over her skin woke her. Iris fought the weight pulling against her eyelids and forced them open. A washcloth, thick with lather, ran over her breasts and stomach, beneath her arms, and along their length. The motion wasn't a rough, heavy-handed scrubbing, but instead tender movements, as if her body was made of porcelain. She let her eyes close again.

"There we go." The man's voice was gentle. "That's better."

A soft dry cloth ran over her, tamping the moisture from her skin, and then, a moment later, Iris felt warm, wet pressure daubing at the cigarette burns on her arms and cool air as the sensation moved on. Again, after hands gently lifted and spread her legs, warm soapy cloth washing her vaginal lips and anus. The soft touch of a caregiver.

Hands reached beneath her arms and pulled her body along the cot until her head tilted backward off the edge. Iris heard the sound of something heavy scraping along the floor, and then felt the sensation of humid heat beneath her head.

Warm liquid poured over Iris's hair and she felt the water running along her scalp. She smiled at the feeling. The clean smell of shampoo exploded around her, as fingers massaged her head and worked up a lather. The hands moved away and more warm water cascaded onto her hair. She felt the weight of the shampoo wash away.

The hands gathered her hair together and squeezed. Iris listened to the sound of droplets falling against a pool of water, and her hair was ruffled dry with a towel. She was pulled back onto the cot so her head rested against the canvas once more.

Iris swallowed dryly, opened her eyes, and tried to talk. "My… my name is Ir—"

"Shhhh." The man put a finger over his lips and shook his head. *"Shhhh, no.* It's better if you don't talk." He had short-cropped, white hair. His face wasn't hard angles and worn edges, but instead appeared soft—a grandfather's face. A man who played golf on the weekends and slipped money to his grandkids when no one was looking.

Iris swallowed and fought inside to keep focused on the man's face. "My name is Iris Sa—"

The man reached forward and rested his index finger against her lips.

"Let me speak very clearly and slowly, so you don't misunderstand anything I'm saying." His voice was soft, but his tone was condescending and slightly raised in pitch, as if he were trying to keep patient while speaking stern words to a child. He smoothed Iris's damp hair away from her face.

"If you speak again without being asked to, I will punch the side of your face very hard, okay? Every time you say something without being asked, I will hit you again. *Very hard."*

A river of ice ran through Iris's body. She opened her mouth and her lips trembled. Iris closed it again.

She felt like throwing up. Beads of sweat broke out across her face. Her temples throbbed. She looked at the man, who was turning her hand over in his and studying it, inspecting her ragged fingernails.

The scream rose inside her like bubbling water, and there was nothing Iris could do to prevent it from bursting free. She lifted her left hand, balled into a fist, and swung at the man's face. He flinched, and the punch rolled off the side of his cheekbone.

A strong, calloused hand flew to her throat and squeezed, immediately cutting off her scream. Iris clawed at the constriction, trying to dig her bloody, chewed-to-the-quick nails into the meat of his hand. Her eyes bulged and her pulse rang in her ears.

A heavy fist rocketed down, hard and fast, and slammed the right side of Iris's jaw. The world became lit sparklers, millions of them, all around her.

CHAPTER TWENTY-TWO
AUDREY: now

"So, you had no idea where your husband had been going, every single day, for seven years?"

Audrey shook her head and reached for the water bottle on the desk.

"No idea where the money was coming from? And never thought to ask?"

"Ask what? Did you ever ask your wife and double-check where she said she worked? Are you sure she even worked where she said she did?"

"I'm sure." Blevins nodded. "Didn't need to ask. Went to enough shitty Christmas parties."

"So did I, Detective. Parties and events where all the supposed executive team attended. Important men. Wealthy, powerful men. I was introduced to them as part of the company where my husband worked."

Blevins leaned back. "But it was all a lie."

Audrey nodded.

"Did you ever find out who they were? I mean, if they weren't part of the business your husband said he worked for, then who were they?"

She sighed and drank from the bottle. "When I was a kid, my dad worked as a cop in Baltimore. Tough man, my dad. He'd come home, every day, telling Mom and I how bad the streets were. Sometimes, late at night, I'd sneak out of bed and listen to the things he would tell Mom when I *wasn't* around. Drugs. Murder. Corrupt cops and politicians." Audrey took another quick sip and set the bottle on the desk again. "He got promoted to Detective, and later, to Internal Affairs."

"I.A.'s not well liked, but even police need policing."

"My dad broke open a corruption case involving the District Attorney, the mayor, and four senators."

"Back in '76, '77 maybe?" Blevins nodded. "I read about it when I was in the academy, but not in detail. Brave man doing that, especially back then. How'd he do it?"

Audrey adjusted her jacket and looked at him. "You're the detective, you tell me."

Blevins smiled at her, glanced at the wall and sighed, and then turned back to her. "If I had to guess, it was probably the way all crooks and politicians get caught. A money trail."

Audrey nodded affirmation, but there was no amusement in her eyes at the detective's answer. "He followed the money."

CHAPTER TWENTY-THREE
AUDREY: then

Audrey flipped through her closet until she found the specific style of black dress she was after—attractive without being sexy. She pulled it from the rack to appraise it, and then pulled it over her head before moving on to do her hair and make-up. Simple silver hoops graced her ear lobes. Audrey checked herself in the mirror. She looked strong. Professional.

She nodded at her reflection and headed down the hallway toward the front door, grabbing her purse from the counter as she did. Audrey glanced at the open doors to Paul's office but never broke stride. It was time for some answers and she had a good start in mind.

Their joint account was at Sweet Water Credit Union, a small community institution with less than six branches in the area. Audrey knew the corporate office and main branch was nestled at the end of a commercial business cul-de-sac barely fifteen minutes away, outside the city.

Even with typical mid-day traffic on the highway, Audrey made it to the credit union in less than twenty minutes. She parked, glanced at herself in the rearview mirror, and exhaled slowly before she got out of the car. That crossroads sensation filled her, making her question whether or not she should proceed. Audrey ignored it and walked inside to the counter.

"Hello, I'd like to speak to a manager."

The woman behind the counter frowned. "Is something wrong, Miss? Maybe I can help?"

Audrey shook her head. "No, no. I'm sorry. It's… a private matter. My husband passed away recently and I just need to speak with a manager, please."

"*Ohhhh.*" The woman's face changed from concern to sympathy. "I'm so sorry, Miss. Our manager is out sick today, but I'll have someone help you." She picked up a phone and pressed several buttons on the keypad. "Hello, David? This is Lindsey. I have a member who needs to speak with someone."

The woman shifted in place, listening to the other end of the conversation. "No, it's..." She lowered her voice. "Her husband passed away and... yes. Okay."

The woman hung up the phone and turned back to Audrey. "Our Vice President, David Schmidt, will be right with you. I'm sure he can help you with whatever you need."

Audrey nodded and stepped away from the counter, walking toward a thick wooden display shelf bolted to the wall. There were plastic racks on top of it with a range of color-coded brochures arranged in order with bold titles: *Mutual Funds & Investment Accounts, Financing A Home, College Funds, Teaching Children to Save.*

It was all the type of things Paul had taken care of.

"Hello."

Audrey turned to the sound of a man's voice and saw him standing there in a charcoal gray suit. He wore silver glasses in rounded rectangular frames. The man stuck his hand out to shake and Audrey took it automatically, gripping his soft, uncalloused skin.

"I'm David Schmidt, Vice President of Loans and Operations."

"Audrey Dugan."

He paused, and then lifted his hand, indicating a hall leading away from the lobby. "Please, Mrs. Dugan, come with me. We'll go to my office."

David led her away to a wide flight of stairs leading up to the second floor and then opened the stairwell door for her. "First office on the right, please."

Audrey walked several feet and turned into an office space, pausing as the man closed the door, and then sat behind his desk in a plush leather chair almost the same as Paul's. She sat in the chair opposite his desk and glanced around the room. There were two bookshelves behind the desk, one of them holding binders with titles like *Credit Union Compliance* and *Understanding the Impact of Federal Loan Rates,* while others showed blank plastic spines. Audrey glanced at the framed photos resting on top of the shelves. Several photos of a boy and a girl, both in their teens, and a complete picture of a family, showing Mr. Schmidt and two teenage children, and a dark-haired woman with a sincere smile.

"Mrs. Dugan, I'm so very sorry to hear your husband passed away. Lindsey mentioned it when she called."

Audrey nodded. "Thank you. It's…" She looked away from the man and out his office window. The tops of weeping willow trees and the hillsides in the distance were the only things in view. Now that she was here, she wasn't sure how to begin. Audrey tapped her fingertips against the chair. "Mr. Schmidt, my husband, Paul, he took care of everything financially related. I'm responsible now, and I need to get a… a handle on things."

"I understand. It's unfortunate, but we see it a lot at the credit union with our members." He turned his chair toward a computer monitor. "I'll pull up your account and see if I can help explain things."

Mr. Schmidt looked over the information on screen. He glanced at her and then focused on the screen again. "Your husband was the primary account holder, and you're obviously on the joint account." He made a few deft moves with his mouse, clicked the button a few times, and keyed in some information. "Mrs. Dugan, by law, we can't take your husband's name off of the account until…" His expression softened and he looked apologetic. "I'm sorry, but until there's a death certificate. But in the meantime, you still have full access as the secondary."

"Of course, yes. I understand that. It's just… I need to know some information. There are some things I'm unclear about on the account."

"Such as?"

"There are…" Audrey ran the question through her head, thinking how it would sound to someone else.

Well, you see, there are deposits and withdrawals for thousands and thousands of dollars, and gee, the thing is, I have no fucking idea where the money was coming from and where it was going to and oh, silly me, I believed my dead husband when he said he was going to a nonexistent job for seven years.

"I'd like to verify some information on specific deposits and withdrawals on the account."

The man's focus lingered on her face and he nodded. "Of course. There are trace numbers associated with each deposit and withdrawal." He turned to the computer monitor again. "Let's take a look."

Audrey leaned onto the desk. "The deposits seem to all be from the same source and I'd like to know what that source is."

Mr. Schmidt clicked his cursor on the first large deposit and the screen changed, enlarging and singling out the transaction. "Okay, this has a Federal Reference Number, so that means it's a wire transfer."

He sighed and lightly tapped his hands against the top of his desk. "Mrs. Dugan, there are things we can do to dig a little deeper into this, but they might take a little time."

"I'd appreciate that. The deposits say they're from the Hawkins Group and I don't know…"

"Your husband was a businessman?"

Audrey nodded and Mr. Schmidt sighed. "We see it a lot. Businessmen involved in this LLC or corporation or whatever. Successful people have a lot of irons in the fire, so to speak, but it makes it very difficult for their loved ones when they're suddenly not here."

"Will it take long? To track the origin of the deposit?"

"Shouldn't take very long." He stood from the desk. "Can I get you something to drink? We have water, coffee and I think there's a few cold ginger ales."

Audrey shook her head. "No, thank you."

"Okay. I'm going to let this search run and I'm going to grab a coffee. That mid-afternoon slump is creeping up on me." The man walked from his office, leaving the door open behind him.

Audrey's focus returned to the family photo.

Cute kids. The daughter has her mother's eyes and cheekbones. The background of the photo looks like a park, or maybe their back yard, all out of focus foliage, saturated with green.

Do I really want to know this?

Audrey chewed on her lower lip and fidgeted with her purse.

"Here we go." Mr. Schmidt walked back in and closed the door. He carried an aluminum travel mug with steam rising from the coffee. Walking around his desk, he paused, still standing, and looked at the monitor. He set the cup of coffee down and eased into his chair. *"Ooookay…"*

He grabbed the mouse and maneuvered the cursor to select some things on screen. "It looks like…" He reached for his cup of coffee and took a sip as he silently read the screen. "The wire transfer came from a Western Union out of Philadelphia, on behalf of the Hawkins Group. Beyond that, there's not much else I can find out at this point. Now, these deposits and withdrawals are all over ten thousand dollars, which automatically—"

"You can't tell me where it actually came from though? Only the company name itself, same as I can see?"

Mr. Schmidt sunk back against his chair. "At this level, I'm afraid not…" He looked away from her, tilted his head side to side, and then focused on her again. "If there was some question of legality, for example, the Federal agencies could go farther, but at our level right here, no."

Audrey felt herself wilt. *A dead end.*

She sighed, nodded, and pushed her chair away from the desk to stand. "Well, thank you for your time, Mr. Schmidt."

"You're welcome, Mrs. Dugan, and again, I am so sorry for your loss. If there's anything else we can help you with, please don't hesitate to call."

Audrey nodded and left his office. When the heavy stairwell door closed behind her, she paused, leaned against the wall, and took a deep breath. She ran a hand over her head and through her hair. Tears tried to rise to the surface and Audrey fought them back.

Well, that was that. One mystery left unsolved. But with Paul dead, the deposits should stop.

So be it.

Audrey walked down the stairwell and returned the sympathetic nod from Lindsey, the woman at the front counter. Outside the exit doors, Audrey walked around the brick building to the side area where she had parked.

She heard a vehicle drive into the lot, hard and fast. Audrey turned to see a side door in a van slam open. Two men with black ski-masks over their heads jumped free, and Audrey had time to register gloved hands gripping the lower half of her face, and a sweet-smelling rag pressed over her mouth and nose. A cloth sack was yanked over her head and strong arms pulled her inside the van.

Then there was nothingness.

CHAPTER TWENTY-FOUR
AUDREY: then

"Is anyone there?" Audrey could hear the soft whisper of fabric against fabric as someone—no, multiple people—shifted in place. The sound of their shoes scuffing against a gritty floor. There were murmurs but too far away for her to understand what was being said.

"Hello?" Her voice echoed, the sound in a large empty space. Audrey's mind swam as if she had downed too much wine.

The cloth sack around her head had been gathered into a tight bunch around her neck, and Audrey felt something wrapped around the cloth, keeping it tightly in place. The fabric was rough against her mouth and chafed her lips. She shifted on the chair she sat in and felt the hard-edged bite of thin cord or plastic around her bare wrists, bound to arm rests. Her feet were free to move, though she only had one high-heel remaining, and felt a cool hard floor beneath her bare foot.

Footsteps headed in her direction and then maneuvered behind her. The pressure of hands working behind her neck and the release of the tight constriction. The bag was jerked off her head and Audrey squinted at the sudden light. The footsteps moved from behind her and walked away as her vision adjusted. Her world was distorted like the reflection in a fun-house mirror, but Audrey blinked her eyes and tried to study the men watching her.

Four men in business suits stood roughly ten feet away. Their expressions were solemn as they stared at her. Two wore glasses and two did not. Three of them were gray-haired with receding hairlines, and wore neckties. They looked like an executive board of directors, expecting bad profit report. The last man had a thick head of black hair, slicked back from his forehead in a shining sweep. He held a hood made of black cloth in his hands.

One of the older men wearing glasses turned to the younger dark-haired man and spoke in a low voice, but loud enough for Audrey to hear. "That's Paul Dugan's wife."

"Who?" The dark-haired man replied, and then looked back at Audrey.

"Paul Dugan. Paul *fucking* Dugan." The older man's face was flushed. "That's his wife. What in the fuck has Schmidt gotten us into?"

Behind her, Audrey heard the sound of a door opening, and two men walked past her to join the others. Everything she saw was distorted, warped like a reflection in a funhouse mirror. The room consisted of a bare cement floor with painted white walls and thick support columns every twenty feet. It looked like a vacant floor of an office building.

The two new men were young, closer to the age of the man holding the cloth bag than the older men. One of them spoke. "He'll be here in a second. He had to take a call in the parking lot." He looked at Audrey and grinned. "What do we have today?"

"Shut the fuck up, Tom." The older man with glasses said, and the leering smile left the younger man's face.

Audrey's head hammered inside. She wanted to talk, but even the thought of speaking swirled in her head and ended in tired resignation. She felt like her words would come out stretched like boardwalk taffy. The muscles in her neck didn't want to work properly and the weight of her head kept tilting her neck backward.

The door behind her opened again and fast footsteps approached and passed her. Her vision was beginning to correct itself and she saw the back of this man, wearing slacks and a perfectly creased charcoal gray suit jacket. He walked to the others and spoke in a voice low enough that Audrey couldn't make out any of the words. Some of the men nodded their head as they listened. The dark-haired man glanced over the speaker's shoulder and looked at her for a moment before he turned his attention back to what was being said.

The speaker turned around to face her.

His face was twisted, skewed like the model in an abstract painting. Audrey blinked slowly and concentrated on forming words. "I...I know you. You're David Schmidt."

The group of other men glanced at Schmidt, and then back to her. Audrey's neck muscles stiffened and she straightened her head. The distortion in her sight was fading as whatever they had given her wore off. She turned her gaze to the two older men wearing glasses, and narrowed her eyes at the one wearing a striped, out of date necktie. "I know you, too. You're Marcus Keller. I met your wife at a party last year."

Audrey's gaze leveled out on the faces of the men. "I know almost *all* of your faces. And yes, I *am* Paul Dugan's wife." She jerked at the binding on her wrists, looked to see the plastic zip-ties holding her in place. "What the hell is this? What do you want?" She yanked her arms again, *hard,* and the chair rocked with her effort. Audrey gritted her teeth and screamed. "Let me go!"

Mr. Schmidt nodded at Audrey, cleared his throat, and then stepped close to her.

She watched as he withdrew a rag from his suit jacket, and felt him press it against the lower half of her face. Audrey's world swam in chemical sweetness again, turning everything into a rainbow oil slick. He pulled it away from her face, crouched down to one knee, and dropped the rag to the floor.

Audrey felt him slapping at her cheeks, not hard, but enough to get her attention.

"That's it. Calm down, now. No need for all that." Mr. Schmidt stared at her and then stood and stuffed his hands into his pants pockets. He bent forward slightly, like a grownup scolding a toddler.

"Mrs. Dugan, your husband Paul, was a..." He pursed his lips. "...very sad loss for all of us. He had a rarely seen talent in both sales and procurement. A gift, really. He was an absolute genius at turning bad products into unique ones. Sought after. And he was very well paid for it."

Mr. Schmidt cleared his throat again. "Now, there are two ways you can look at your situation." He took a step away, and then swiveled back toward her, an amused expression on his face. "The first is... admittedly, rather difficult for you. You can dig into where your husband's money came from and the reasons why." He smiled and shook his head. "I don't recommend that option."

Audrey heard his words through a long tunnel.

"The second option, which I highly, *hiiiighhhly* recommend... is this." He stepped closer to her and crouched to one knee. "Let this go. Stop poking around with things you know nothing about."

He raised a hand to raise his glasses, pinched the bridge of his nose, and blinked several times before putting them back in place. 'Tomorrow, by the close of business, there will be a deposit in your bank account. Let's call it a… severance package, so to speak, for a valued employee. After seven years, it comes to roughly…"

He swayed his head back and forth, seemingly doing calculations in his head. "Five and a half million dollars. We'll make it look like it's coming from a life insurance policy so it'll appear completely above board and legitimate."

Mr. Schmidt stood up and put his hands in his pockets again. "It'll be good for you. New life for you and Sarah. She's a *very* pretty girl by the way."

He smiled and Audrey felt her insides grow cold.

"Don't…" She heard her words, slurred and slow. "Don't you hurt my daughter."

"Hurt her?" Mr. Schmidt grinned and glanced back at the other men before returning his attention to Audrey. "Why on Earth would we do that?"

The man with the slick dark hair stepped forward, moving to Mr. Schmidt's side.

"We wouldn't hurt her. She's… what, four months shy of her twentieth birthday? Oh, she must love Ireland right now. Beautiful country."

Audrey felt her fists tighten. She swallowed hard.

"Stop digging around, take the money and keep your fucking mouth shut or we take your daughter and you'll never, *ever,* see her again." Schmidt stepped closer and leaned down to Audrey's face, looking into her eyes. He looked thoughtful for a moment, and then spoke in a soft voice, his tone intimate and gentle, as if he were saying secret things to a lover.

"I will personally make sure she ends up in Colombia or somewhere in the Middle East. Do you have *any* idea what kind of kinky fucked-up shit they do to women in the Mid-East?" He shook his head and turned to the dark-haired man. "They don't age well in this line of work over there."

"Not at all." The dark-haired man smirked.

"I've seen twenty-two-year-olds that look sixty."

"Harsh country."

"And after... what, twenty-four?"

The dark-haired man nodded. "Twenty-five, maybe."

"Twenty-five." Mr. Schmidt nodded at the man's reply and turned to Audrey. "They tire of the *old* girls and that's it. Good-bye."

The dark-haired man whistled and made an airplane motion with his hand, flying away.

"And if she misbehaves for a sultan over there, or a prince..." Mr. Schmidt put his hands out as if to frame a scene. "Sometimes they heat up crude oil right from the field, get it good and hot, boiling, and they pour it on the women's faces to mark them for being rebellious." He glanced to the dark-haired man. "What's it smell like? It's like... like..."

"Fried chicken." The dark-haired man said.

"No, no. Fried pork! That's it!" Mr. Schmidt nodded and refocused on Audrey.

"Don't." Audrey shook inside, quaking with anger and fear at the same time.

One of Mr. Schmidt's hands went to her neck and wrapped around it, squeezing off her breath. His face was a red grimace, eyes deadened, as he gripped her.

"Don't you ever, *ever,* presume to tell me what to do."

Mr. Schmidt kept his focus locked on Audrey's eyes as he leaned in closer, his fingers still squeezing her throat. "Her body will be dragged to an empty oil field and buried in the sand. It will never be found. Not *ever.*" He smiled thinly. "Not in a million years."

CHAPTER TWENTY-FIVE
IRIS: now

"What's the matter, Doctor? Run out of questions?" Iris watched the man stare absently at the corner of the table.

"Hardly." Doctor Walker gave the slightest shake of his head. "My mind is just having trouble *not* focusing on one question in particular."

"What's that?"

"Why a girl like you, beautiful, highly intelligent, doctor's degree… no drug problem. No former arrests, not even a traffic violation. You say your fiancé was killed, and you were abducted. You're telling me you were human trafficked and sold. And yet you're here now. You escaped, and you're here now."

The doctor leaned forward. "You're telling me *all* of this is true. Well explain why you never told a single soul until today? Explain that to me, Iris. Why would you hide something like this? Why not go to the police as soon as you possibly could?"

Iris stared at him with her one visible eye. The corners of her mouth turned up slightly. She reached for her pack of cigarettes, quickly pulled one free from the box, and took her time lighting it, taking a long drag and slowly releasing the smoke on her exhale. "Did you know I wanted to be a reconstructive pediatric surgeon?"

The man nodded at her. "I just read that in your file."

"Do you know what kind of child isn't absolutely terrified when they look at someone like me, who has burn scars across half of their face?" Iris put the tip of her right index finger against her tongue and dipped it into the ashtray

The doctor shook his head.

"Children who have burn scars like me, that's who." Iris's eye glistened as she glanced at him. She used her ash-coated fingertip to write on the table.

The doctor reached out to the manila folder, flipped through some sheets of paper, and then sat back in his chair. "You were involved in an accident as a child, badly burned, but not…" He looked away from the file folder and back to Iris. "You weren't burned like this."

Iris shook her head and dipped more ash on her fingertip as she continued to write. Next to the ashtray, in thin gray strokes: FUCK YOU.

Doctor Walker's eyes flitted to the wording and then he stared at Iris and sighed. "How did those burns happen?"

CHAPTER TWENTY-SIX
IRIS: then

The cells in Iris's body were shredding themselves with a frantic need.

Her hair and scalp were soaked with sweat and she'd thrown up twice during the night. The muscles of her stomach contracted into hard stone fists one moment and opened to an empty cavern the very next.

"How bad is it?"

Iris opened her eyes and craned her head backward against the cot to see where the voice had come from, and saw a tall section of chain link fence. When she had been brought in, she was out of her mind on drugs. It didn't surprise Iris that she hadn't noticed the chain link before the rusted razor of withdrawal had given her clarity again.

Peering at Iris, through the fence, was the upside-down face of a young black woman wearing a hospital gown. Her skin was patched with vitiligo like a palomino horse. The woman put her fingers through the openings of the chain link separating them.

The side of Iris's face felt as if it had been hit with a sledgehammer. Pain blossomed from her cheekbone and throbbed in pulses along her temple. Her mouth was dry and she felt her lips split open as she replied. "How bad is what?"

"My mother was a junkie. I know the signs of withdrawal."

Iris coughed and shook her head, but she knew the process. The girl was right. The days and nights before getting here had blurred and she wasn't even sure how long it had gone on, but it had been long enough to get her hooked on heroin.

Her stomach clenched and Iris brought her knees up tight against her body. She hugged her legs, rocked against the cot, and prayed this hell would pass quickly. Her eyes and nose dripped tears and mucus, and random waves of goose bumps washed over her skin in painful chills.

"Think of your favorite memory."

Iris heard the woman whisper.

"Whatever that is, get that memory in your mind and hold

onto it. Remember the details, how it smelled and felt. How the air tasted on your tongue. How it sounded. Put yourself back there until you're not *remembering*, you're *living* there again."

Iris felt the muscles in her arms twitch on their own, like beetles clamoring over one another beneath her skin. She shook on the cot and hugged her legs tighter.

"Put yourself back there. All of this will pass soon."

The woman's hands moved away from the chain link fence and Audrey heard creaking sounds as the woman settled down on a cot of her own.

Iris thought of the beach again, of Nathan. But even the thoughts of the summer sun couldn't warm her inside.

***

The night stretched on, and through the agony of withdrawal, the man gave Iris Pedialyte and Gatorade. Sometimes he would lift her head up to help her drink from the bottles, and other times she found the strength to swing her legs over the edge of the cot to sit up and hold the bottle herself.

Sometimes, she kept the liquid down.

True sleep was sporadic and blotchy, but when it came, it was a blur of dreams, much like it had been when Iris had first been injected with heroin. Images of the black woman, her face a beautiful quilt of brown and pale white.

The sensation of heaving over the edge of the cot and the sour stink of bile.

The man, washing her body and rinsing the shampoo from her hair.

"Please…"

The man ignored her whisper as he poured another cup of hot water over her hair. He stood and pulled her body onto the cot, without wringing the moisture from her hair, letting it drip into the canvas beneath her. He stared down at her blankly, and Iris opened her mouth.

Before the first full syllable escaped, the man swung his fist against Iris's jaw.

Later, she woke completely turned around on the cot in the opposite direction, and found herself staring at another wall of chain link. Iris saw part of another person's face, though this was more a girl than a woman. Her dark hair was pulled back from her young Latina face, and she sat on her cot like a statue, knees tucked against her chest, draped with a loose-fitting hospital gown. Her arms hugged her legs as she rested her chin against her kneecaps.

Iris lay still on the cot and went in and out of consciousness. Every time she opened her eyes, the girl was still sitting in the same position. She always looked on the verge of crying, but through the snapshots of her dreams, Iris never saw a tear slide down the girl's cheeks. She never heard the girl whimpering.

On the third side of Iris's cage was a woman with skin the exquisite hue of polished marble. She sat on her cot sideways, her gown ruffled down her arms and bunched around her waist. Iris noticed the woman's red hair reached down to the middle of her back. Her body was void of freckles and moles and blemishes of any kind, except for the bright pink birthmark at the dead center of her chest. It was shaped with ragged, spiked edges into the skewed form of a Valentine's Day heart.

Iris felt herself trembling inside almost constantly, but the need to throw up had subsided. The man came with a fresh bottle of Gatorade, and she took three long gulps until he pulled it away from her and told her that was enough.

Later that night, he returned, applying medicine to the wounds on her arms and back and in between her legs. While this was happening, the quaking inside of Iris grew stronger, threatening to shake pieces of her off onto the floor, but she squeezed her hands into tight balls of iron. She looked away from the man the entire time, focusing on the chain link ceiling of her cage. The patterns met in the right-angle corners like an M.C. Escher painting, absent of origin, but enmeshed in an illusion stretching on in an endless loop.

The man pulled a fresh hospital gown over Iris's bare body, and let it lay, untied, over her. He stood, stared at her for a moment, and then bent down and patted her head. He whispered and nodded. "Good little thing."

CHAPTER TWENTY-SEVEN
IRIS: then

Iris woke to the high-pitched creak of metal hinges.

The man stepped inside her cage and handed her a paper plate with a small pile of scrambled eggs and two sausage patties. He watched her as she scooted back on her cot, and then he backed away, locking the cage door behind him. Iris folded the paper and tilted it, shaking the eggs toward the edge of the plate into her mouth. She chewed and swallowed, and angled the plate again for another bite.

She couldn't believe how amazing the plain, unseasoned eggs tasted. The sausages tumbled against her lip and Iris leveled the plate again and picked up a sausage. The meat was peppered and though it made her lips sting, she closed her eyes and savored the flavor.

The whine of metal on metal rang out again, and Iris opened her eyes to watch the man opening the other cages and giving plates of food to the other three women. The black woman and the redhead dug into their food as enthusiastically as Iris, but the young Latina girl didn't even move her head to acknowledge the man's presence as he held the plate out.

The man said something under his breath, and the girl immediately lifted her head and took the plate from him. He stepped out of the girl's cage, locked it, and then left the women alone.

Iris swallowed the last bite of her first sausage patty.

The Latina girl held the plate in front of her for a moment, and then softly put it on the floor. She scooted back onto the cot and pulled her legs up to her chest again, gently resting her chin on her kneecaps.

Iris finished her breakfast and put the empty plate beside her on the cot. The hospital gown hung loosely on her body and she glanced down at the gaping front, seeing the lines of her ribs.

Outside, Iris could hear the sound of a vehicle starting its engine, and then footsteps. A large overhead door rose on tracks from the cement floor and Iris could see trees outside through the opening, framing a large yard of green grass. The silhouette of a man stood in the frame, and then he walked off into the light.

Iris saw the red brake lights and white reverse lights of a large panel truck as it backed up and stopped inside the entrance of the building. The man cut the engine, got out of the driver's side, and walked to the rear of the truck. Iris heard the popping sound of a heavy latch at the rear of the truck, and then the rumble of an overhead door being raised.

The man walked from the rear of the truck and stopped to look over the row of cages.

"Time to go." He removed a pair of gloves from his hands and stuffed them into a rear pocket of his jeans. Iris watched him reach toward a small holster at the side of his hip and remove something as he stepped toward the cage where the black woman was kept.

The man worked the metal latch on the door of her cage and paused. He held up a small device in his hand, the size of a TV remote, and pressed a button on the side. Iris heard a crackling sound and watched a purple arc of electricity appear at the end of the man's device. He released the button and it went quiet and when Iris blinked, she could still see the bright sparks behind her eyelids. She saw the man press his thumb down on the device and the small lightning bolt snapped in the air again. He was making a point. A warning.

He opened the girl's cage and she stepped forward, leaning away from the chain link ceiling. She stood straight after she exited the cage, and he put a hand out. "Stay."

Next, the man walked past Iris's cage to the redhead and repeated the same process except he gripped the girl's arm and led her to stand beside the black woman.

Iris felt the shaking inside her begin to swell.

The man went into the cage of the young Latina girl, shook his head and cussed at the untouched paper plate of breakfast. He jerked her by the arm up from the cot, and walked her toward the other two women, planted her in place, and then stood in front of Iris's cage.

"Now, you." He flipped the latch on the outside of her cage, and for one brief moment, Iris thought about charging the door, just rushing into it with everything she had and barreling into him, knocking the man to the cement floor and praying the other girls would help her.

And then what? You don't even know where you are. Run outside and... then what?

Iris stepped free of her cell, and the man gripped her wrist tightly as they stepped toward the rest of the women. He motioned with his hand for all of them to move forward toward the truck and waited until they were all in line. "Stop."

He let go of Iris's arm and motioned to the redhead. She stepped forward, and he took her hand to help her climb up inside. The black woman was next. He grabbed the small Latina girl at her waist and lifted her to sit on the platform. The girl turned away and crawled inside.

"Come on." The hand that held the stun gun pointed at Iris and waved her toward the truck.

She stepped forward and he took her hand, helping her inside like the others. Iris crawled several steps inside and looked down. On both the bed and walls of the truck, and also when she looked up to the roof, Iris saw a layer of charcoal gray padding, lined with angled ridges.

Acoustic foam to dampen the sound.

The man slammed the rear door shut, and she heard the lock fall into place.

CHAPTER TWENTY-EIGHT
AUDREY: now

Detective Blevins opened a desk drawer and withdrew a short connection cable. He plugged it into an outlet at the base of his desk lamp, hooked the other end to the recorder, and leaned back into his chair. "You knew these men?"

"I recognized most of them, knew some of their names, but not all."

"Mrs. Dugan, why didn't—"

"Press charges? Scream at the top of my lungs? Call the police?" Audrey shook her head and drank from the bottled water. "They threatened my..." She looked away from him and chewed on her lower lip. "These are *powerful* men, Detective. Wealthy men who *know* people."

"Yeah, I know the type." Blevins' voice sounded tired, somewhat drained.

"The next day, right before five o'clock, I got a notification on my phone from my banking app. A deposit was made."

"How much?"

Audrey glanced at him and then focused on the water bottle in her hand. "Five point four million dollars."

The detective slowly leaned forward, studying Audrey. "So, you were a rich widow, your daughter was safe, and all you had to do was keep your mouth shut and have a good life?"

She nodded without looking at him, and the detective remained quiet for a moment. He stood and walked to a small counter by the refrigerator. A coffee pot and column of foam cups were lined up beside it. The man poured himself a cup and came back to sit.

"Alright. So what happened then? What happened after they let you go?"

CHAPTER TWENTY-NINE
AUDREY: then

Audrey watched with a sickness as Mr. Schmidt pulled into the driveway of her home. He had never asked for a single direction to get there.

Not once. He knew exactly where he was going.

He brought the car to a stop and parked near the entrance. Audrey pulled the door handle but it wouldn't open and she turned to glare at the man. He had a hard-edged amusement in his eyes as he held her gaze for a moment, and then pushed the unlock button on his door panel.

Audrey had kicked her remaining high heel shoe into his floorboard and left it there as she got out without saying a word. The stones of the gravel driveway felt sharp beneath her bare feet.

Vehicle headlights turned into the drive and Audrey saw that someone had driven her car from the credit union lot. She watched as the car pulled behind Mr. Schmidt's and parked. The younger man with slicked back hair stepped out of the driver's seat, shut the door behind him, and approached her. He smirked and offered his hand, palm up, to Audrey.

"Your keys."

She gripped her purse in one hand and grabbed the keys from him as she headed toward her front door. From behind her, Audrey heard Schmidt's car door open and close. She didn't bother to watch his car's taillights as they left.

Inside the house, Audrey closed the door and locked it. She let her purse and the keys fall to the floor, leaned her back against the door and slowly slid down to the floor. Tears wouldn't come, and somehow that was worse. Her body was freezing and she couldn't stop shaking. Audrey sat like that for a while and then gripped the knob to the front door and struggled to stand again.

Putting her hands on the walls to steady herself, Audrey walked through the living room and down the hallway to their, *her*, bedroom. She removed her earrings and tossed them to her dresser. The slit on the side of her dress had been torn, and she angrily grabbed the cloth with both hands and yanked it apart, tearing the fabric up to her waist. Audrey pulled the shoulder straps until they snapped and she yanked the dress down, letting it fall to the floor in a tumble. Her chest heaved and she felt sobbing tears erupt to the surface.

She went to the bed, crawled onto the mattress until she reached her pillow, and collapsed into the soft cushion. She pulled Paul's pillow close and clutched handfuls of it, pressed it against her face to take in his smell. In that moment, she hated him for whatever he had done, and hated herself for needing him right then, needing to breathe in his scent because it was the only thing familiar in her life.

Why? Why, Paul? Why aren't you here to take care of me?

A single sob of agony escaped her, and Audrey held her breath, rocking against the mattress. She lay like that for a long while, as silent tears boiled down her cheeks, and then she pushed Paul's pillow away from her until it fell to the carpet.

***

Sunlight shifted through the blinds of the bedroom and Audrey blinked slowly, willing herself to sit up. The corners of her eyes felt gritty, crusted, and she supposed it was dried tears.

She dressed in jeans and a t-shirt and thought of ignoring the pile of torn dress on the floor, but stopped and picked it up. In the kitchen, Audrey stuffed the dress into the garbage can, pulled the bag free, and yanked the plastic strings tight to tie it off.

The absolute silence of the house struck her and she looked around at the kitchen, realizing she couldn't remember when she had last eaten, but had no appetite. Audrey glanced at the wooden wine rack nestled in between the kitchen cabinets, and withdrew a bottle from the top, a chardonnay by Francis Ford Coppola. Not great, but not bad either.

The vodka was... *awful.* That had been Paul's poison of choice.

I'll pour it down the drain. The house will never have vodka in it again.

She withdrew a corkscrew from a kitchen drawer and worked the top of the bottle, popping the cork free of its prison. Audrey peeled the remaining foil from the neck, tossed it to the counter, and then reached into her purse to grab her phone. Carrying the bottle of wine and her phone into the living room, Audrey sat down heavily on the couch.

After several healthy swigs of chardonnay, Audrey put the bottle down and scrolled her phone screen to the favorite numbers list. She let her thumb hover over Sarah's name for a moment, and then pressed it to make the call.

Two rings. "Mom!" Sarah's voice, excited and happy.

I have become a sparrow, a harbinger of death.

Audrey closed her eyes, felt the hot grit at their corners. "Hey honey."

"I'm *sooo* excited to come home, Mom! I love it here, but I miss you and Dad and I can't wait to tell you and —"

"Honey?"

"Dad is going to *love* the photos of the castles! I found the one he told me ab—"

"Honey, is Gloria there with you?"

Audrey heard some laughter in the background of the call and then Sarah's voice again. "Yeah, she's here, why?"

"Of course, she is. You two are joined at the hip." Audrey smiled.

My God, I sound tired. Broken.

There was a beat of silence on the phone and Sarah's voice leveled and became serious, the excitement replaced by caution and worry. "Mom, are you okay?"

"Honey… I have some bad news. It's um…" She turned away from the phone and took a deep breath. Her vision blurred. "Sarah, honey, your father… Dad died."

After the words were spoken out loud, Audrey floated away from her body. The conversation continued without words, only the sound of Sarah screaming on the phone. Audrey listened as her daughter cried and sobbed and then calmed to a somewhat reasonable level as her own numb acceptance kicked in.

There was talk of return flights and informing her college

advisor. Audrey was aware of it all, but from arm's length, drifting away from it like a kite with a broken string.

They said their tearful goodbyes, and Audrey hung up the phone and drank from the wine bottle, cradling it between her breasts. She took another big swallow and took care to gently set the bottle down on the coffee table. Audrey sat forward and screamed, loud and furious. The sound bounced off the walls and back at her, and Audrey's hands tightened into fists. She shrieked louder, the effort tearing at her throat and grating it raw. Rage and fury galvanized her body and she screamed more, directing her wrath at the open entrance to Paul's office.

Leaping from the couch, her fists still clenched, Audrey charged into the office. She swung her hands and swept the top of Paul's desk. Papers and a stapler and a wire mesh pencil holder fell to the floor. She swung her arms again, and his flat-screen computer monitor crashed against the wall and tumbled to the carpet.

Audrey turned to a bookshelf and grabbed the sides of it. She yanked at the shelves and they popped free of their pins. Family photographs fell, along with books, hardbacks about war and cheap paperback spy novels. Audrey wrenched at another shelf and the fiber-board construction creaked and snapped loose as a shelf broke free on one side, sending books spinning to the carpet. She punched the leather loveseat sitting beside the bookshelf, clenched the cushions from the frame and tossed them aside.

Audrey screamed again until it felt as if something tore loose in her throat. She charged the other side of Paul's office, grabbing plaques from the wall and hurling them against his desk. Glass shattered in a shining hail.

An old weathered baseball bat leaned against the wall near the pocket doors, and Audrey grabbed the handle and lifted it high overhead. She swung it against the drywall, punching a hole beneath a metal wall clock. She brought it back for another swing, and the smooth hickory handle slipped from her hands, slamming the thick end against a framed Beverly Doolittle print of an Indian stalking game through a cluster of birch trees. The bat bounced off and somersaulted toward Paul's desk. The print tilted and crashed down at an angle against the trashcan beneath it. A long curling seam ran over the now broken glass.

Audrey collapsed to her knees on the carpet. Her lungs heaved with exertion. Blood coursed through her veins, pulsing and ringing in her ears, but the rage had subsided for now, blown away in a violent tornado.

Her head was down, hair hanging around her face. Audrey's throat felt blistered and raw, as if she had gargled with chips of stone from the driveway. She pushed her hair from the right side of her face, and then ran a hand over her face and head.

Audrey looked up at the wall where the framed print had hung.

Embedded flush with the surface of the drywall, there was a dark gray rectangle the size of a manila folder. In the dead center of the panel was a circular shape with several rows of buttons.

A safe.

CHAPTER THIRTY
AUDREY: then

You have to think like Paul. What was important to him? Easy to remember?

Audrey had tried Paul's birthday, her own birthday, Sarah's birthday. Their anniversary date. None of them were the correct combination.

What if it the combination was already programmed when he got it? Some random series of numbers?

Audrey drank from the bottle of chardonnay as she glared through the open doors at his trashed office.

No. That would never sit well with Paul. He would want the combination to be his own. Military training had been beaten into the core of his being. The strength to adapt. Efficiency. Control, control, control.

Audrey brought the bottle to her lips again and paused. She set the bottle on the kitchen counter and slowly walked back into Paul's office. On the wall behind his desk was his framed honorable discharge certificate. Audrey's gaze filtered down to the smaller text in the middle stating the exact date. April 2, 2012.

She turned and stared at the LOCK ENGAGED on the small black screen.

Can't be.

Audrey typed on the keypad: 4-2-12 and the red letters changed status from LOCK ENGAGED to LOCK DISENGAGED.

A sharp exhale escaped her and she flinched. Audrey hesitated a moment before gripping the small handle, and then she squeezed and pulled the door open.

The interior of the safe was about the size of two shoeboxes placed on top of each other. It was mostly empty except for a short stack of envelopes and papers, and she picked up a navy-blue case resting on top. She flipped it open to reveal a tri-fold portfolio of gold coins behind plastic sleeves, all of them gleaming and untouched. Audrey dropped the case to the carpet and withdrew a manila envelope. Her breath caught as she saw what lay beneath it. Four stacks of cash—hundred-dollar bills—all gathered with mustard yellow bands of paper with $10,000 printed on them.

Audrey turned her attention back to the envelope and bent the metal clasp to open the flap. She withdrew a glossy 8 x 10 black and white photo of a military Humvee flipped on its side. The ground where it rested was scorched, and the vehicle was a mass of twisted metal on what would have been the passenger's side. The tires were missing, the wheel rims charred black and caked with melted rubber.

Audrey let the envelope and the photograph fall to the floor. She moved the cash to the side and took the only thing remaining in the safe—a short pile of squares a little larger than playing cards.

Polaroids.

CHAPTER THIRTY-ONE
IRIS: now

"Did you ever watch SpongeBob SquarePants, Doctor?"

"I've seen a few episodes, yes."

"When I was a kid, it was my favorite. I mean, I had posters on my walls. I had a stuffed SpongeBob and a Patrick I slept with. *Loved* that show." Iris cleared her throat and reached for another cigarette. She lit it, exhaled, and then sniffled and shook her head. "I begged my parents for SpongeBob pajamas one Christmas. That was it, the only thing I asked for. I was eight years old, but I was old enough to understand my parents didn't have a lot of money back then, and I figured pajamas couldn't be *that* expensive, right? And honestly, it was the only thing I wanted. A pair of damned SpongeBob pajamas."

Iris shifted in the chair, turned sideways, and rested her arm around the back of the chair. "We were living in a trailer, this shitty little trailer in a mobile home park that was..." She shook her head. "Money was tight even though both of my parents were working. Hell, my dad had two jobs at the time. But, anyway, these pajamas were all I asked for. So, it's about a week before Christmas, right? I'm in bed and my nightlight's on, but I'm awake, and I hear my parents talking in the living room."

She glanced at the doctor. "No such thing as privacy in a trailer. Most of the kids I knew there got their sex education from living in a trailer and hearing their parents." Iris coughed laughter and shook her head.

"Anyway, I hear my parents talking, my dad telling my mom he couldn't find a kid's pair in medium, only large. I was no dummy, though. I knew they were talking about the pair of pajamas I had asked for, and truth was, I didn't even care if the pajamas fit or not.

"But Mom was upset. I couldn't make out what she said, only the tone of her voice and it was sad... so very sad, and then I heard her crying. It wasn't like they were arguing, right? I mean, Dad's voice wasn't loud or even had that hissing kind of anger people make when they're pissed but trying to be quiet."

Iris took a drag on her cigarette and rested her arm back in place. "But Mom was crying because they couldn't get a pair that would fit me, and I couldn't even be excited anymore. I didn't want her to be *sad.* I didn't want Mom to cry. I wanted to run out into the living room and hug her, just hug her and tell her it was okay, that I didn't care what size they were. I'd grow into them. It was the thought that counts, Mommy.

"So, I got out of bed to go do that. Except there was this loud popping sound outside and the power went out in the trailer. My night light, the lights in the hall. Pitch black." She motioned with her hand, pointing out the visuals of the memory. "Well, then it became an event, right?"

The doctor adjusted in his chair as he listened.

"I made my way down the hallway to the living room, and Mom heard me, pulled me with her up on the couch. She hugged me and I hugged her back, and for the moment, the SpongeBob pajamas were forgotten. Dad had stepped outside to see what was going on and it seemed power was out in the whole neighborhood. If it had been in the summer, no big deal, but this was a few weeks before Christmas, right? It was twenty-nine degrees outside and our trailer didn't hold heat worth a damn."

Iris puffed on her Winston. "We had this little shed in the back yard, small, just big enough to store the lawnmower and some tools. Dad put some summer lawn chairs in there, shit like that.

"But he went outside to the shed and came back with a small kerosene heater, about the size of a camping cooler." Iris took a fast drag on her cigarette and exhaled just as quickly.

"He brought it inside and a few minutes later, Mom was holding the flashlight while Dad lit the heater. It's been years, but I still remember how it smelled, that kerosene heater.

"Dad looked at me, and then leaned closer to Mom and mumbled something, and Mom whispered to me I could stay home from school the next day. We were all going to camp out in the living room." Iris smiled and flicked her cigarette ash into the tray.

"Somehow, my parents made having the power outage fun. The kerosene heater didn't give off much light, but Mom squatted down on the floor beside it and read me *Rikki-Tikki-Tavi* by Kipling. She never read Dr. Seuss or anything like that. It was always something she enjoyed as a kid. Kipling or E.B. White, some Emily Dickinson once in a while. Not many books specifically for kids.

"Anyway, she read to me, and then her and Dad sat on the couch, sharing a beer." Iris sniffed and shook her head again. "Laughing, I remember them laughing about something, some shared joke between them. I was on the living room chair, this big, cushy, beat-up thing, but I was twisted up on it, upside down. I was holding up the Kipling book to catch the glow of the heater so I could read more."

She cleared her throat. "My legs were up in the air against the wall, doing that stupid feet tapping shit that kids do, and my feet were against the living room curtains. Mom and Dad were teasing each other, joking and laughing, and I was upside down on the chair, reading, and... this was the greatest night, ever, right?"

Iris puffed on her cigarette and glanced at the doctor. "I guess I pulled at the curtain with one of my feet or something but the whole damn thing, curtain rod and all, fell on me. I twisted and fell off of the chair, trying to stand, and the tail of one of the curtains somehow hit the inside of the heater."

She stared off into the distance, lost in the memory. "I was tangled up in the whole thing and got tripped up and the next thing I know, I'm lit up like a human torch.

"The fabric of the curtain turned to a syrup of flame. My nightgown was long and..." She glanced at the doctor. "I tried to wipe the fire off of me, but it didn't matter, it was...

"My father grabbed this crocheted quilt from the back of the couch, this ugly thing with all sorts of different colors. Dad hated the thing, but anyway, he grabbed the quilt and threw it over me. I just remember holding my arms up, screaming for him, for him to help me."

Iris was silent for a few moments, and then she let out a long breath. "Took a long time to heal. Had to wear the scuba suit, the compression suit, you know? Salves and ointments and getting my burn scars massaged. It was hell."

The silence of the memory hung heavily in the room until the doctor broke it.

"Your father saved your life."

"He did." Iris smiled weakly and looked at the doctor. "I remember the first time we went to the beach after that, when I was finally out of the hospital and healed up. I had fought and cried with my mother before going on vacation because she wanted to buy me a one-piece swimsuit, and I wanted a bikini. I was nine-years old. I was old enough for a two-piece, right? Like all my girlfriends at school."

Iris held the glowing cherry of her burning Winston in front of her face and stared at it. "I won the argument. So, we got to the beach and Dad set up this umbrella while Mom laid out the blanket and stuff. The sun is absolutely blazing, and I took off my t-shirt, Mom slathered me up with sunblock, and I head for the water. The sunlight hurt my skin, I remember that." She brought the cigarette to her lips and took a drag, flicked ash into the tray.

"In many ways, it was like the sun was waking up the pain of the burn somehow, burning my skin deep down below the surface, like fire had gotten a taste of me and wanted a second helping. So, I ran into the ocean to avoid the sunlight.

"I remember these two boys on the beach, one a little older than me, one a little younger. They were staring at me and talking to each other in low voices.

"And then it hit me all at once, why Mom wanted me to wear a one-piece. I looked down at the melted pink swirls and burn scars on my right side, collar bone to hip." Iris leaned on the table.

"The boys kept staring as I walked back from the wet shoreline up to the dry sand and sat down on the blanket again, beneath the shade of the umbrella. I pulled my t-shirt back on to hide my body, and had my first grown-up realization. I was different than everyone. I'd been marked."

The doctor nodded, glanced at his iPad, and then returned his focus to the woman.

"My father never graduated high school. Never went to college. But he was a smart man. He was very…" Iris took a breath and waved her hand with the cigarette, seeming to search for the right word. "Aware... *cognizant,* of his surroundings and people.

"I saw Dad glance at the boys and then back to me, and he put it together pretty quickly. We nibbled on beach snacks Mom had packed, and after a while, Dad stood up and held his hand out to me. I didn't want to take my shirt off. No way. Not after being ogled at like I was some sort of circus freak.

"I don't remember what Dad said to me, but I remember him squatting down and speaking in his calm, gentle voice. I remember eventually, but reluctantly, I took my shirt off and dropped it to the beach blanket."

Iris flicked ash in the tray and sighed. "Dad held my hand and we walked down, close enough to let the waves catch our feet. He picked me up and I wrapped my arms around his neck. I glanced back over his shoulder and saw the boys, now openly pointing at me as they talked, and then, as Dad walked us into the ocean water, I saw their mouths drop open and they looked at each other. One of them started laughing and bent over, holding his stomach. Now, I wasn't sure exactly *what* they were laughing at, I just knew it wasn't me."

Iris smiled, a sincere smile, but one tainted with an emotion other than happiness. "I didn't know until years later when Mom told me, but my father had dropped the rear of his swimming trunks on purpose, exposing more than a little of his pale rear end and giving the boys something else to focus on."

The doctor grunted a small laugh. He smiled and nodded. "Sounds like he was a good man. Good father."

"The best." Iris swallowed and turned her cigarette over in her hands. She stared at the glowing ember of her cigarette as the smoke drifted toward the ceiling.

CHAPTER THIRTY-TWO
IRIS: then

Iris heard a scream pierce the pitch-black interior as the truck began to move. She knew it was the young Latina girl but the sound was swallowed up by the foam lining. They were in a prison that even restrained their sounds.

Moving in the direction the scream had come from, Iris reached out and felt the girl flinch away for a moment before grabbing onto Iris. She pulled the girl close, put her arm around her, and they held onto each other with their backs against a sidewall. At some point, even though the ride jostled them repeatedly, Iris drifted to sleep as she listened to the slow breathing of the girl in her arms.

The truck braked hard, snapping Iris awake. The vehicle reversed and they slowed to a stop. Iris felt herself tighten up inside as the vibrations of a running engine ceased as well.

She heard the heavy clink of the metal door lock, and the rear panel rose with a loud rattle. Iris braced for harsh sunlight but saw the dim fluorescent glow of what looked like the inside of a large warehouse.

Then she saw the cages.

These weren't made of chain-link fence, but from strips of metal bolted together to create eight-foot cubes.

Not cages, Iris thought. *These are stalls. Livestock stalls.*

A woman in a tight-fitting maroon dress stood by the man at the rear of the truck. Her short hair was slicked back from her face, and she held a clipboard in front of her as if she was checking a shipment manifest.

The man snapped his fingers twice, and waved his hand at the four of them. "Come on."

First, the black woman moved, followed by the redhead. Iris started forward and felt the Latina girl pull at her hand. She stopped and turned, whispering to the young girl. "You have to. It'll be worse if you don't."

The girl still appeared on the verge of crying. Her expression tightened and changed. Iris watched the last pieces of the girl's childhood float away like rising embers from a burn barrel. The two of them made their way to the edge of the truck and the man helped them down to the pavement.

The woman with the clipboard stepped forward, jotted something down, and studied the women. She walked to the door of the first metal stall and motioned for the black woman to go inside, waited until she was completely inside, and then closed the door. The woman continued with the redhead and then Iris.

Though she had a death grip on Iris's hand, the young Latina girl let go and Iris stepped inside a stall. She stared through the openings between the metal slats and breathed a sigh of relief as she watched the girl comply and step into her own stall. The woman marked something off on the clipboard, and she and the man walked away from all of them, deeper into the building.

"You been to one of these before?"

Iris turned to the sound of the black woman's voice, and saw the woman's eyes staring through the metal slats of the stall. Iris shook her head. "I don't know what you mean."

"A stage auction. I can tell that's what this is by the way..." The black woman looked around the stalls and the warehouse. "That's what this is."

"What does that mean exactly?" Iris stepped closer, inches away but divided by the metal wall.

"It's run like any auction. Get you up on a stage and parade you around in the center. People bid on you or they don't."

"What happens if they don't?" It was cold and Iris pulled the cloth of her gown against her body and crossed her arms.

The woman raised her eyebrows and shook her head.

Footsteps approached and Iris moved to the front of her stall. Two men stopped in front of the redhead. One of them wore a clean black suit and had something draped over the crook of one arm. The other man was casual, wearing jeans and a brown flannel shirt. He wore a black knit hat and had scruffy brown facial hair. A walkie-talkie, clipped to his belt, protruded over his shirt, and he gripped something in his right hand.

"This one." Suit-man said.

Mr. Casual unlatched the front of the redhead's stall, and Iris watched him raise a stun gun in front of him. He gave a nod and the redhead stepped free of her stall and stood beside him. Reaching for the gown ties at the back of the redhead's neck, the man tugged at the fabric and it fell to the cement floor.

Suit-man looked her up and down, selected something from the crook of his arm, and handed it to her. "Put this on."

Iris watched the redhead dress in a dark green bikini.

The two men went through the same motions with the black woman. She stood, naked in the chill, until she was handed a bright magenta bathing suit, and the men moved to the front of Iris's stall.

Mr. Casual pressed a button on the stun gun and Iris watched the crackle of electricity at its tip. She nodded at him and stepped from the stall when he pulled the door open. The man's fingers worked at the back of her gown and it slid away from her skin. She attempted to cross her arms and Suit-man grabbed her arm and stopped her.

"Ohhhh." His gaze lingered on her body. "You should call—"

"Was thinkin' the same thing." Mr. Casual wet his lips and nodded.

Suit-man handed Iris a copper-colored bikini. "Put this on."

Iris stepped into the bottoms and pulled them up to her waist. After fastening the bikini top behind her back, she brought the strings around her neck and tied a bow. Suit-man looked over, his attention again resting on the scarred portion of her body. He pursed his lips together and the two men stepped past her, moving on to the next stall.

The Latina girl was handed a dark blue bikini. She put it on as the men watched her, and then she stood still, arms limp at her sides. Her eyes were distant and Iris got the feeling she somehow wasn't even seeing the men in front of her.

The two men walked to the side of the redhead, and Suit-man turned around to the four of them. "Okay. We're going to—" His eye level gaze dropped downward on the black woman's body and an expression of disgust washed over his face. "Oh, for Christ's sake, can someone clean her up and get this fixed?"

Iris's attention went to the woman and saw the patch of blood in her bikini bottom and several dark lines dripping down her inner thighs.

A man dressed in a sweatshirt and jeans approached from the recesses of the warehouse. He took the black woman by her arm and led her off into the building.

"Mark today's date down in her file!" Suit-man yelled and put his hands on his hips. "And get her another bikini! Same fucking color!"

Releasing a heavy exhale, Suit-man turned to face the women and continue addressing them. "We're going to walk, single-file, toward the rear of the warehouse to the entrance door. It will be much warmer inside. We'll be waiting there for a little while, but not long." He shook his head dismissively. "And then we'll proceed."

He put his hands in front of his chest and clasped them together, like a teacher outlining rules for a fieldtrip. "My associate will be with you the entire time. So, please behave or there will be repercussions."

Iris watched the man scan each of their faces for comprehension, rebellion, *something*, and then the son of a bitch actually smiled, pleased with himself and their lack of reaction.

The three girls walked onward.

CHAPTER THIRTY-THREE
IRIS: then

The air was humid and Iris felt beads of sweat on her scalp, trailing down her spine, but it was better than the cutting chill of the warehouse. Mr. Casual waited with them in a long black-painted hallway with a single fluorescent fixture overhead casting harsh light over their glistening skin. The black woman was escorted back to them after a short while, wearing a different style of bikini in the same color. Her shoulders were slumped, her face an unimportant page torn from a book. Angry fingerprints stood out on one arm.

Iris glanced at a closed red door ahead of them in the hallway on the left. Beyond the door, she could hear the murmuring of a crowd.

Mr. Casual's walkie-talkie squawked and a voice spoke through static. "Navy Blue."

He unclipped the walkie from his belt and raised it toward his face. "Copy." The man held the Latina girl's upper arm and led her to the red door. They paused and the young girl glanced back at Iris. Her expression could have been cast in stone for all of the emotion it held. Mr. Casual opened the door and gave her a slight shove through the threshold. He pulled the door most of the way closed, leaving it cracked open.

Iris couldn't make out the muffled words over the loud speaker past the door, but after a moment, the sounds were the rapid-fire pattern of an auctioneer. The tone of the voice rose, excited. There was a pause, another fast-paced spew of speaking, and then things dissolved back to the low white static noise of a group of people.

The sight of what lay beyond the door caught Iris's attention. It looked like a ramp angling upward and the glow of distant bright lights. She chewed at her lower lip, peeled skin away, and tasted her own blood.

Several minutes went by and the walkie squelched again. "Pink."

"Copy that." Mr. Casual stepped past Iris and led the black girl to the entrance and through the doorway to the ramp. The woman straightened herself and marched up the ramp as the man closed the door completely this time.

Iris waited.

She studied the burn scars along her side. The lines of her ribs were more prominent and she wondered how much weight she had lost. In the cold overhead light, her twists of scar looked dark and shiny. She brushed strands of hair away from her forehead.

There was a single whimper from behind Iris and she turned to see the redhead's face. The girl's lips were parted, trembling. Tears flowed down her cheeks and the lids of her eyes matched the color of her hair.

Iris took a step toward the girl as static from the walkie-talkie broke the silence. "Copper."

"Copy." Mr. Casual lowered the walkie and raised his hand toward Iris. He motioned with the fingers of his free hand. "Come on."

Mr. Casual grabbed her upper arm and led her to the red door. He placed a hand at the small of Iris's back, gave her a slight push through the doorway, and she continued up the slope of the ramp toward the glow of the lights ahead.

CHAPTER THIRTY-FOUR
AUDREY: now

"What were the photographs of?"

Audrey tilted the bottle of water to get the remaining drops. "Could I—"

"Sure, of course." Blevins stood and retrieved a fresh bottle of water. He sat back down in his chair and glanced at his own water, barely touched.

"How long have you been a detective?" Audrey unscrewed the cap on the bottle, placed it gently on the desk. Her voice had taken on a faraway quality, almost as if she were waking up from anesthesia.

"Coming up on fourteen years. Before that, ten more as a traffic cop." Blevins shook his head. "A long, damned time."

"Have you ever..." Audrey drank from the open bottle and leaned back in her chair. "What's the worst thing you've had to investigate?"

Detective Blevins laced his fingers and rested them on the table. "The world can be a terrible place at times, Mrs. Dugan. Spend enough time in this job and you get to see some truly awful things." He ran a hand over his face and sighed. "I suppose it would be a call regarding a mother and her boyfriend, both heroin addicts. Open and shut case."

Glancing at his water bottle, Blevins chose his foam cup of coffee, drank from it with a pinched expression, and put it back down on the desk. He cleared his throat, and drank from his water bottle. "He was jonesing for some heroin and discovered she was holding out on him. He found her in the bathroom shooting up and got pissed off. As retaliation, he put their two-month old daughter in the oven and turned it on."

"Christ." Audrey closed her eyes.

"I've seen a lot of bad things, Mrs. Dugan. Best I can do is gather all the facts and try to let the courts find justice afterward."

"Do you think it does?"

"Does what?"

"Find justice?" Audrey shifted in her chair.

"Sometimes." Blevins sighed. "Other times, I think justice comes much later, when they stand before God."

A short buzz came from his jacket and he reached to the inside pocket, checked his phone with a sigh, and put it back in place. He leaned forward in his chair and rested his elbows on the desktop. "The photographs you found in your husband's safe, what were they of, Mrs. Dugan?"

CHAPTER THIRTY-FIVE
AUDREY: then

Audrey felt the cold curl of disgust and repulsion that floods through your system when you've seen something you know you weren't supposed to, something you shouldn't *ever* see. Something you can never *un*see.

There were eight photographs, a deterioration broken down on instant photos.

The first showed a girl, a young woman, naked and on all fours. Her back was bowed, her hair smeared away from her face, head hung low. The woman's eyes were raw, pink at their edges. Her shoulders were slumped, her hands cropped out of frame. In the dark background of the photo, it looked like wooden panels and a rack of something Audrey couldn't make out.

Audrey looked at the side of the girl's body, along her mid-section, at the scarred flesh there. She recognized it immediately for what it was—how many nights had that same mottled skin slept beside her?

Burn scars.

She slid the top photograph to the bottom and looked at the next.

The same girl, slightly closer than the previous picture, only this time, her arms were out to her sides, a length of pipe separating them. Even though the girl's body was vertical, her head had tilted backward as if she had passed out. A black strap and ball gag wrapped snugly around her face.

Audrey studied the photograph and saw a square patch of skin on the girl's hip was darker than the scarring above it on her side. This looked like a fresh burn—a new wound. And there, on the girl's inner thigh, another patch, the same size and shape of the burn on her hip.

Shuffling the photograph to the bottom, Audrey flipped to the next picture and brought a hand up to cover her mouth. The girl in the photograph was sitting on a short stool. Audrey stared at the girl's body from a head-on point of view. Several squares of newly burned flesh adorned her body, spaced out like a chessboard.

Her face had changed. There were circles of shadow beneath her eyes and even though she stared directly at the camera, her focus was on something else entirely beyond the photographer on the other end.

Audrey flipped to the next photo, and the next.

Each photograph was a brief jump forward in time. A time-lapse of torture.

She paused and covered her mouth. Audrey wanted to vomit. She wanted to throw up and scream and shatter everything in the room, turn it to dust, destroy it all to absolute and utter nothingness.

She breathed in and out, slowly, and flipped to the next photo. The paler squares of flesh had been burned to match the others, though as the older wounds healed, they were becoming lighter once again. The pattern stopped at the girl's right collarbone.

Audrey slid to the next photo. Her breath caught in her throat as she saw the close-up of the girl's face, some of the skin charred and cracked. The girl's eye is what made Audrey tremble inside. The cornea was damaged, the moist highlight against the eye's surface was rippled, and the outside corner was blistered and oozing.

That icy wave inside Audrey crested higher. She immediately flipped to the last photograph because she was certain if she didn't do it right then and there, she wouldn't be able to.

This photo was another close-up of the girl's face, the image cropped at the top of her head and the bottom of her throat where it met her collarbone. Her hair had been pinned back to unveil the patchwork of burns, from her chin up to the edge of her hairline. The scorched flesh reached close to a quarter of an inch from her lower right eyelid, so the hollow circle of shadow that had been living there could no longer be seen.

Audrey's gaze drifted to the girl's right eyeball. The rippled surface had tightened, pinching the shining flesh of her eye and the cornea itself, which had lost its natural color and turned the pale color of a beached sea animal, rotting beneath the sun.

The urge to vomit hit her again and Audrey's stomach convulsed, but she swallowed and tightened her body and the feeling passed. She threw the photographs into the safe and stared at the open door. Her legs abruptly felt too weak to stand. Audrey slammed the safe door closed.

LOCK ENGAGED

Backing away, she rested a hand on Paul's desk to stable herself. Her jaw ached and the world felt as if it was tilting on its axis. Audrey took a timid step toward the doorway and then another. Putting a hand against the doorframe, she took one step at a time, slowly, focusing on the motion itself. Her breath came ragged and heavy, and Audrey kneeled on the floor, crawling the few feet to the living room on all fours. She lay on the carpet and rolled onto her back.

She heard her phone vibrate on the coffee table, but ignored it. Audrey forced herself to slowly breathe through her mouth and calm down. From here, she could see the peak of the high ceiling above her. Her gaze followed the seam at the top and bottom as far as her eyes could track it, tracing it back and forth.

After a while, Audrey's body stopped shaking inside. She rolled onto her stomach and did a half push-up to get to her knees and picked up her phone from the coffee table. She tapped it awake and saw the notification from Sweet Water Credit Union:

DEPOSIT NOTIFICATION

She checked the time on her phone. It was ten minutes before five o' clock.

Right before the close of the business day.

CHAPTER THIRTY-SIX
AUDREY: then

Audrey woke to the sound of jingling keys outside the front door.

At some point during the night, Audrey had crawled onto the sofa to sleep, and now she forced herself to open her eyes and focus on the foyer. She squinted as the door opened and light in the front hall was flicked on, her eyes adjusted to the brightness as two figures walked inside her house. Her body felt like wet cement and she continued to look at them from a sideways point of view.

"Mom?"

I'm dreaming, Audrey thought. She didn't reply, and then heard a man's low voice.

"Well, I'm going to go. Again, I'm so very sorry."

Audrey blinked and swallowed hard at the man's voice. She grabbed the back of the couch, pulled herself up, and her head swam. Sunbursts dotted her vision.

The taller figure leaned down, and Audrey watched the man hug Sarah. As he held her, the man ran a hand over the back of Sarah's head and smoothed her long hair until it rested against her back.

Mr. Schmidt turned to smile at Audrey. "It's going to be okay."

Audrey's heart raced. That inner tremble stuttered inside her.

He pulled away from Sarah and put a hand up in a wave. "Hi, Audrey. Get some rest, okay? It'll be good to have your daughter back home."

The front door opened again and he walked through, closing it behind him on the way out.

Sarah walked quickly through the foyer, her expression crumpling in on itself. She knelt in front of Audrey, and they clung to each other. The sobs came then, racking Audrey's body and making her frantically clutch at Sarah's back as if she might be yanked away.

The sobs leveled to tears, the desperate embrace easing to shared solace, and Audrey straightened to see Sarah's face.

"What…" Audrey glanced at the front door and then back to Sarah. "How did you get home?"

"I moved my flight up, Mom. I had to be here. I *had* to."

"That's not what I mean." Audrey's heart slammed in her chest as she heard a car outside drive away on the gravel. "I would have—"

"How did you know I was flying back, anyway?" Sarah wiped her face with her hand and then swiped it against her jeans. "I mean, thanks for sending me a driver and all. It was way better than taking an Uber, and it was better getting a ride from someone who *knows* you and Dad, but how—"

"What did that man say to you?" Audrey heard her voice and didn't care that the sound of panic was bristling in its tone.

"I don't know. He... Mom?" Sarah shifted away. Her expression changed. Worry crossed her face. "Mom, you're scaring me a little. Didn't you send that man to pick up me? He knew my birthday, our address. He knew I'd been in Ireland and which castles I—"

"Yes, honey." Audrey shook her head and hugged her daughter again, tightly. "Yes, I... I sent him to get you. I'm sorry. It's been... You're here." She closed her eyes and bit her lip. "You're safe. That's all that matters now."

Sarah held her mother and cried against her chest, all of their emotions advancing again in a second wave. When the crying eased again, Audrey released a heavy exhale, pulled away and stood. She went to the kitchen pantry, withdrew a box of tissues, and set it on the kitchen counter.

"How did it happen, Mom?" Sarah walked toward the kitchen and sat on the high-top stool on the other side of the counter.

Audrey tore open the top of the tissue box and tossed the cardboard flap into the garbage can. She withdrew a sheet for herself and then another, before sliding the box toward Sarah.

"Your dad was having lunch by himself at a restaurant downtown and...it just hit him." Audrey wiped her nose and rested her hands against the counter. "The waitress called 911 and they got him to the hospital pretty fast. The quicker they're able to treat a stroke victim, the better, but..."

She crumpled the tissue and threw it away, and then raised

the second sheet in her hand. "I was with him at the hospital for a while, until he came to and then..." Tears sprung to her eyes. Thinking of Paul on the hospital bed, Audrey couldn't help it, despite everything since. "I was there when he...when it happened."

Sarah had remained still and quiet, listening and letting tears spill down her cheeks. "Did he—" She started to speak and choked on her words. "Did Dad say anything? You know...before?"

Audrey stared at her and swallowed hard. She gave a soft nod.

"What did he say?"

He apologized to me, but I didn't know what for, and now, dearest daughter, now I still only know part of the hellish things your father was doing.

"He said..." Audrey put her hands to her sides and tightened them until she felt her fingernails biting into the flesh of her palms. "He said he loved you very much and..."

Sarah's face broke and she leaned forward, putting her elbows on the counter, laying one hand across her forehead, holding her temples.

"He said to live your life to the fullest." Audrey continued, knowing her daughter needed this.

Sarah's body shook as she cried, but she reached out for the box of tissues and drew one out. A long, weary sigh escaped her as she wiped at her eyes and then blew her nose. She crumpled it in a fist.

It felt like the pressure had been let out of the room.

Tears did that sometimes, Audrey thought, *like destroying an office.*

"Are you thirsty?"

Sarah shook her head.

"Hungry?"

"No, Mom. I'm okay."

Audrey walked around to stand beside her. "Honey, listen, this... this might sound crazy, but you know your father didn't want any funeral or service."

"I know."

"I was going to talk to you about it but I... we're going away, you and I." Audrey rested a hand on Sarah's shoulder. "I know you just got back from Ireland, but I think…"

Audrey looked at her daughter's face and then around the living room. Her gaze landed on the bag of Paul's things on the kitchen counter, and she turned back to Sarah. "I just…" The trembling had been rising inside Audrey, the quaking that seemed to originate from her very core.

"What do you mean we're going away?"

"We're going to Italy for ten days." Audrey forced a small smile and reached out to brush Sarah's hair from her forehead. "You and me. Just the two of us."

Sarah looked down at the counter and cleared her throat. "*Dad just died.*" Her gaze returned to her mother. "And what, we're going on a vacation?"

Audrey let her hand drop from her daughter's shoulder. She could feel the shaking inside her threatening to drain all of her strength again. She took a step back and put her hands flat against the counter. "Sarah… I just don't think I can be here right now. Not with your dad…" She heard her voice raise, cracking with raw emotion and from the screaming she had done recently.

"I can't fucking be here right now! I just can't!" Audrey hated the pain hidden inside her scream like a venomous sac. Audrey hated herself for it. She put a hand up over her mouth and squeezed her eyes shut tightly. She whispered, "I'm sorry."

Sarah's eyes went wide as she stared at her mother. Her expression, only moments ago full of grief and sadness, had been painted with worry and fear. Sarah nodded gently and lowered her voice. "When?"

"Tomorrow morning." Audrey opened her eyes. Her voice sounded drained, absent of energy. "A car will be here in the morning to pick us up." Audrey straightened and locked her knees so she wouldn't fall. "Just take the luggage you came home with, honey. If there's anything else you need, I'll buy it when we get there."

"Okay, Mom." Sarah's voice was soft and resigned, timid as if she'd been scolded.

Audrey closed her eyes and felt her daughter's hand, smooth

and warm, against her cheek. That almost broke Audrey in half. Sarah used to do that all the time as a toddler, and even then, Audrey had thought it such an unusual motherly gesture for a child to do. She reveled in the warmth, and forced a small smile as she opened her eyes again.

"I couldn't sleep on the flight. I kept thinking…" Sarah sniffled and pulled a fresh tissue from the box. "Of *things*, you know? Memories."

"Go try and rest." Audrey patted Sarah's shoulder and watched her walk from the kitchen and down the hallway toward her bedroom.

Audrey waited a few moments, biting back her body's desire to collapse right where she stood. She gathered herself together, and walked toward the entrance of Paul's darkened office. Part of her was stunned Sarah hadn't noticed the open doors, but Audrey also thought maybe it had been such a private part of the house for so long, the space itself didn't even register to her.

After easing the office doors closed, Audrey walked to her bedroom and sat down on the bed. It took less than half an hour to book the trip and the driver for morning.

Fuck the cost.

Exhaustion weighed her muscles and she wanted to lie down on the bed, but instead Audrey pulled a suitcase from her closet. Hoisting it onto the bed, she unzipped the side and started to gather things from her dresser. Audrey stopped, sat on the bed, and stared.

I can't change whatever Paul was doing. It's already done. The only thing I can do is move forward. Me and Sarah. I'll never speak of this, not to her, not to anyone, not even on my deathbed.

Just move forward.

Audrey lay back on the mattress and stared at the ceiling for a long while before her eyes closed on their own.

CHAPTER THIRTY-SEVEN
IRIS: now

"It's true when they say beauty is all a matter of perspective." Iris exhaled smoke through her nose. "Eye of the beholder and all that. What's terrible and ugly to some, others might find wonderfully alluring and...beautiful."

"I would agree," the doctor nodded. "But what makes you say that?"

"No reason." Iris smiled. "Just...thinking out loud." She leaned forward and propped her elbows on the table. "Did you know, on average, a human body has three thousand square inches of skin?"

"No."

"If you break that measurement down into five by five-inch squares, and average...*ohhhh,* say, one or two of those squares a day..." Iris took a quick drag on her cigarette. "It would take approximately five weeks to cover all of those squares."

Doctor Walker gave a slight shake of his head. "I'm not sure I understand."

Iris's smile grew wider.

CHAPTER THIRTY-EIGHT
IRIS: then

The ramp was made of rough plywood, and Iris felt it flex slightly as her feet padded up the incline. As she neared the top, it leveled out onto a circular stage with a ring of overhead spotlights, glaring down on the platform like they should be highlighting a show car. Beyond the stage, a high curving wall encompassed the area. To her left, Iris saw the shine of glass on floor to ceiling windows like box seats at a football stadium. The glass was dark, but she could see silhouettes moving behind it.

Suit-man was waiting for her on stage. His face shone with a layer of sweat beneath the overhead lights. Stepping closer, he placed a hand at the small of her back. In his other hand, he held a wireless microphone, and as he turned toward the windows and spoke, his voice amplified through speakers around the room.

"Verified age of twenty-five, though it appears like a much younger product. Partial, natural, customization on right side. Bidding starts at seventy-five hundred."

Iris looked at the surface of the stage. She could see a path worn on the plywood from the footsteps that had walked here before, and wondered just how many there had been.

"Do I hear a starting bid for seventy-five hundred?" Suit-man stared at the window. "Six thousand?"

Iris thought of the black woman's expression when she asked her "What happens if no one bids on you?"

Suit-man waited, sniffed, and scanned the window. "How about five thousand to start things off?"

Iris saw movement behind the window, a raised arm and a brief flash of a red light.

"Five thousand to start!" Suit-man pointed toward the window, smiled, and began to speed through his words, raising the price to five and a half thousand, then six thousand, and a jump to eight. Each time, Iris saw a pinpoint flash of red light behind the window before he moved on to a higher bid.

Suit-man's hand rested against Iris's back again, and he pulled the string-tie on her bikini top. His hand moved to the back of her neck, undid the bow, and the cloth fell away to the floor, exposing her bare breasts.

The bid jumped to ten thousand, and then twelve. Thirteen. Fifteen. Suit-man repeated fifteen and a half thousand several times, and stopped. "Fifteen thousand. Going once, going twice! Do I hear fifteen and a half thousand?"

There was a flash of red behind the glass. Suit-man smiled and pointed again. "Fifteen-five!"

Iris could hear the excitement grow in his voice as the bid jumped past sixteen thousand, and then to eighteen. His words stopped carrying meaning, an incessant drone from somewhere far away.

I can't be here. How is this happening? How am I here?

"Sold for twenty-one thousand!" The woman from earlier, with the maroon dress and clipboard, stepped from the darkness, picked up the discarded bikini top from the stage, and led Iris away toward the shadows. Iris glanced back to see Suit-man withdraw a walkie-talkie from his suit pocket and hold it to his mouth, away from the microphone. "Green."

The woman brought Iris forward, and a door beside the glass window opened for them. Iris stepped into a linoleum-tiled hallway, and the woman turned to face her.

"Take off the bottoms."

Her insides had become a barren permafrost. A tundra of dead things. Iris felt herself slide the bikini bottoms from her hips and she let them fall to the floor. She stepped free, and the woman with the clipboard handed her the same hospital gown she had arrived in.

Iris put it on, and the woman pulled a cloth bag over Iris's head. She felt herself being guided farther along the hall, heard the metallic sound of heavy latches being opened, before she was nudged forward and hands helped her upward. Cold metal met the bottoms of her feet, and she put her hands in front of her. Reaching out, she touched the familiar pattern of chain-link fencing, and Iris eased herself down to sit as the sounds of latches being closed clanked out around her. Through the chain-link bottom, she could feel a thin carpet beneath her feet.

She heard the soft *thunk* of a vehicle's door being closed. Not a commercial truck though—this was gentler, like a soccer mom's SUV. Iris heard the sound of an engine starting up, and felt the vibration as it idled in place. A radio turned on, and jazz music began to play.

Another vehicle. She was getting transported again.

Her stomach roiled.

Dear God, what now? I just want to go home.

Please, can't you take me home?

CHAPTER THIRTY-NINE
IRIS: then

Iris dozed in the gray twilight sleep as she jostled during the ride.

After what felt like a couple hours of driving, she felt the vehicle come to a stop. The engine shut off and a moment later, the rear of the truck opened up.

Iris felt her cage being dragged, the bottom of the chain-link sliding against the carpet as it moved. The latches were flipped open.

"Come on. Closer."

It was a man's voice, but one she hadn't heard before. Iris still wore the bag over her head as she blindly reached out in front of her. A large hand encircled her right wrist, tugged her forward, and then released her. A pair of hands held her along the sides of her rib cage, and Iris felt herself being lifted, and then set down on her feet.

It's one man, Iris. Only one.

Her right arm was held, and Iris felt herself being led forward a short distance. She heard the sound of rusted hinges and felt the movement of air as a door swung open.

"Take it slowly."

Iris was led inside a structure, and then down a short flight of stairs. The wood beneath her bare feet felt dull and gritty. At the bottom of the stairs, her feet touched rough cement, and they walked forward for several paces before stopping. She heard the man's shoes scuffing as he moved, and then the sound of chains.

This might be your only chance, Iris. Sometimes happy tears come with a little blood

The hospital gown was pulled away from her, tugged down her arms until she stood, naked and bare. She heard a soft gasp of breath from the man and in that single moment of surprise, Iris swung blindly toward the sound.

Her balled right fist connected with his flesh, and Iris felt his lower jaw shift from the impact. She twisted, swinging her left foot straight up, hard and fast, aiming for what she hoped was his crotch, but she missed and hit nothing but air.

With the bag over her head, Iris felt something smash against the side of her face and rocked her sideways. A hand reached out and caught her by her throat, encircling it tightly.

"Now, now." His voice was low, a father comforting a child over night terrors. "Time to settle down."

He held her there, by the neck, and behind the bag on her head, Iris saw black sunspots in her vision as his hold cut off her air. She clawed at his hand with her blunt-nailed fingers, but his grip may as well have been a steel vice. Her pulse pounded in her ears and heat flooded her eyes.

Iris let her arms fall to her sides again and the man eased her down to sit on the cement floor and released her throat. She choked and gulped in mouthfuls of air, but sat still, feeling the pain coursing through her face.

"That's better. *Shhhhh...* sit there like a good girl."

First one wrist, and then the other, Iris felt something wrapped around them and buckled tightly. Links of heavy chain rattled against each other and her arms felt weighted. She moved her arms slightly, and felt her hands move in sync, connected somehow.

"Now, then."

The bag was pulled from Iris's head, and she blinked at the Man in front of her. The light here was dim—cast from a yellow bulb in a wire cage mounted on a wall to her left. He was tall—easily a foot taller than she was—and broad in his shoulders and chest. His hair was brown, graying at the temples, and his face showed the lines of middle age.

He studied her face, and then the Man's gaze dropped down to her breasts and the scars on her body. Staring, he released a heavy exhale, and then looked at her face again. "There's a...a place to sleep. Blanket if you're cold." He motioned with his hand toward a wall. "There's always water if you're thirsty, and some days I'll bring you orange juice."

Iris saw a row of large white translucent bottles—all of them secured to the wall with thin metal straps. They were upside down and had a bent metal tube protruding from black caps.

They're water bottles for animals, the kind used for hamsters and rabbits.

"I'll be back in the morning to feed you, and tomorrow... tomorrow, we can begin."

Iris watched his Adam's apple move as he swallowed. His voice was shallow, words slightly breathless. She noticed his gaze had returned to her burn scars.

There was *excitement* in his eyes—a new toy to play with.

He gave a slight nod, and put his hands in his pants pockets— *Nathan used to do that when he was upset. Or excited about something.*

—and walked away toward the stairs. She heard hinges creak as a door opened and closed, and then it was silent.

Iris looked overhead and noticed thick wooden beams and the underside of narrow wooden slats from the floor above. Cobwebs swayed in the corners. On three sides of her, Iris saw horizontal wooden boards making up a stall. At one point, the boards must have been worn and weathered, but they had been painted over in a chalky white. The floor beneath her was rough cement, full of pockmarks and stained patches.

Iris looked down. Her wrists wore thick leather cuffs with two buckled straps on each band. Connecting them was a stiff black rod that looked like a piece of plastic PVC pipe. There was a chain threaded through the pipe that rattled when she moved, and Iris realized there was no way for one hand to reach the other and undo the buckled straps. She raised her hands toward her mouth, wondering if she could use her teeth to undo the straps, but they were buckled tightly against her inner wrists and the pipe prevented her from reaching them.

She moved her arms and watched a length of chain ripple against cement. Iris followed the chain with her eyes and saw it led to a metal square bolted into the wall at the rear of the stall.

The place smelled used—earthy and slightly sweet, and of something else rich and unsavory she didn't recognize. Iris walked toward the mattress in the back of the stall and sat down on its thin cushion. The fabric was stained in places and she didn't want to think about what had caused them.

In the corridor, just beyond the stall, stood a bare wooden

workstation, like a gardener's bench, and above it were two closed cabinets. Past that, in the shadows, Iris saw the end of a thick chain laying on the cement, snaking away toward the dim shape of a mattress similar to the one she sat on.

It was so quiet the silence made her ears ring.

The plastic pipe between her wrists forced Iris to reach with both hands, but she picked up a thin blanket from the edge of the bed and shook it open. Iris swung it around and maneuvered the slightly damp cloth until it covered her like a cloak, and she pulled it tightly around her.

Iris waited.

She woke to the sound of tearing paper, but the noise stuttered like Morse Code. Iris opened her eyes and saw the Man, crouched on one knee as he ripped a strip from the top of a large bag. He wore faded jeans and a long-sleeve light blue shirt with the cuffs rolled up to his elbows. Tossing the piece of paper aside, he moved the now open bag into her area, positioning it beneath the water bottles against the wall.

Iris sat up on the mattress pad, still holding the blanket around her body.

The bag was bright yellow with a swirling circular design in the center, framing a photo of a smiling bulldog. *Ol' Roy Dinner Rounds* rested in a banner beneath the phrase *Now with More Beef Flavor!*

"I figure you'll be hungry...after." The Man stood before her, his hands on his hips. He licked his lips. "You are *so very special.*"

He had a light sheen of perspiration on his face though it wasn't warm. He went to the workstation, opened a cabinet, and pulled something free. "I hate to do this, but in my experience, it's..." He glanced away from her, and flicked his tongue over his lips again. *"Necessary."*

The Man knelt down in front of her. He didn't look into Iris's eyes, only focused on her mouth. He made a face, reached into his shirt pocket, and retrieved a small tube of lip balm. He uncapped the end, held the back of her head with one hand, and then ran balm over her cracked lips.

Iris tasted mint and vanilla.

"There, that's better." The Man nodded, appraising his effort.

Iris watched as he recapped the tube and returned it to his shirt pocket. He lifted something from the floor at his side, and stretched forward, bringing a strap across the front of Iris's face. A spongy ball pressed against her lips.

"Open."

She did as she was told, and the ball nestled into the depression of her open mouth. Iris's tongue tested the surface of the ball gag. It tasted salty. *Used.* Grit from the floor speckled its texture. There was no choice but to breathe through her nose.

He finished buckling the contraption behind her head, nodded to himself, and walked toward the rear wall of the stall. "Stand up."

Iris did as she was told and heard the sound of chain links being pulled against metal. She felt a tug on her arms and turned to watch the Man pull the length of chain like a cord on a flagpole, drawing her back against the wall and raising her arms above her head. He hooked a link of chain onto a bolt set into the wall and walked back toward the workstation.

Iris looked down at her leather-cuffed wrists as she heard the Man moving things around in the cabinet.

"Beauty is a strange thing. It's all a matter of perspective, really. What is terrible and ugly to some, holds such beauty and allure to others." He withdrew items from the cabinet and returned, stopped in front of her, and his work boots—clean and unmuddied—came into Iris's line of sight.

In his left hand, the Man held a narrow blue tank the size and shape of a coffee thermos, except for a small pipe extending from the end. He adjusted a dial near the pipe, and Iris heard a slight hissing noise.

He moved his right hand to his shirt pocket and withdrew a wooden match.

Iris glanced at the small blue tank.

God, no.

The world turned on its axis. Iris's chest ached, her heart clenched in a fist of ice. Frost grew over her bare skin. Urine streamed down her legs as her bladder gave way.

The Man's gaze snapped back to her, flashing down to her lower half at the liquid dripping to the cement. "*Shhhh,* it's okay. That happens sometimes."

He ran the match along the length of his jeaned thigh and Iris watched the tip of the wooden stick burst into flame.

I can't be here. This isn't happening to me.

The Man held out the match to the end of the cannister's pipe, and blue flame at the tip *whuffed* to life. He waved the match in the air, and dropped the sliver of wood onto the cement floor.

He was breathing faster. His tongue flicked out over his lips.

One hand held the blue canister, and in his other hand, the Man held a piece of cast iron the length of a fly swatter. A handle of dull, aged wood was at one end, but the Man angled the other end toward the blue flame of the torch. That side had been shaped into a flattened square roughly the size of a slice of bread.

"Transformation can sometimes be...*painful.*" He nodded slightly as he watched the torch lick the surface of the cast iron. "But when you're finished, on the other side of it all, you realize it was all worth it."

Iris's body shuddered. Her fingers were ice-covered branches. She stared at the flame of the torch and watched the cast iron begin to take on the color of sunset. Orange and yellow spread over the square shape, until the entire surface glowed.

"It takes time, yes." The Man set the cannister onto the floor, and moved closer. "Effort."

Iris shook her head at the Man. Her breath was ragged panic-soaked hitches through her flaring nostrils. She bit down on the rubber ball against her mouth.

His free hand gripped Iris by her throat. The Man held her there as he pressed the red-hot piece of iron against the smooth, unmarred flesh of her sternum.

Her world detonated with agony.

CHAPTER FORTY
AUDREY: now

"If you had come forward back then, you could have had protection, you know? From all of this. You and your daughter, both."

"I couldn't risk it, Detective." Audrey shook her head, raised the crumpled tissue in her hand, and wiped at her nose. "Couldn't risk my daughter. She's—"

"You had her and a few million dollars." Blevins' expression was sympathetic but distant, a look of observation, waiting for her reaction.

"It was never about the money," she whispered. "Yes, it made life easier, but I'd give it all away, every penny, if none of this had ever happened."

"Mrs. Dugan..." The detective looked away from her, sighed and nodded. "Random crimes happen every day for one reason or another. Terrible, *horrible* things. But something like this? Not so much. Not without motive. This kind of thing...is personal."

Blevins leaned his elbows on the table and steepled his hands together. "I'm going to ask you this once more, and I want you to answer truthfully. I *need* you to answer truthfully."

Audrey wiped at her eyes and nodded.

"Mrs. Dugan, did you know the assailant?"

Audrey stared at her hands resting in her lap. She picked at the tissue.

"Audrey?"

"No." She shook her head slightly as she whispered. "I didn't know her, but Paul..." She swallowed, and the glare in her eyes sharpened. "I'm certain my husband did."

CHAPTER FORTY-ONE
AUDREY: then

Audrey zipped her luggage bag closed and stared at it.

If there was anything else she or Sarah needed, Audrey would buy it in Italy.

Money certainly isn't an issue now, is it? The cost of booking an immediate trip to Italy was a small fortune, at least it used to be. Now? It won't even be missed.

A bitter laugh escaped her, almost degrading into a sob before Audrey bit it back.

She set the luggage on the carpet, extended the handle, and wheeled the bag out into the hallway, stopping at the line where the carpet met the kitchen linoleum.

It was early, and Audrey went through the routine of making coffee. She crossed the living room floor and stopped at the sliding glass door to the back yard. There was a moment of hesitation, and then Audrey opened the door and stepped outside.

The early morning air was warm, but the chair felt cool against her skin as she sat down. Audrey glanced at the bottle of vodka, and at the burner phone on the other side of the table. She stretched forward, picked it up, and then flipped it open with her thumb as she rested back against the chair. The screen showed nothing new since she had last inspected it—no text messages or calls. She used the arrows on the small keyboard of the phone and navigated to the icon for PHOTOS, took a deep breath, and selected it.

Empty.

Audrey closed the phone, put it on the table, and stared overhead.

The sky was a rich, cloudless indigo with the faintest glow of predawn light. Audrey stared at the stars. The Polaroid images of the girl looped through her mind like a film reel. Her scarred flesh, some of it charred black in spots. The vacant expression on the girl's face, experiencing an agony so deep, her mind had drifted away from it all. Audrey thought of the girl's hair, framing her face in oily strings. She thought of the wooden slats in the background behind her, corralling her like some kind of animal.

Audrey thought of the first time she'd held the photographs. How her hands shook when she saw the account deposit notification on her phone. She thought of Mr. Schmidt, hugging Sarah, comforting her.

Motherfucker!

She stood, grabbed Paul's burner phone, and flipped it open once more. Audrey gripped the phone in both hands and twisted, gritting her teeth as the two halves of the phone cracked apart. She raised her hands and took a step toward the pool, but stopped.

The lawn sparkled with morning dew, and Audrey ran from the deck out into the grass, continued running until she reached back where the honeysuckle vines and wild raspberry grew in thick tangles, and the woods began. She stopped, raised her right hand, and threw, as hard as she could, toward the underbrush. After the first half, Audrey shifted the other portion of the phone into her right hand and made a second throw into the undergrowth.

She heard whispering noises as the phone flew through leaves and greenery, and then it landed with a dull thud. Audrey's chest heaved, as if she had just finished a marathon, and she stared into the patch of shadows, catching her breath again. When the crickets resumed their interrupted chorus, she finally turned and walked back toward the house.

Wet footprints from the moisture of the grass marked her trail on the cement surrounding the pool but began to fade as Audrey got closer to the sliding glass doors. The smell of freshly brewed coffee greeted her and she withdrew a single mug, put it on the counter, and then grabbed the creamer from the refrigerator.

Shuffling steps caught her attention, and Audrey saw Sarah, yawning and rubbing one eye, as she approached from the hallway.

"Good morning, Honey." Audrey reached for the cupboard and paused. "Coffee?"

"Yes, please." Sarah sat down on a stool on the other side of the kitchen counter.

Audrey pulled a second mug from the cabinet, filled them both and added cream. She slid a mug in Sarah's direction. "How'd you sleep?"

"Okay, I guess." Sarah sipped from her mug. "Woke up a few times, but I was exhausted. But then again," she glanced at the clock on the microwave. "Normally, I would have already been awake for about four hours."

"Well, you won't have to try to get used to a time zone difference just yet. Italy's five hours ahead, same as Ireland." Audrey sighed. "You hungry? Want some breakfast?"

"Still not very hungry." Sarah raised her mug in a *cheers* motion. "Coffee though. Coffee and a shower. Something about being on a flight that long with so many other people just makes me feel *yecccchh.*"

"Then you'd better hurry up with that coffee and get moving. We've only got about forty minutes or so until the cab gets here."

Sarah nodded, her eyes half open. She got off the stool and carried her mug as she walked back toward her bedroom.

Turning toward the fridge, Audrey opened the door and scanned over the contents. She grabbed the half-empty jug of milk and poured it down the kitchen sink, setting the container to the side. After that, Audrey withdrew a deli bag of sliced turkey, half a head of lettuce, and a plastic container of leftovers from three days ago. None of it would still be good by the time they got back from their trip.

All of it went into the trash and Audrey tied the bag off and pulled it free from the can. She shook open a fresh bag and lined the inside of the can, picked up the trash, and walked toward the door to the garage.

Three large plastic garbage cans rested against the wall of the garage. Audrey walked to the first one, only half-full, and tossed the trash bag inside it. She put her hands on her hips stared at them for a moment, and then turned, slowly, toward the garage windows.

Paul's barn stood in the distance, roughly a hundred yards away.

The girl in the photos. The slats of white boards in the background.

Audrey stared at the large building. Paul's barn.

Off limits, just like his office.

Audrey's gaze remained for a moment longer, and then she

hurried inside the house and walked directly to her toolbox on the pantry floor.

CHAPTER FORTY-TWO
AUDREY: then

Audrey swung her hammer against the padlock on the barn door latch. The lock bounced against the steel hoop and swung back in place, unharmed. She planted her free hand against the wooden door to stabilize her stance, and slammed it again, twice. She could see glints of dented metal along the edge of the lock.

She stopped and turned the hammer over to slide the claw end beneath the latch attached to the wooden door. The hammer was small, a tool for basic household chores, but the physics still applied. She levered the handle down and the nails on the metal strap began to pull free of the old barn wood. A few adjustments and more pressure, and the latch pulled free, hanging limp and useless with the lock still intact.

Audrey eased the door open.

A metal box with a light switch was attached to a wooden beam on her left, and Audrey flipped the switch. A row of low-wattage lights flicked on overhead and she paused. The old poker table Paul had bought sat off to the right, covered with a dusty canvas drop cloth. A refrigerator emitting a soft hum sat close to it, nestled against the wall. She knew Paul had gotten a second fridge out here, probably still stocked with cold beer, and her gaze ran over the collection of liquor bottles on top of it.

A silver boom box rested on a bench to the side of the fridge, and she could see several CD cases stacked on top of it. Audrey took a few steps inside the barn. Even though it hadn't been used for farm work in years, it still smelled sweetly of old hay.

The riding mower was parked on the left side of the barn, and Audrey saw a stack of lawn chairs beside it. Paul's bag of golf clubs. Sarah's mountain bike. Inflatable floating chairs.

There was a quick flutter in the rafters overhead, and Audrey flinched reflexively. A series of excited chirps broke the quiet, and the dark blur of a startled barn swallow flew past her and through the open doorway.

Hand-hewn beams stretched the width of the barn, with

wooden rafters as thick as her waist, all shaped and notched by hand to fit together like a jigsaw puzzle. Above those, Audrey saw the underside of the rippled tin roofing panels, angling down to meet the tall vertical beams and wooden slats of the barn's exterior. Thin yellow light of sunrise filtered in between the boards.

Gathered around the base of a support beam, Audrey saw a cluster of drip-streaked paint cans. Some of the boards at the far corner of the barn were painted white, though she could see a thick coating of cobwebs and dust on them even from a distance. She remembered the unfinished job and the cans from when they had moved in. Paul had made the comment that painting the barn's interior must have been a much bigger project than the farmer had considered.

Lengths of rough-cut lumber lay across the beams overhead, along with several oddball pieces of plywood.

I'm not going to throw that stuff out. Maybe one day I'll use that old barn wood to make a bookshelf or a bench, maybe. Paul had said that to her the first week after they had moved in, and they had never been touched since. It had started with Paul calling the barn his man-cave. At the start, there were poker nights once or twice a month—a boys only club.

Then one day Audrey had discovered a lock on the door when she wanted to retrieve her and Sarah's bikes for a ride. Paul had shrugged it off as protecting the lawn mower and tools, though he had moved the bikes to the garage soon after.

But no, Audrey thought, *the barn had become off-limits, same as his office.*

Thinking back, Audrey realized she hadn't so much as stepped foot in the building since a few weeks after they had moved in, seven years ago.

But I didn't care. I have my greenhouse and an entire upstairs room I do oil paintings in. Or did, at least. Even that has been months ago.

Paul never invaded those spaces—my spaces—not once.

What did I care if he had his own spots for him and him alone?

Audrey stepped farther into the barn as the sunlight outside grew stronger. It was a sturdy structure, built right from the start—there was barely any give in the old floorboards. Cobwebs decorated the right-angle junctions of almost every wooden beam, and Audrey saw movement in some of them, their spindly builders hard at work.

The barn was off limits, like his office. Like the wall safe I didn't even know about.

Audrey stopped and looked around. The card table and summer things, the lawnmower—normal things any family might have in a storage shed or garage. She sighed and realized she had been gripping the wooden handle of the hammer so tightly the palm of her right hand ached.

What did you expect, Audrey, some kind of horror movie?

She let the hammer drop to the wooden floor and it landed head first and fell onto its side. The cab would be here soon, and she had to gather everything to get ready. Audrey turned toward the door.

Just move forward, Audrey. You and Sarah both. Put it behind—

A cough, raspy and harsh, stopped her.

Slowly, Audrey turned toward the rear of the barn. She swallowed hard, and noticed the section along the wall, the cut-out in the floor revealing a set of stairs leading below.

Audrey took her time, choosing each step carefully to be quiet, and she slowly made her way to the top of the stairs. She paused, cocked her head, and listened.

She heard the faintest noise of chains rattling against cement.

CHAPTER FORTY-THREE
IRIS: now

"There isn't any..." Doctor Walker put a hand to his mouth and cleared his throat. "There's no documentation or, uh..." He glanced at her uncomfortably and flipped through the folder aimlessly, before staring at the papers.

"Iris, how much of your body..." He looked up at her with a helpless and confused expression.

The woman leaned forward on the table, the better for him to see her. "Everything except what's left on my pretty little face, Doctor."

"How..." The doctor's hands tightened to fists, and he kept running his thumbs back and forth over his closed fingers. The color drained from his face. He cleared his throat again. "How... how long did this continue?"

Iris shrugged and leaned back, bringing the cigarette to her mouth for a puff. "Hard to say, really. The days all sort of blended together, but if I had to guess, I'd say it was close to a month and a half."

"Christ," he whispered and ran a hand over his head.

"*Every day*, sometimes once in the morning and once at night." Iris nodded and shifted in her chair. "He would put burn ointment on me in the evening and give me painkillers."

She pointed at the doctor with her hand holding the cigarette. "He never tried anything sexual, though, I'm not sure if he planned to eventually or not. Closest he came was taking his shirt off one night. I saw his skin, scarred and twisted like strawberry taffy."

Iris tilted the Winston in her fingers, watching the smoke rise into the air. "He had been burned too. I don't know, maybe he was waiting until I was complete, you know? Like he was some fucking artist refining his work until it matched the vision in his head."

Iris stubbed out the end of her cigarette in the ashtray. "The first three or four times, he used the ball gag and tightened the chains against the wall so I couldn't move. After that, it just became something happening to me. Another experience like anything else, like...eating a popsicle or brushing my hair.

There was no need for it anymore."

Her voice lowered to a whisper and she raised her hands to pantomime the actions matching her words. "That hot iron would come down against my thighs or breasts and I would *hear* it sizzle. It would make me shake in place, that sensation, but I didn't try to scream anymore. I didn't cry. Didn't react."

"Why not?"

Iris watched the smoke rising from her stubbed cigarette butt, and then glared at the doctor. "Because *fuck him*, that's why."

She let her gaze remain on the doctor and then snatched her pack of cigarettes to shake loose a fresh one.

CHAPTER FORTY-FOUR
IRIS: then

The Man stood at the edge of Iris's stall, his chest heaving, damp ovals of sweat soaking his shirt beneath his armpits. He stepped toward the row of water bottles, and Iris watched as he pressed a fingertip to the ball bearing at the bottom of one of the metal tubes. Water flowed from it in a weak stream, and the Man held a hairbrush in his other hand beneath the flow.

He moved closer and brushed the right side of her hair away from her face. Earlier, he had tried to use a thin silver barrette to pin it back, but it wouldn't stay in place. Moving back and forth from Iris to the water bottle, the Man continued to soak the brush and run it through her hair. He finally offered a grunt of approval.

His eyes scanned over her body and he frowned. "You uh…" He walked toward the workstation and knelt to the lower cabinets. "I have things, supplies, but you have to…" The Man shut the cabinets and stood, carrying a small stool in one hand and a tampon in the other. He sat down in front of her on the stool and opened the tampon wrapper.

"Spread your… spread your legs more." He leaned forward and slid the plastic applicator inside her with a practiced move. When the Man's breath quickened, he paused, and then pushed the plunger all the way down, hesitating again before slowly withdrawing the applicator.

He swallowed hard, picked the plastic wrapper from the floor, and walked to the workstation again. Iris watched him put his palms flat on the tabletop and take several deep breaths. After a moment, he went through the cabinets and brought out the implements he had come to use on her daily. He walked back, sat down on the small stool, and lifted her left arm. "Now then, let's have a look."

Iris watched him inspect the blistered patch of skin at the center of her arm, along the crease of her inner elbow. The square of flesh was an angry red, cratered with raised, pale-colored pustules. Reaching into his pants pocket, The Man withdrew something the size and shape of a travel tube of toothpaste. He uncapped the end, squeezed a blob onto the first and second fingers of his right hand, and delicately screwed the cap back on before returning it to his pocket.

"This will help." He gingerly smeared the yellowish cream onto Iris's inner arm. His breath quickened as he ran his fingertips over her damaged flesh.

It felt like molten-hot razors dragging over her arm, but Iris wouldn't let herself be there. In her mind, she was standing behind him, staring over his shoulder, watching the expression on her own face, carved of stone.

He let go of her arm and shifted on the stool, straightening his left leg and reaching into his other pants pocket. This time, he drew out a box of matches.

Diamond Strike Anywhere Matches. Same kind Dad used to bring on camping trips.

The Man picked up the blue canister, and hell began again.

It was almost ritualistic by now, the process of it all—a gentle turn of the dial on the canister, the low hiss of escaping pressure, the sharp flick of the match as it caught light, and the glowing sapphire flame huffing to life. Like a sunrise emerging from a black sky, the square of iron shifting in color to an orange blaze.

The agony the heat brought to her was so intense it broke through the other end of the spectrum into the void. Iris felt like she was being plunged into a frozen river for a split-second, and then there was nothing—no sensation at all.

Iris watched his tongue flick out several times and the Man bit his lower lip and adjusted how he sat on the stool. He put his left hand at the back of her neck and used his strong thumb beneath her chin to lift her head toward the ceiling.

"Okay. You should…" He swallowed hard. "You should close your eyes."

His words were a breathless whisper as he moved the hot square of iron toward Iris's face. When it was close enough to feel the heat, Iris closed her eyes and tried to let herself dissolve into nothingness.

Tears swam along the bottom edge of her eyelids, making them flutter. Iris felt the Man's grip adjusting the angle of her head as he pressed the iron against her skin, crisping the hollow of her right cheek and the angle of her cheekbone above it. The scorching heat adjusted with her position, and she felt the Man repositioning the iron along the outer ridge of her skull, against her temple.

Her legs began to shake.

The boardwalk, with its endless path of weathered gray wood. Nathan, floating in the ocean. His smile. Faint tan lines on the sides of his face from his sunglasses. The smell of saltwater. Watching the drops run down his body as he stepped onto the beach. The coconut scent of suntan lotion. The feel of the sun on my skin. The way it made my skin—

She smelled her cooking flesh, acrid and metallic, but mildly sweet. Iris's breath hitched in her chest and her eyes shot open as she flinched in reflex. Her right eye saw the briefest flash of glowing orange and she snapped her eyes closed tightly. Her mouth opened on its own, trying to gulp in lungfuls of air.

Everything she had experienced before was insignificant. *Nothing.*

Now, the ground had opened up and swallowed the very definition of what pain was. This was something else entirely.

Her mouth gagged, hands bound, Iris's mind rebelled against the sensation. A loud ringing exploded in her ears and she felt detached from herself. Floating.

"Fuck!"

Iris heard the Man curse and the tumble of the wooden stool as it fell back away from him. She squeezed her eyes shut and shook her head. Her right eye was a hunk of charcoal, a burning ember living in the house of her skull. She wheezed, tried to breathe, and lurched at the leather cuffs holding her wrists.

The hot iron clamored to the cement, and Iris opened her left eye to watch the Man running away from her. He grabbed one of the water bottles from the wall rack and wrenched it free of its metal bracket.

Then his hands were on her face, pushing her head backward so she was looking skyward. Iris felt a stream of water at the bridge of her nose, pooling in both wells of her eyes. She blinked and felt the cool liquid wash across her right eye. It flowed and swirled and Iris blinked again, seeing flashes of the Man's silhouette against the caged wall light behind him.

More water, and still more, flushing her eyes. Iris thrashed against it and the Man clenched a fist full of hair on the back of her head, holding her in place. She heard the water splashing against the cement below, and finally, the Man released her and threw the bottle toward the workstation.

"Why did you do that?" He gritted his teeth and raised his voice. *"Why?"*

Iris opened her left eye, ignoring the drops of liquid hanging from her lashes. She blinked and the waterdrops fell free. She stared into the Man's face.

A rictus of anger washed over his face and his arms became rigid steel bars with clenched fists at his side. His cheeks were flushed, and he screamed. *"Why did you do that?"*

He walked away, stopped at the workbench with his back to her, and put his hands on his hips. Iris saw him shake his head. Reaching into one of the cabinets, the Man picked something up and returned to her. He stooped down to lift the water bottle, and then looked at her face. His expression had changed to disappointment now, almost on the verge of tears, and his voice lowered to a whisper. "Why did you do that?"

Holding his palm out to her, Iris saw a group of four pills, but her hands didn't want to cooperate with her mind. They lay, dead as river stones, like any chance of her giving him a response.

Her right eye was the embodiment of the sun, a volcano on some distant island, a mansion with a foundation built in hell. Her face throbbed and pulsed with the new burns, but Iris's eye was the core of it all. A seething, raging furnace.

The Man nodded and fed the pills to her one by one, pushing them between her lips and teeth. He lifted the water bottle stem to her lips to give her a drink.

Iris forced her right eye to open, and the Man's face was warped, the sight of him rippled like heat waves off of asphalt. Hot liquid flowed from her eye over her cheek, and she felt the salty sting against the inner pulse it had developed.

The Man grimaced and turned his gaze away. He chewed on his lower lip and sucked air between his teeth. His arms hung loosely at his sides and he looked like a child who had broken something important while their parents were away, and had no idea how to fix it.

He walked away without another word, and Iris crawled toward the mattress. She was cold all the time lately, a shiver to the core of her bones—she knew it was her body rebelling against the Man's *sessions* with her.

She lay there as the painkillers filled her with white static, and her mind drifted in and out of the shadows. The sensation of silk ribbon pulling through her fingers woke her, and Iris looked down to see a slender, gray snake wriggling between the first and second fingers of her left hand. Its thin forked tongue flicked out, tasting the air, and Iris continued watching as it slithered on, smooth skin like a whisper against hers.

There was a flash of movement from the space beyond her stall, and she saw another snake of the same coloring, this one the length of her forearm and bulging in its mid-section as it crawled across the cement floor. She watched its tail disappear as it went behind the workstation.

The sounds of the man entering the building and walking downstairs made Iris turn her head. The painkillers were thrumming through her body, but she saw him kneel down beside her. He took her hand and she felt the soft crinkle of plastic press against her palm. It was cold, and Iris opened her left eye to see a zip lock baggie half-filled with crushed ice.

The Man walked away again, leaving her alone in the dim light.

BURNER

180

CHAPTER FORTY-FIVE
IRIS: then

Iris sat up on the mattress, smelling her own filth. It had been four days since she had last seen the Man. The bag of *Ol' Roy* dogfood was almost gone. Except for the last in line, the row of water bottles was empty, and even that container was less than half-full.

Her stall stank of urine and bowel movements. And blood. Her menstrual blood.

After the first day of the Man's absence, she had struggled with the bar between her wrists, but eventually she had removed her tampon. She didn't believe he was coming back to give her a fresh one.

Iris coughed. Her throat was dry, and she glanced at the remaining water.

The burn on her inner elbow had crusted over, and thin fissures in the flesh leaked a weak yellow pus. When she flexed her arm, flakes of skin sifted from it like ashes from charred firewood.

Weak tears leaked from her right eye constantly, as if it had been lanced to dribble away the gift of sight. The vision had passed beyond dim and warped to barely anything at all. Even when Iris crawled close to the white-washed slats of the stall, the sight through that eye was nothing but smears of charcoal. Opening her eye felt like unfolding an old dry-rotted leather wallet.

Slow footsteps padded in her direction, and Iris listened to their cadence. These steps were soft and cautious. These were timid and lacked confidence.

The footsteps paused, shifting on the slight grit of the cement floor.

Those footsteps aren't the Man.

Iris lurched from the mattress and crawled across the stall floor, yanking at the chain connected to the wall behind her. It snapped her wrists and arms, jolting her to a stop, and as she looked into the hall, Iris felt the breath flood from her lungs.

A woman stood in the corridor beyond her stall. She flinched, took a step backward, and raised a hand to cover her mouth.

Iris saw the woman's expression, her eyes wide with shock.

"Pleaassseeee..." Iris's voice was a foreign sound—dry wind rattling cornhusks in a field. She couldn't remember the last time she had spoken out loud, could barely recall screaming her throat into raw rags behind the ball gag. *"Help meeeeee!"*

The woman released a heavy exhale of air. A thin whine escaped from her mouth.

Iris recognized the expression—the woman couldn't accept the reality in front of her. Iris pulled at her chains, hearing them clink against each other as she yanked them taut against the anchor in the wall. *"Pleeeassse!"*

The woman took a step forward, and then stopped. Her gaze began to shift back and forth over the stall and the mattress, the row of water bottles strapped to the wall. She shook her head and the noise in her throat deepened, shaping into a low mantra. *"Nononononononono."*

She turned her back to Iris, took a step, and then another. And then the woman ran down the corridor with her arms stiff and straight at her sides, swinging them like a spooked child in a darkened wood.

"Come back!" Iris screamed through the ruined tatters of her throat. *"Pleeasse!"* She lunged at the end of her chains and her wrists snapped back over her head. *"Hellpp meeee!"*

The woman's footsteps thumped up the wooden stairs, and Iris listened to the distant dull sound of a door slamming shut.

Iris fell to her knees on the pavement and slammed her fists, and the connecting bar, against her scarred thighs. Her heart was a lumbering machine in her chest. The noises from her throat filled with primal grief.

She screamed but there was no longer anyone to hear.

CHAPTER FORTY-SIX
AUDREY: now

"Mrs. Dugan…" Blevins loosened his necktie and then pulled on the knot itself, taking the entire tie off. He tossed it on the side of his desk, undid the top button of his dress shirt, and exhaled. There was a brief vibrating noise from his suit and he reached inside, withdrew his phone and checked the screen, then put it back in his jacket pocket.

"Do you need to call someone?" Audrey's voice was timid, resigned.

"No, I…" He ran a hand over his face and back over his head. "I don't know what the fuck—" He stopped himself and cleared his throat. "Mrs. Dugan, you *fired* your attorney and—"

"That *wasn't* my attorn—"

"You should probably get one." The detective sucked on his lower lip, and waved his hand, dismissing her interjection. "You *intentionally* walked away from a woman chained up in your barn." He moistened his lips with his tongue. "You're telling me all of this and I—"

"Detective Blevins," Audrey leaned forward and spoke directly to the recorder on his desk. "I'll admit all of this again in a confession, an official one." She stared into his eyes a moment, and then leaned back.

"Christ." Blevins held his hand against the lower half of his face, his gaze on the woman. He held it for a moment, and then pulled it away. "And you just left? You and your daughter just… flew off to Italy?"

Audrey looked down at her lap. "Every single day, I think back to that moment, Detective. Every single day. I think about her eyes, pleading with me, *begging* me to save her. I hear her voice, full of pain. How absolutely… *tortured* she sounded. I cannot begin to imagine the hell that girl was put through. Everywhere I could see, her body had been *fucking burned* and—"

Her voice broke. Her eyes glassed over and she sniffled and daubed the tissue beneath her nose. "I would trade everything to go back and do the right thing."

"Why the hell didn't you?" Blevins shook his head and he turned away to stare past her. Both of them were silent for a few moments. His eyes were tired. He tapped the desk with his fingertips.

Audrey tilted her head slightly and stared at the detective. She looked worn and weathered. The light in the room made the shadows beneath her eyes even darker.

After a moment, the man nodded. "Yeah, sure...your daughter."

"The cab came to get us. Sarah and I flew away."

"For ten days?"

She nodded.

"And when you got back?"

Audrey blinked slowly at him and turned to her hands again. "After we got back, that was when the start of *my* hell began."

CHAPTER FORTY-SEVEN
AUDREY: then

She wasn't real.

By the fifth day of the trip, the thought had settled in Audrey's mind. It came to her on the streets, at the hotel, and on tours, the three words repeating like a tribal drum.

She wasn't real.

On the first full day, she and Sarah had visited Vatican City and the Sistine Chapel. They had stared so long at the ceiling, Audrey's neck had begun to hurt. The mural was beautiful beyond words, but soon after leaving, Audrey couldn't even conjure the image of God and Adam reaching out to touch each other's fingertips. It was as if she was seeing and hearing everything through a haze of static.

When bedtime of the first day arrived, and they readied for sleep, Audrey's thoughts turned to the girl again. Her voice, pleading and frantic. Desperate.

Once, Audrey reached for her phone, but then wondered who she was going to call. The police? Then what? *Everything* would come out. The Hawkins Group, Paul's involvement—*whatever that was*—and however deep it may be.

The girl is still in your fucking barn, Audrey. You can't just throw her in the fire pit and pretend she never existed.

A heavy, breaking sob almost escaped before Audrey capped her hand over her mouth. If everything came out, if she went to the police, how would she and Sarah be protected? These weren't small-time criminals, these were wealthy men—lots of money was involved, and they wouldn't take this lightly. She swallowed hard and listened to Sarah breathing peacefully in her sleep.

Audrey stared at the ceiling.

Even if they *could* be protected, if everything came out, it would follow Sarah forever. Her entire life would be stained. It was doubtful Sarah would even talk with her again, knowing her mother knew about the girl in the barn and did nothing. If everything came out, about Paul, about this, it would kill Sarah, shatter and break her like carnival glass.

Audrey drank wine each night to help her sleep, but when rest finally came, it was fitful and uneasy. She dreamt of waves crashing against Italian beaches, but in her dreams, it was the sound of chains being dragged across weathered cement.

It had taken a little convincing, but on the seventh day Sarah talked her into renting Vespa scooters and driving to the Colosseum. Sarah had taken the lead on the drive, and Audrey was thankful for it. They arrived and parked, and Audrey realized she had no memory of the route they took to get there. It was as if she had been dreaming the entire time, observing as a spectator in someone else's life, and then awoken as Sarah had come to a stop at a cobblestone street.

They toured the Colosseum and Sarah marveled at the structure. Audrey heard the early part of the tour guide's words, explaining how the structure was completed in 80 AD and held anywhere from fifty to eighty thousand spectators at a time.

She wasn't real.

The mantra in Audrey's head drowned out the rest of the guide's words for the entire tour, and when it was over, they drove the scooters back to the hotel. Audrey imagined this is how a concussion had to feel—dreamy and confusing and faraway.

On the eighth day, they had eaten breakfast and drank espressos at an outdoor café. Sarah said it was the stereotypical Italian movie scene, and they just *had* to do it. Afterward, they took a tour bus to Pompeii, photographing and admiring the sites.

Audrey felt out of body as the bus drove on, as if she was a kite adrift in a high wind.

It had been 2,000 years since the volcano left Pompeii in ruins, and Audrey watched Sarah trail her fingertips along the ancient walls, her expression enthralled, fascinated. A thriving community at one time, and so many people, dead and buried beneath fire and ash in moments. The tour guide led the group through the narrow streets, and spoke of the rich culture and developed city that once thrived.

The tour ended in a covered pavilion, showcasing a series of cast plaster figures in their last moments before death. The guide said they had been created by pouring plaster into the small cavities of the ash-encapsulated remains of the humans who had perished. It was a time capsule of death. Some of the figures appeared to be crawling away. Others were lying down in the gray pebbles and ash.

Audrey crossed her arms and paused in front of a pale figure. Its hands covered the lower half of its face and its knees were drawn up like a frightened child during a thunderstorm. She stared at the figure, the rough plaster surface, the terrified position, the hopelessness. Her heart hammered in her chest. Her vision blurred, and her lungs struggled for breath. She stumbled to get away from the crowd and get some air, backing away and staggering to a bench. Audrey put her palms on her knees to steady herself, and closed her eyes as she breathed.

"Mom?"

Sarah's voice was in front of her. Audrey lifted her head, opened her eyes, and forced a thin smile. "I'm okay. Was too warm with all those people…" She waved a hand at her face and exhaled slowly. "I needed some air."

Sarah sat down beside her and gently rubbed her back. "You sure?"

Nodding, Audrey gave her another smile and faced forward, willing her breath to slow. Her heart was calming. She nodded toward a wooden pavilion where tourists had already begun to gather. "Almost time for the cheese and wine tasting."

"We don't have to, Mom." Sarah's hand rubbed soft circles. "If you don't feel—"

"No, no. I'll be okay." She inhaled through her nose deeply, and then let it out slowly through her mouth. "I'm fine, Honey."

Sarah's expression was filled with worry. "You sure?"

"Absolutely." Audrey stood from the bench and felt stable again. She put her hands out to Sarah and forced a smile full of mischief. "Come on. It's legal for you to drink here, and you and I are going to get giggly in public."

Sarah grinned and took her mother's hands. As the two of them walked, hand in hand toward the wine tasting pavilion, the thought pulsed in Audrey's mind.

She wasn't real.
Audrey almost believed it.

CHAPTER FORTY-EIGHT
AUDREY: then

"Do you remember when Dad got me that doll for Christmas I wanted *sooooo* badly? I think it was called Talking Tiffany or something."

"Oh, I remember. Three years old and he was wrapped around your little finger."

It had been an unplanned day and, as they sometimes turn out, resulted in some of the best moments. After some quick shopping in a food market, they had gone to see the golden sand of Serapo Beach stretching out to meet the turquoise waters. It was postcard beautiful, even more so in contrast to Pompeii and the location of so much death the previous day. Audrey smiled at Sarah, pulled the cork on a bottle of red wine, and put it and the corkscrew beside the small basket of meat, cheese, and fruit she had brought.

Sarah's expression broke into a smile, and she went on. "Did you know Dad went to like... *five different department stores* trying to buy it for me? He told me about it years later when we went for my driving test."

"That damn doll was sold out everywhere." Audrey pulled two wine glasses from the basket and offered one to Sarah. She poured some into her daughter's glass, and then filled her own. "Your dad came home after shopping that night and had a glass of Scotch out in the back yard by himself. I think he was close to murdering people at the mall."

Sarah sipped from her glass. "And then," she sputtered laughter. "Then the doll freaked me out so bad when I heard it laugh, I threw it—"

"In the damned hallway!" Audrey joined her daughter, laughing at the memory. "Your father and I walked out of the bedroom that morning and saw it laying there! He glanced at it and kept on walking."

"It sounded demonic!" Sarah shook her head, laughing, and then looked out over the sparkling water. Her voice softened, the amusement and humor dimming. "Dad never said a word to me about throwing it in the hall and never playing with it again."

The rays of the setting sun caught strands of Sarah's hair, turning them golden. Her eyes were afire with light, and as Audrey looked at her daughter, she thought she had never seen her more beautiful. She felt emotion swell inside her and Audrey turned away, knowing if she continued to look at her, she wouldn't be able to speak.

"He loved you very much." Audrey glanced back at her then, the words her daughter needed to hear out in the open.

Sarah opened her mouth to speak, and then shook her head. Her eyes brimmed with tears along their lower lids, and she drank from her glass instead.

Scooting closer, Audrey gently leaned against her shoulder. "We're going to be okay, Honey."

"*Are* we, Mom? I mean…it's weird and serious to talk about, but you can, you know?" Sarah raised her free hand up to wipe her eyes, but fresh tears spilled over her cheeks. "Mom, if we need to sell the house or I need to drop out of—"

"Hey?" Audrey put her wine glass down on top of the picnic basket, and turned to Sarah. "*Heyyyy*. Come here." She spread her arms and hugged Sarah, bringing up a hand to smooth the girl's hair along the back of her head. Audrey whispered to her. "Honey, *nothing* like that is going to happen. There's nothing for you to worry about. Your father had things in place to take care of everything. To take care of *us*."

Audrey felt Sarah's breath hitch in her chest, and knew her daughter was fighting the urge to completely break down into sobs. She eased away from Sarah and held the sides of her daughter's face in her hands.

"We're going to be okay." She wiped her daughter's tears from her cheeks and stared into her eyes. "Really."

The moment passed, and they sat on the beach enjoying the wine and each other's company. Warmth of the sun and the breeze coming off the water made it magical, and for the first time since arriving, Audrey felt present and in the moment. Audrey listened as Sarah talked about old memories and things her father wouldn't be present for in the future. Some memories brought laughter with them, and others ushered a fresh bout of tears.

There was a bittersweet feeling about it being the last night before they had to fly back. Yes, it had been a wonderful, amazing experience, but Audrey knew the truth—the trip had been an escape, a *denial* of the reality back home.

Cathartic, Audrey thought. *An unburdening of grief.*

But how do I unburden what I hold? Is that even possible?

Audrey put an arm around her daughter, and they stayed there sitting close to each other until there were no more words to say. The bottle of wine was empty and the sun had descended past the horizon.

The world back home waited patiently.

BURNER

CHAPTER FORTY-NINE
IRIS: now

"Did you know the woman you saw in the barn?"

"No." Iris shook her head as she exhaled cigarette smoke through her nose. "Never saw her before that moment.

The doctor ran a hand over his face and pushed his iPad aside. He leaned forward on the desk and then pushed his chair away from the table and stood up.

"She saw you, chained up like that, and she just…" He put his hands in his pockets and looked at the ceiling. "She left you there?"

"Absofuckinlutely." Iris flicked her tongue out over her lips to moisten them.

"I…Iris, I don't…" Doctor Walker shook his head, glanced at the two-way mirror, and then back to her.

"Think you could ask your naughty little puppy on the other side of that mirror if I could have some water?" Iris smiled sweetly and the doctor turned to look at the mirror and gave a nod.

"Iris, I'm…" He cleared his throat and took a heavy breath. "None of this is in your file and I'm not exactly sure—"

"No rulebook on *this* shit, is there, Doc?"

"If what you're telling me… this woman, the mother of—" The doctor cut himself short, cleared his throat again, and straightened his posture. "She left you there, shackled in the barn, and… what then?"

Iris stared at the burning tip of her cigarette as the smoke drifted upward. Doctor Walker stepped to the table and sat back down. He flipped the folder closed, appearing to be disgusted with its contents and pushed the material to either side of him, opening a clear path on the table.

The door swung open quickly, and the detective from earlier stepped inside, set a Styrofoam cup of water on the table. He smiled and gave a wink at Iris and then left the room again.

"Humans can go without food for…" Iris shifted her head side to side. "Around three weeks, give or take a few days."

She shifted in her chair and crossed her legs. Aside from her state-issued uniform, she could have been sitting in a job interview.

"Water, though… that's less forgiving. A good rule of thumb is, *on average*, we can go without water for about a hundred hours."

Iris took the foam cup and stared at its surface, at the floating patch of small bubbles more solid than the rest. A glob of spit. She made a display of noticing it, turned to the mirror, raised her cup in a cheers motion, and drank. When Iris was done, she winked toward the detective on the other side, and set the cup on the table.

Holding the cigarette in front of her, Iris took another drag and then her gaze returned to the glowing ember as it dulled to ash. "So, you want to know *what then*, Doctor? I'll tell you, what then."

CHAPTER FIFTY
IRIS: then

Youbitchcuntmotherfuckerhowcouldyouleavemelikethis!

Iris fought against the chains holding her in place. She tried to scream but only produced the hoarse, gruff sound of an animal in distress.

Tears she thought she could no longer cry sprung to her eyes, and she let her arms fall in front of her, the chain jangling against the concrete.

Four days. It's been four fucking days since I've seen the Man.

And today, the woman shows up.

Something is wrong.

The woman wasn't coming back. Iris saw it in her expression. The fear. The shock. *The refusal to believe.*

Iris knelt on the cement, arms in front of her, and stared forward. For a while, she dared to believe the woman had run away to call the cops, the FBI, *anyone* to come help her.

She waited.

From outside, Iris heard the faint sound of a car engine, and the slightest flicker began to swell in her chest, igniting Iris's heart and a lamplight of hope. She found the strength to rise from her knees and stand. Tears blossomed at her eyes and she ignored them, allowing them passage to fall down her face.

The noise of the car engine grew louder, and then softened again—from a distance—as the vehicle drove away.

She isn't coming back. No one is.

CHAPTER FIFTY-ONE
IRIS: then

After a while, Iris crawled on her hands and knees toward the bag of *Ol' Roy* and pulled it closer. She shoved one hand inside the package, the tube of PVC at her wrists catching the paper and crumpling it as she reached down to the bottom. Iris tilted the bag and the remaining kibble slid to the corner of the waxed paper liner. She gathered up a single handful—almost all that was left—and brought it to her mouth.

The Man is not coming back.

The pellets of food were dry as dust and tasted of cornmeal—unseasoned and bland, like plain scones left to grow stale and hard. Her mouth was void of moisture, and as Iris chewed, the dog food thickened to a wad of paste. She made her way to the row of water bottles on the wall and tilted her head beneath the one at the end of the line, lapping at the ball bearing stopper at the bottom of the metal tube. Drops of water flowed into her mouth, and Iris swirled it around to dissolve the mouthful of *Ol' Roy.*

The Man is not coming back.

She reached for the top of the plastic bottle, able to grip it with only one hand because of the PVC pipe, and wiggled the bottle back and forth in the hose clamp attaching it to the wood. Iris pulled upward and the water bottle rose with her motion, sliding free from the clamp. She flipped it upside down, held the bottle between her bloodied knees, and twisted the lid until it came free. Letting the cap fall to the cement, Iris lifted the plastic container to her mouth, tilting it to take a drink of water.

Tears sprung to her left eye, and they burned as they spilled down her cheek, gritty and wounded, like dried saltwater chafing sunburned skin. Her right eye was crusted shut, barren of tears.

Iris took another swallow and held the container up in front of her. There was barely two fingers worth of liquid remaining.

A half-days' worth at most, even if I ration it out. Then what, Iris? It's been days since I've seen the Man and the woman saw me and fucking left!

She's not coming back. There is NO ONE coming.

A seeping cold filled Iris, slow and creeping, like tree sap in an autumn chill. She sat the water bottle beside her on the floor and stared at the crumpled bag of dog food. Her gaze turned to the line of water bottles and the now empty hose clamp at the end of the row, wide and open like a surprised mouth.

Iris crawled toward the wall and stood. Up close, she studied the circle of metal, and saw the rear of the strap had been secured to the wooden wall with four Phillips head screws. She reached out to trace an index finger around the edge of the circular strip, arriving at the small bolt in the strap responsible for loosening or tightening the clamp's grip. The bolt connecting the ends of the band together was thick with a sharp edge to it.

Iris looked at the leather cuffs on her wrists. The wraps were roughly five inches wide and the leather was thick as one of her little fingers and as stiff as plywood. She studied the four thinner straps on the undersides of the cuffs, buckled tightly and cinched through rectangular metal loops.

After pressing the outer edge of the cuff of her left wrist against the metal, Iris moved her hands in sync, pressing hard against the edge of the bolt and sliding the leather back and forth.

The hose clamp held in place, but flexed and moved with her motions. Iris stopped after the fifth stroke against the bolt, bent her elbows, and pulled her hands up toward her chin. She put the tube of PVC pipe tight against her throat in order to crane her neck and see the edge of the cuff. There was a line—a scratch in the leather lighter than the surrounding material.

It was a start.

Iris took a deep breath and adjusted her stance. She repositioned the leather cuff against the bolt and dragged it back and forth. The sound deepened to a dull grinding noise, and Iris kept going. A sheen of sweat broke out on her face, and her shoulders began to ache from the motion.

She began to think of questions to occupy her mind. Iris ran through her memories.

How many times have I had lobster?

First time was in Baltimore's Inner Harbor when I was ten years old. I thought it tasted like bad fish. Second time was in Massachusetts, right before I left for college. Dad, Mom, and I had a mini-vacation in Salem, checking out the witch museums and the new age vibe. And dogs. Everyone in that town seemed to be walking a dog.

The third time was when Nathan and I were on the date when he asked me to move in with him, and he wanted it to be special. He arranged it ahead of time because his cousin knew the owner of the restaurant—table reserved with candlelight and a bottle of wine. Nathan had ordered before we got there, salad and bread, then a lobster for each of us. So cheesy but so sweet, he thought that's what it took to impress me.

Three times for lobster.

One, two, three.

She ground back and forth three full strokes on the clamp, as she thought of the next question.

How many pairs of shoes does Nathan own?

In her mind, Iris counted the shoes in their shared closet, running through his sneakers, and dress shoes, winter gear, and a pair of flipflops with a braided hemp strap she had busted his balls for. So, seven, including the flipflops.

One, two, three, four, five, six, seven.

Back and forth, against the bolt, Iris kept moving her arms.

How many pets did I have as a kid?

Images and names of various animals ran through her head.

Rufus the cat, Lox the goldfish, Fuzzy the hamster. Another cat Dad named Edgar. Fuzzy II, the revenge of hamster. Molly, the golden lab.

One, two, three, four, five, six.

Her shoulders burned, but Iris pressed onward. Cramps twisted inside her biceps like angry eels fighting to escape, and she breathed through the pain. Sweat beaded on her face and began to drip down her naked body. A fine dust sprinkled against her bare feet, and Iris saw specks of leather floating down. She pushed harder, and the pain in her arms caught fire, hot coals burning beneath her flesh.

Her legs, already weak, felt numb. Beads of sweat ran down from her scalp, over the freshest burns on her face, like lines of liquid fire.

How many times did the Man burn me?

The images flashed through her mind. The torch. The stool he sat on, the DIAMOND STRIKE ANYWHERE matches. The hiss and blue flame coming from the torch. The bright orange glow of the cast iron.

Iris's left knee jerked and almost buckled completely before she caught herself. At the sudden drop, her wrists changed angle on the backward stroke against the bolt. She felt the sharp bite of metal along the outer ridge of her left hand. The pain was an explosion of fireworks—fast and hard—and she fell backward against the wall. Her mouth opened in a silent scream, and Iris's breath froze inside her heaving chest.

Her left little finger twitched with the sudden throbbing pain in her hand. Iris knew however she had hurt herself, the damage was bad. She twisted her wrist as far as she could inside the cuff. The outer ridge of her hand was laid open like a butterflied shrimp. Blood poured from the edges of the wound and slicked her palm, dripping to the cement with soft, pitter-pat sounds.

The slice was deep and ragged, as if the sharpened metal had stuttered its cut along multiple ridges of her skin. Her little finger flicked on its own again, and Iris watched as movement inside the exposed meat of her hand twitched in sync.

Her stomach turned and both of her knees threatened to buckle. Iris turned her hand away so she couldn't see the wound, grit her teeth together, and took slow controlled breaths.

This is bad, Iris. This is really *bad. That hand is* beyond *fucked.*

She lifted her hands, tucked the PVC pipe tight against her throat, and twisted so she could see the progress on the bottom of the leather cuff. Hot trails of blood ran down her wrist and fell against her bare breast.

Iris's gaze landed on the light-colored scratch on the leather where she had been grinding against the bolt for close to an hour. She smiled at the sight of it, but her expression held no shine, only a bitter poison. It was the humorless smile of someone who has given up on hope and is barely clinging to desperation.

The result of working the cuff against the bolt for as long as she had was so insignificant, it was almost incalculable. Iris glanced at the thickness of the leather and a new counting question ran through her mind.

How many hours would I need to spend, grinding against that bolt to cut through this leather cuff?

A hundred? A thousand?

A thousand. Yeah, Doctor, that seems about right.

Doctor.

The mere thought of being a doctor made laughter erupt from Iris's mouth. The sound of it was high and alarming. She leaned against the wall and let herself slide down the rough wooden slats until she sat on the floor next to the puddle of her blood.

Iris looked up at the hose clamp and gave it a thumb's up with her right hand.

A for effort, pal.

It's not you, it's me. Really, I mean that. Apparently, I have a cuff made of fucking rhinoceros hide.

She shook her head and grinned at the bolt.

Iris picked up the bottle of water and tilted her head back, taking two heavy swallows, and then poured what was left over her face. It felt heavenly—the water against her skin, trickling over her body. Iris held the container overhead until her already strained arm muscles couldn't handle the effort any longer. She dropped the water bottle to the cement next to its matching cap. Her gaze ran over the thickness of the metal drinking tube, and the metal cap itself.

Sometimes the tears of happiness are mixed with a little blood.

Dad's words. My God, it feels like a million years ago when I heard him say that.

Iris leaned her head back and looked at the hose clamp. There was something colliding inside her thoughts, a sequence of ideas meshing together. That cold tree sap feeling crawled through her body again, and Iris kept staring upward as the idea overtook her.

CHAPTER FIFTY-TWO
AUDREY: now

"So, you and your daughter had a great time in Italy." The detective leaned back in his chair, an expression of disgust on his face. "Well, that's good, Audrey. That's great."

Audrey's eyes glassed with tears and she turned away from him. She fussed with the crumpled tissue in her hands. "You said you were married once, Detective. Any kids?"

He remained silent and then took a deep breath, sighed, and shook his head. "Not a good idea for a beat cop or detective to be a father. I made it clear when she and I first started dating that kids weren't going to be in the picture."

"Then you wouldn't understand." Audrey lifted her head to face the man. "I'm *glad* I have those days to think of, that time shared with my daughter."

Blevins stared at her and then pulled a drawer of his desk open. He reached inside, withdrew an open box of tissues, and slid it in her direction.

Audrey reached forward and took a fresh sheet to daub at her nose.

"You two got back home and then what? I need to hear it out loud, Mrs. Dugan." He straightened in his chair and leaned forward on the desk.

"Yeah, we got back home, and I waited. For the news to break. A knock at the door with red and blue lights flashing outside. A team of FBI busting through the door. For anything at all." Audrey wiped at her nose. "But nothing happened."

"No, no." Blevins shook his head and tapped the desk with his index finger, emphasizing his words. "*Something* happened, all right. You saw the woman in the barn before you left and you said *nothing* to *anyone.* You left her there to die. Tell me what happened when you returned."

CHAPTER FIFTY-THREE
AUDREY: then

As the driver pulled up in front of the house, Audrey opened her eyes, put a hand on Sarah's shoulder, and gently shook her awake.

Audrey got out of the car and walked to the trunk to retrieve the luggage. She thanked the driver, and she and Sarah made their way inside the house. Sarah wheeled her luggage into the foyer and parked it against the wall.

"I'm wiped out, Mom. I'll deal with the luggage tomorrow." Sarah, still half-asleep, shuffled off down the hallway toward her bedroom.

"It's alright, Honey. I am, too." Audrey smiled to herself, thinking of the times Sarah would fall asleep in the car and Paul carried her inside to tuck her in bed. It seemed like those memories were only a few months ago. Oh, how the years had flown by.

She walked from the living room into the kitchen, and pulled a glass from the cabinet. She reached for the kitchen faucet, and her hand froze in mid-air. In the bottom of the sink, she saw drops the deep color of aged rust.

Audrey felt a soft wind against the side of her face, and turned to see shards and splinters of glass across the kitchen counter, beneath the broken window overlooking the backyard. A potted fern from the deck outside laid there, plastic cracked and spilling soil over a black plastic ladle and onto the floor.

Dried smears of red streaked the white vinyl frame of the window, trailing onto the counter and the counter's edge, as if someone had gripped onto it to help lower themselves to the floor.

She's free. Jesus Christ, somehow, she got out.

Audrey slowly set the glass on the counter, and scanned the kitchen. The refrigerator was stained. Below the handle, spatters of red speckled the brushed steel surface. An open jar of olives sat on the counter beside the fridge.

She's been inside my fucking house.

Audrey swallowed hard and looked at the floor, tracing the trail leading onto the carpet and down the hallway toward the bedrooms. She reached for the wooden block of knives at the rear of the counter near the microwave, and withdrew the wide-bladed chef's knife from the top. She crept onto the carpet and down the hall, her eyes searching for more blood. A trail led to the doorway of her bedroom, and Audrey stepped inside, glanced at the open closet and the staggered, open drawers of her clothes dresser. She flipped the bed covers back and crouched down to check beneath the bed, but saw nothing but Paul's bedroom slippers.

Audrey held the knife in front of her as she walked toward the master bathroom and stepped inside quickly, her gaze scanning the empty room. Dried splashes of blood patterned the inside of the sink and the surface of the counter. The medicine cabinet was wide open, and Audrey saw an empty box of bandages on the edge of the sink. A pair of scissors and a roll of white medical tape rested beside the bandages.

The bottom of the shower held swirls of dried filth, and a soggy clump of brown paper stained with red.

Audrey walked into the hallway and rested her hand on the doorknob to Sarah's bedroom. The carpet was clean of any blood and the white door free of any smears. Audrey kept her hand on the metal knob a moment longer before she moved away.

Continuing down the hall, Audrey looked over the living room. Nothing appeared out of place, no additional bloody patches. She glanced at the sliding glass doors to the backyard, and stopped. They weren't closed all the way.

Audrey went to the junk drawer at the end of the kitchen counter, and rummaged in it until she closed her hand on the small flashlight she knew was there. Holding the knife in one hand and the flashlight in the other, she quietly left the house and headed toward the barn.

CHAPTER FIFTY-FOUR
AUDREY: then

A smear of blood marred the pale wood of the frame. The wooden door was partially open, leaving a gap of darkness. Audrey reached forward, stuck the knife in the opening, and used the blade to swing the door wide. She flicked the light switch and stepped inside, training the beam of her flashlight onto the wooden floor ahead of her. A trail of blood, heavier here than inside the house, dotted the aged planks, and Audrey walked further, toward the rear of the barn.

Audrey walked over the creaking boards until she reached the top of the stairs, and then shone her flashlight downward. The sharp scent of urine and fecal matter hit her as she descended, and Audrey paused at the bottom of the stairs. She walked slowly down the corridor between the stalls, farther and farther toward the workbench at the end.

It was quiet down here except for the low hum of the lights. Audrey's palms were sweat slick and she tightened her grip on the knife. She aimed the beam of her flashlight ahead of her in the corridor, and continued until she reached the last stall.

What she had left behind was no longer there.

CHAPTER FIFTY-FIVE
IRIS: now

Doctor Walker glanced at Iris's left hand.

She gripped her cigarette lighter tightly, but sideways, pinched between her index finger and thumb. She flicked a spark, and for a moment, the flame cast light on the bottom three fingers of her hand, which hung limp.

"How did you escape, Iris?"

She coughed a harsh laugh, and curls of smoke drifted toward the ceiling.

"Mental fortitude." Iris leaned back in the chair and twisted her head to one side and then the next, popping bones in her neck. "My dad told me his father took him raccoon hunting once when he was a kid. He grew up on this big farm in Maryland and I guess the raccoons had been picking off the chickens one by one. So, my grandfather baited some logs in the woods around their house."

Iris took a drag from her Winston. "He went out into the woods and bored holes into fallen trees, and around each hole, he made my dad smear a little oil from a can of sardines. Then my grandfather hammered nails around the edge of those holes, all of them down at an angle, like some tiny punji stick trap."

She held her cigarette out in front of her at a forty-five-degree angle to illustrate. "My grandfather drove them about halfway in, so you could still see the point of the nail if you peered down, and then he dropped a little ball of tin foil into each hole. Then they left and went back home."

Iris sniffled and used the back of her right hand to scratch her nose. "A couple days later, the two of them went back out to check on their traps, and you know what my dad said, Doc? What he told me he saw out there?"

Doctor Walker shook his head.

"He said he walked with my grandfather from hole to hole, five of them in all, and at four of the five holes, there was a raccoon, standing and snarling, ears laid back, ready to tear up anything that got close.

"My grandfather knew a little something about *mental fortitude*, Doctor. He knew how stubborn raccoons can be." Iris put her elbows on the table and leaned closer. "Even with the threat of death, there was no way in hell they were going to let go of those shiny little treasures they found in the holes. My grandfather just went from log to log and shot all of them, as easy as you please. Just a completely worthless ball of foil, but enough to catch them right where they stood."

She flicked ash in the tray. "Before my grandfather could take their carcasses home, he had to cut off their clenched paws and leave them behind in the hole. They wouldn't let go, even in death." Iris shook her head slowly.

"My dad never went hunting again. *Not ever.* Not after that night. But he remembered the lesson and so did I."

The doctor cleared his throat. "And what lesson was that?"

"If you want something bad enough, whatever that *thing* is, sometimes you have to deal with pain. Sometimes you have to look past the pain and the threat of death... go beyond it. Keep focused on whatever that thing is, and never, ever, loosen your grip until you get it."

"But if they had let go, they could have simply walked away."

Iris smiled and leveled her gaze at the doctor. "That's the other part of the lesson." Before you grab hold of that little treasure... make sure it's worth dying for."

CHAPTER FIFTY-SIX
IRIS: then

Iris tore a wide strip of paper from the bag of *Ol'Roy*, and brought the edge of it to her lips. Using her teeth, she held it in place, pinched with her fingers, and separated the layer of lamination from the paper. Iris let the plastic fall away, and kept the dull brown sheet.

Her hand throbbed with an inner pulse. The wound had the color and appearance of strawberry preserves smeared on fresh bread. She grit her teeth and wrapped the paper around her hand, the brown absorbent surface against the bloody opening.

Scooting along the cement, Iris picked up the discarded seam from the dogfood bag, the half-inch strip of paper that had been triple-stitched with thread to seal the package. She put one end of it between her teeth, clamped down, and wound it around the layer of paper on her hand. After several wraps, she brought the other end around again and looped it, pulling it with her teeth to tie a knot. She repeated the process, and doubled it. It wasn't nearly as constricting as it should be, and it wouldn't absorb much blood, but it was something.

Iris took a deep breath and let it escape in a hiss between her teeth. She leaned her head back against the wall for a moment and then noticed something on the cement floor. Reaching out with her right foot, Iris nudged the lid of the water bottle back toward her until she could pinch it between her fingers. She raised the lid to her mouth, and slowly bit down. Adjusting it slightly, Iris bit down on the rim of the lid again, moving little by little until she had flattened a section of metal.

Holding it between her teeth, Iris's gaze centered on what she could see of the lid. She tilted her head, studying it. Iris pushed off the cement with her right hand, and moved closer to the empty hose clamp. She eyed it for a moment, and then put her entire left hand inside the circumference until the metal band was across her palm and below her knuckles.

Iris leaned her face forward, the lid still held tightly between her teeth. She lined up the flattened area of the rim with the flathead slot in the screw of the hose clamp, and pushed forward, feeling the lid fit into the groove.

Clamping down hard, Iris tilted her head to the right, and felt the screw turn with her efforts. She pulled back and adjusted the position of the lid, lining it up with the head of the screw again.

Over and over, Iris twisted and then realigned, turning the head of the screw a fraction at a time. It was tedious, but not taxing, and eventually, she felt the constriction of the hose clamp against her skin, tightening around the middle of her palm and the lower joint of her thumb. She realigned and turned again, watching the grip of the metal against the paper of the dogfood bag bandage.

Several more turns of the screw, and the clamp was tight enough that Iris thought it would be a struggle to pull her hand free. Iris bit down on the lid and continued. The pressure from the clamp became painful, beyond someone stepping on your hand, and closer to running over it with a car.

Iris paused, and twisted so her right hand could hold the metal lid. She stared at the fingers of her hand in the clamp. They were turning red at the second knuckles and lower, the pressure great enough to blanch the tips of her fingers white. They looked plump and swelled with captured blood. Her thumb joint had flattened, the digit red and constricted.

You're almost there, Iris.

She clenched down on the lid again, adjusting it to the side so she could bite down on it as far back in her mouth as possible. The tighter it became, the more difficult it was becoming to twist. She pressed the lid against the groove, and jerked her head in small bursts, forcing the screw to twist a little at a time. The metal of the lid began to bend under her effort. Iris pressed further, and when she gave another hard twist, the edge of the lid suddenly caved and buckled back against her upper lip.

She tasted the warm salt of her own blood, but ignored it.

The middle of her hand was filled with a dull ache like a bad tooth. Iris knew she was close. *She had to be.*

Lining up the bent lid with the flathead slot again, Iris inhaled through gritted teeth. She twisted her head harshly and she *felt,* more than heard, a crack in the large knuckle of her thumb. It felt as if a high voltage current coursed through her hand. There was an explosion of misery as the inner mechanics of her hand released.

Iris screamed as her knees buckled, and her weight pulled her and the clamp holding her into a grand snarl of pain. It snapped in place, wrenching her shoulder as she hung there. The lid fell from her mouth and hit the cement. She watched its lopsided wobble into the corridor outside her stall, past the length her chain would reach.

The small bones in her wrist strained to pull apart from each other under her weight, and Iris wanted nothing more than to stand and relieve the pressure. She kicked and scrambled against the cement.

She heard a faint, tender noise above her and glanced up to see the *Ol' Roy* paper wrapped around her hand crinkle and bunch up. There was a dull popping sound, and abruptly, as her weight continued to pull her down, Iris watched the center of her hand in the hose clamp fold in on itself.

Iris's body dropped to the cement and she shrieked in pain.

Striped cuts from the notches of the hose clamp lined the skin of her crushed hand. Her first finger wiggled when she tried to move them, but the rest of her hand looked like the distorted flipper of some strange sea animal. Each half of her hand seemed to move independently from the other, cascading waves of torture as the pieces inside ground against one another.

The width of her palm had almost been divided in half, and she knew the bones of its midsection had broken from the pressure. Her wound had reopened and blood dripped to the cement. It wouldn't take long before her hand began to swell, her body trying to protect the damage as best as it could. There wasn't much time.

Iris straightened her arms in front of her and braced her knees behind the PVC pipe. She closed her eyes tightly and pulled backward, pushing against the bar with her legs as hard as she could.

Her left hand stalled at the edge of the leather cuff, its thick edge pressing into her broken thumb joint, setting off road flares of pain. Iris leaned forward and jerked back with all the strength she had left.

It happened so quickly, she fell flat to her back on the cement, and the PVC pipe and left wrist cuff swung wide to her right, smacking the floor with a clatter of chain and plastic. Iris's skull thudded against the cement and black spots flickered in her vision.

She lay still and stared at the wooden rafters.

Iris moved her right arm and smiled to herself when there wasn't any forced, in sync motion of her left arm. Rolling over onto her stomach, she began to rotate her wrist inside the right leather cuff, turning it so the buckled straps faced her.

Leaning down, she bit the end of the top strap and pulled it to the side, working the leather back and forth until the prong popped free of the hole.

Repeating the process, Iris undid the second strap. She bit down and peeled the cuff open enough to slide her right hand free. A cry escaped her. Iris pushed up with her right palm, got to her knees, and then stood, cradling her broken hand.

She walked the length of the corridor and climbed the stairs to the first floor. It was dark, but she could see a thin light shining through the wooden walls. Iris made it to the door, shouldered it open, and stepped outside. Her bare feet touched cool wet grass.

The stars in the indigo night stretched on and on, and she felt the breeze against her bare skin. Iris stood there and smiled, reborn.

CHAPTER FIFTY-SEVEN
IRIS: then

The potted fern bounced off of the sliding glass door without so much as cracking the pane. Iris picked it up with her good hand and slung it against the glass with the same results. Her chest heaved with effort. She was weak. She trembled as waves of pain flowed through her body.

Iris turned to her left and saw a small window on the house, a bit higher than she was tall. She picked up the potted fern and walked closer, throwing it dead center of the glass.

The window shattered inward, and Iris dragged a chair from beside the pool and stood on it to peer inside. Reaching through the window, Iris grabbed a long-handled plastic ladle from a glass container of cooking utensils. She flipped it around and ran the plastic handle along the edges of the window frame, knocking loose the remaining pieces of jagged glass.

She dropped the ladle and crawled through the window, taking care not to press her hands down on a glass shard waiting to bite into her skin. Her wounded hand shrieked with pain and drops of blood fell onto the windowsill and the counter top below.

And then Iris was inside a house, standing in a kitchen, her feet on clean linoleum instead of filthy cement. She turned to look at the kitchen faucet and stumbled toward it, scrambling to turn the water on with her filthy hand. She leaned her face into the sink, putting her mouth directly into the stream of fresh cold water, and gulped it down like a newborn pup. She used her good hand to cup the water and splash it over her face.

Cool liquid flowed into her stomach. A few more swallows, and Iris pulled away and shut the water off. The pain was still there, roiling inside, but the water alone made her feel somewhat better. Her stomach growled and she looked behind her at the modern stainless steel refrigerator, thinking of the food it might contain.

Later. You can eat later, after you've washed the animal stink off of you.

The house was quiet.

Iris's attention shifted beyond the open kitchen counter to a living room.

Sofa. Loveseat. Big screen television. Framed art on the walls.

It may as well have been a set display from a science fiction movie. Everything seemed foreign to her—things she had heard of, maybe dreamed about.

How long has it been since I've seen these things in real life?

Iris walked from the kitchen onto the carpet, ignoring her bleeding hand, and relished the sensation of soft padded fibers beneath her feet. She walked down a hallway and stopped at the end, in front of two doors. On the right, Iris saw a bedroom, clean and tidy, and she went inside and turned immediately toward another doorway. She could see the edge of a sink in the small room, along with a toilet.

Iris smiled.

The shower was heaven. Hot water cascaded over her head and face as Iris squeezed liquid soap onto her skin from a bottle of body wash. In the close confines of the shower, Iris could smell herself—the wild scent of a sick, feral animal. There was a green plastic loofah hanging from the bottom of a corner shower rack and she used it to lather the soap on her skin into a thick froth.

At her feet, the water was a swirl of filth around the drain, but the soap smelled like fresh air and the ocean. Iris could feel the bubbles of lather popping against her flesh. She moved beneath the spray of water, rinsed, and then lathered again, this time close to sobbing at the silky feel of soap against clean skin.

She grabbed a bottle of shampoo and squirted a thick dollop directly onto the top of her head. After setting it down, Iris used her right hand to work it into her scalp and slick it back through her hair.

Beneath her, blood dripped from her damaged hand, polka-dotting the water. She used her teeth to untie the makeshift bandage around her hand, and then let the paper fall to the shower floor. Suds from the shampoo cascaded over the wound, and Iris gritted her teeth at the burning sensation, though it was minor and distant from the pleasure of the shower. After rinsing the shampoo from her hair, she held her face beneath the spray, feeling the sting against her skin. She moved away from the showerhead, blinked the water droplets from her good eye, and turned off the water.

Iris stepped from the stall and grabbed a rolled-up towel from a shelf on the wall next to the mirror. The fabric was thick and soft against her skin, and she thought about the stupid, normal, everyday things most people take for granted.

Iris sniffled and sighed and let the damp towel drop to the floor.

Two toothbrushes protruded from a dark blue cup on the sink, and a half-empty tube of toothpaste sat beside it. The mere thought of it made a light groan of pleasure escape from between her lips. Iris grabbed a brush and squirted paste onto it, ignored her busted mouth and scrubbed the bristles against her teeth and gums. She spit foam into the sink, saw the blue-white froth tinged with her blood, and brushed more anyway.

When her gums felt raw, and her teeth felt somewhat smooth and normal again, Iris rinsed the brush, tossed it back in the cup, and faced herself in the mirror for the first time in months.

I'm a wax figure left in the summer heat. A freak.

The thoughts lacked self-pity and were simply of acceptance. Tears did not spring to Iris's eyes, nor did she feel pangs of longing for how she used to be. She felt as numb and detached as if she was studying the reflection of an inanimate object. With her right hand, she brushed her hair down, letting the bangs fall over the right side—the *burned* side—of her face. Her hair reached just above her cheekbone, and Iris gave one last look at herself before opening the door of the medicine cabinet.

On the shelves rested a variety of moisturizing creams and hair products, but Iris reached for a box of rolled white gauze. She sat it down on the sink, pulled a roll of white medical tape from the cabinet.

She lifted her left hand, palm up, and began wrapping the gauze around its middle, working her way down to her wrist. Even the gentle pressure made fresh waves of pain ripple through her entire body, but Iris pressed on. The first layer of gauze immediately blossomed red, but she continued layering until she had used the entire roll.

Next, Iris used the medical tape and started the process all over again, taking time to wrap her hand—secure but not tight—to hold the gauze firmly in place. She left the materials on the sink, and moved into the bedroom.

After rummaging through the clothes in the dresser and closet, Iris dressed herself in jeans and ankle socks, a plain brown t-shirt, and a zip-up jogging jacket. The jeans were too long and she had to cuff the legs. They were loose on her hips.

At the bottom of the closet, Iris withdrew a pair of Nike running shoes—a size too big for her, but they felt amazing on her feet. She left the bedroom and walked back to the kitchen. It was time for something other than *Ol' Roy*.

The peach yogurts and sliced American cheese were the first things Iris ate. She struggled for a moment to open the jar, but succeeded, and ate green olives, almost finishing off the entire container. She put the jar on the counter and closed the fridge door, leaned against it, and sighed.

A wave of stomach cramps hit her like a sledgehammer, and Iris doubled over. A shiver ran through her body and her mouth filled with hot saliva. She felt like she was going to throw up, and she closed her eyes, breathing through the sensation until it passed.

Iris walked into the living room and sat on the couch. After cots and cages and the thin mattress in the barn, the plush, deep cushions were as alien to her as the rest of her surroundings. She looked around the living room, at the end tables, photographs on the walls, and then turned behind her to look over the kitchen walls.

No one had landlines anymore. Not a single phone in sight.

The foyer of the house was to Iris's left, along with a set of closed double doors. Iris eased herself from the couch, and slid one of the pocket doors open enough to peek inside the room.

Broken frames and artwork. Books scattered to the floor. The room was trashed.

The scent of old cigar smoke reached her nose, and something else, musky and strong—the *smell* of the Man. Her stomach churned, but Iris stepped into the room. Whoever had done this was in a rage.

Glass shards cracked beneath her sneakered feet. A computer

laid on the carpet, on its side, the plastic case cracked and exposing circuit boards. Iris saw a baseball bat lying behind a desk. Her gaze landed on a busted picture frame, the photograph inside creased and covered in broken glass.

The Man. The woman.

A teenage girl.

All of them were smiling in the photograph. Happy. Content.

Iris crouched to one knee and pulled the photograph from the broken frame, folded it, and stuffed it in a rear pocket of her jeans. She stood up and looked around, noticed an electronic safe set into the wall. Her eyes flitted to the picture frame on the floor below it.

Hidden. Oh, I wonder what you keep in there.

She read the electronic screen, the red letters: LOCK ENGAGED.

Iris ignored the safe and left the office, heading through the living room to the sliding glass door. She flipped the lock, walked into the back yard, and then realized she had automatically slid the door closed behind her without even thinking about it.

Old habits, I guess. How many times have I opened and closed the sliding glass doors at my old apartment? Let's see. Two years together with Nathan, four, maybe five months out of the year it was warm enough to enjoy the weather on the deck.

About three-hundred times? Sounds about right.

One, two, three…

Iris began counting in her head as she walked from the backyard to the side of the house. Even after the scalding hot shower, every joint in her body throbbed and ached. The muscles in her shoulders were thick lumps of clay, and she had to hold her left arm up, because even the slight motion of walking set off detonations of pain.

…twenty-one, twenty-two, twenty-three…

Iris walked down the driveway, past the barn.

…thirty-eight, thirty-nine, forty…

At the end of the driveway, she stopped and stared at the large black mailbox mounted to a thick wooden post. Iris pulled the door open and took out the bundle of mail, letting the catalogues fall to the ground as she sifted through the stack until she found what she was after.

AUDREY DUGAN, along with the address, was in all caps in the envelope's window. Iris folded the envelope, stuck it in her back pocket along with the photograph of the girl, and turned right onto the main road.

...forty-one, forty-two, forty-three...

By the time Iris reached *six-hundred and eighty-three*, a delivery driver had felt mercy at the sight of her outstretched hand, thumb up, in the universal pose for hitchhiking. He pulled to the shoulder, and Iris opened the door to the rig and got in.

"Headed to Collinsville, if you're headed that direction." The driver said.

"Anywhere is better than hell."

CHAPTER FIFTY-EIGHT
AUDREY: now

"How did you explain the blood?"

Audrey stared at the detective with a confused expression.

"On the floor, the carpet. How did you explain the trail of blood to your daughter?"

"Oh," she shook her head dismissively. "After I locked the sliding glass doors again, I… I went to the kitchen and I cut my hand with a piece of broken glass, bandaged it up."

"Clever." Blevins raised his eyebrows and nodded. "But couldn't you have just faked it with a bandage on your hand?"

"Fake a wound?" Audrey wiped her nose with a tissue. "Not with Sarah. The next morning, as soon as she saw the bandage, Sarah wanted to see how badly I hurt myself. Applied fresh ointment and rebandaged it. Fuss over it, you know? That's how she was from the moment she was born, motherly, caring like that."

The detective's suit jacket buzzed repeatedly and he drew his phone out, stared at it and tapped his thumb on the screen. It went silent and he tucked it away.

"And the girl in the barn was gone?" Blevins took a drink from his water bottle and slowly set it down on the desk again.

"Yes."

"You had no idea who she was?"

"No. Not her name, not anything, except the Polaroids in Paul's safe."

"You still have those?"

"I burned them." Audrey put her purse on the edge of Blevins' desk and adjusted in her chair. "I burned them like everything else."

CHAPTER FIFTY-NINE
AUDREY: then

Audrey had closed and locked the doors to Paul's office the morning after getting back from Italy. It had been mentally ingrained into both her and Sarah that his office was off limits, and even now that Paul was dead, Audrey didn't think Sarah would venture into the room, but she wasn't taking any chances.

Three days passed, and each morning, Audrey turned on the television to watch the local news. There were no breaking headlines about a missing woman found naked and stumbling on the highway. No reports of fishermen finding a corpse. Nothing.

Each morning, Audrey watched and held her breath, though she knew the reality. If someone found the girl alive, people would be knocking at her door or *breaking* it down, long before a news anchor ever read a word on camera.

But if the girl's *dead* body was found, it became one more secret on an already tall pile.

Sarah was invited to a four-day beach trip from high school friends she hadn't seen since going away to college, and after lots of reassurances it was okay to leave her mother alone, Audrey convinced her to go.

Standing on the porch, Audrey smiled and waved goodbye to Sarah as the group of girls drove down the driveway, headed for a few days of fun. But the smile on Audrey's face dimmed as she put her hands on her hips and turned her attention toward the barn. She stared for a moment longer and went back inside.

One thing at a time, and Paul's office is first.

Audrey unlocked the pocket doors and slid them into the wall slots. She stared at the trashed office, exactly the way she had left it.

No. Not exactly how I'd left it.

She was in here, in Paul's office. I know she was.

Audrey took a deep breath, and got to task, gathering up the contents of the desk—the sticky notes with unknown phone numbers on them, business cards with names that didn't register to her, everything foreign and only attached to Paul. She stuffed all of it into thick black garbage bags. Next, she began cleaning up the things she had broken and thrown around the room. The photographs and the Bev Doolittle print were carefully picked over for loose shards of glass and dumped into a fresh bag.

She stacked the books, noting she would box them up later and drop them off to Goodwill. There was no need to scan the titles—Audrey knew there was nothing she would ever read. Simply touching things in here made her feel grimy and unclean, as if she was sorting through an alley dumpster of maggot-ridden food instead of her dead husband's belongings.

Three full garbage bags later, Audrey half-carried, half-dragged them down the hall and into the garage. She paused and wiped perspiration from her face with her forearm, and headed back through the living room and out into the yard.

Time for phase two.

Paul had hired landscapers to install the firepit not long after they had moved in. It was a wide circle of beige and gray stones blending perfectly with the landscaping, and appeared as if it had been there forever. Audrey remembered saying the pit was large enough to roast a small pig and Paul had laughed at the time, saying they just might do that someday.

They had mostly used the firepit in the late fall when the night air turned crisp. The three of them would sit around the orange glow of the crackling flames and talk. Sometimes, Audrey and Paul would share a bottle of chardonnay, and enjoy the night with a soft buzz.

Now, those memories seemed like they were from someone else's life.

Audrey walked to the side of the house and gathered up an armful of the split oak logs for the pit. The stockpile was depleted somewhat from last year, but it still reached to her mid-thigh, and was more than enough for what she had planned. After stacking a pile of wood into the center of the pit, Audrey appraised it, and retrieved a cardboard box from the garage. She tore it apart, stuffing pieces along the base of the logs, lighting them as she went. Minutes later, the fire was roaring, flames waist high. Audrey walked inside the house, leaving the sliding glass door wide open.

She carried Paul's computer back with her, and stepped over the low stone wall before tossing the electronics onto the burning logs. She waited and watched as the gray plastic cover began to liquify from the heat. Whatever information was on the drive was being melted away.

Burned.

As the logs popped in the fire, Audrey smelled the mixture of charring wood and the acrid stink of burning plastic. The combination of exertion and the high heat brought more sweat to her face and she took a step away from the pit. For a moment, she thought of stripping her clothes right then and there, down to her bare, naked skin, and jumping into the pool.

But no, Audrey thought. *I have to keep going. I have to get through the next part of it.*

From the back of the house, Audrey could see a thin sliver of the barn. Her gaze followed the rippled tin roof, down the vertical siding, and farther, to the stone foundation.

She let her hands fall to her sides and headed to do what needed done.

CHAPTER SIXTY
AUDREY: then

I should have worn gloves.

Her insides shook as Audrey walked toward the stall at the end of the corridor, but she knew it had to be done—a means to an end. She stopped and surveyed the small space.

The stink of piss and shit had dampened but was still thick in the air, like an animal's cage that had recently gone unoccupied. There was something else as well, almost sweet, like fried meat. Her stomach clenched and she wanted to heave. Audrey opened her mouth and breathed slowly, fighting her reaction.

Against the rear wall, a thin mattress cushion showed stains like brown chrysanthemum flowers across its quilted surface. A thick chain was secured to a metal plaque on the wall, and Audrey's eyes traced the length to a pair of leather wrist cuffs and a plastic tube separating them. One of the cuffs lay there, its straps and buckles splayed open like the underside of a dead horseshoe crab. The other cuff, Audrey saw, was blotched with dark stains and had a thin line scratched across its width.

She scanned the wall and saw a row of water bottles mounted with hose clamps. The last metal strap in the line was twisted and empty and coated with dark grime. Her gaze fell back to the stained leather cuff and Audrey had to pull her focus away from all of it. She stared at the wooden beams overhead and watched cobwebs shift slightly.

How long was she here? What had Paul done to her during that time?

He spent time in here and then crawled into bed with me every single night.

Every single fucking night.

Waves of nausea hit her again and Audrey moved, trying to ignore it. One by one, she withdrew the water bottles from their holsters on the wall, and let them fall to the cement floor. She stepped into the corridor and stood by the wooden bench and cabinets. A hand-held blowtorch rested on the bench platform, next to a box of matches. An iron rod, ending in a wide, flattened square, lay across the wood behind the torch. The surface of the square looked aged. Small tufts of something clung to the outer shape.

That's what Paul used.

That's what he used to burn her.

Oh my God, is that her skin? Her burned skin?

IT'S HER FUCKING SKIN!

The urge to vomit hit her, fully and completely, and Audrey put a hand against the wooden bench to balance herself. She bent, coughed, and threw up her morning coffee. Pale liquid splashed against her feet and ankles, and she heaved again. Her eyes watered and her nose began to run. Audrey shook her head, and spit the sour taste of vomit to the cement floor.

She straightened, spit again, and slowly opened up the cabinet doors. There was an uncapped tube of Neosporin ointment resting in front of a black Polaroid camera, and an opened box of film cartridges. An opened box of tampons sat beside the film.

Audrey walked back to the house carrying the camera, the matches, and the tube of ointment. The small pile was added to the bonfire, and she noticed the casing of Paul's computer had melted down to a square metal frame, dripping gobs of flaming plastic to the logs beneath it.

On the return trip to the barn, she paused in the pantry and grabbed her screwdriver and the case of bits. She took a step to leave and paused, picking up the retractable utility knife from her toolbox as well.

In the barn, she removed the screws attaching the hose clamps to the wall. The plaque anchoring the log chain came down next, and Audrey carried the chain and leather cuffs to the fire pit, tossing them onto the pile with the rest.

The leather straps blackened and began to twist in the heat. The silver buckles and prongs reflected orange from the flames, and then started to darken. She watched the cuffs curl and then straighten out again, exposing the inner surface like flowers opening to the sun.

Or a sick animal, relaxing in death.

The PVC pipe began to smoke and then melt in long stringy drips.

Audrey lost herself for a while as she stared at the flames, and then she broke free from the image, and made her way back to the barn.

Using the utility knife, she made long cuts along the center of the mattress pad. Halfway through the thickness, the blade began to snag on the cloth and Audrey paused. She flipped the blade around in the holder, giving it a fresh edge, and resumed cutting until the pad split completely in half as she sliced through the bottom layer of batting and fabric.

Sweat soaked through her t-shirt and dripped down her face. Audrey thumbed the utility blade back into hiding, and tucked it into a back pocket of her jeans. She grabbed the edges of one half of the mattress and lifted.

The ammonia and copper penny scent of the body fluids and waste wafted from the cloth. Audrey turned her head and gagged, walking quickly in an effort to let the smell trail behind her. She carried the mattress pad to the fire, and then returned to add the second half. Billows of gray smoke lifted into the air, and she stepped away from the heat.

The leather cuffs looked like strips of burnt bacon, and the silver buckles on the straps had turned black as charcoal, like segments of the chain itself. She could distinguish pieces of what remained of the computer, and the flames licked up and around the circuitry.

Audrey opened Paul's safe and gathered the Polaroids, stuffing them into a back pocket of her jeans. Knowing where they had been taken, and the images the photos contained, made her gorge rise yet again, but she tightened her stomach and headed toward the kitchen.

She paused there to grab a corkscrew and bottle of chardonnay—a 2017 *Far Niente* she and Paul had brought back from a trip to Napa Valley. They had set it aside in the wine rack and proclaimed they would drink it on a special occasion.

Audrey stood at the edge of the fire pit and withdrew the photographs from her pants pocket. She flung the group of them toward the center of the fire, and watched as they immediately began to blacken and shrivel up like the blacksnake fireworks she used to get for Sarah when she was a kid. Audrey turned away from the spectacle.

The wine would have tasted amazing chilled, but Audrey decided she didn't really care one way or another at the moment. She sat down in a chair by the pool, used the corkscrew to open the wine bottle, and dropped the corkscrew, cork still attached, to the cement. Tilting the bottle toward her nose, she closed her eyes and breathed in the scent. It smelled incredible—crisp apples and citrus, damp moss and wet stone, roasted hazelnuts and fall leaves.

Magnificent.

She raised the bottle toward the fire in a cheers motion. "This a special enough occasion for you, you son of a bitch?"

Audrey pulled back and then threw the bottle at the fire pit, hearing the glass shatter as it crashed against stone. She sat in the chair and watched the flames until the mattresses were eaten away, until the leather cuffs crumbled to ash and fell away to nothing but the metal buckles from the straps.

She watched until the flames died down to nothing but a group of embers, a glowing collection of secrets gone forever, and future memories lost for good.

CHAPTER SIXTY-ONE
IRIS: now

"So, you hitchhiked home?"

Iris nodded.

"Why not have the driver take you to the police? At least use their cell phone to call your parents? Your mother, at least, to let her know you were still alive. Something. *Anything*."

"I wasn't—"

"Why didn't you call the police, Iris? I don't understand."

Iris sat quietly in her chair, breathing slowly, calmly. She spoke softly, but not directly, to the doctor. "I wasn't sure what I was going to do. I wasn't sure I was going back home."

He leaned on the table, shook his head slightly in disbelief. "Iris, you had been missing for almost three months. There had been people searching for you. Your fiancé is *still* an unsolved murder. The NCIC, the National Crime Infor—"

"I know what the hell it stands for." She glared at the doctor. "I told you already. I wasn't sure if I was going home or not."

"Why?"

Iris lunged upward, knocking her chair to the floor behind her. She grabbed her bangs in her right hand and yanked them to the side. "What's so fucking hard to understand, Doc? I'm an only child. Pride and joy, going to be a doctor, help children and save the world. Take a look. Take a *good* fucking look!"

She snapped her head toward the mirror and marched closer, staring at herself. "If you had been a good little doggy, you'd be in here, but I know you're fucking listening to me on the other side, watching me. I wanted to make sure you got a good, up close look. Didn't want you to miss it."

Iris bared her teeth and glared at the doctor sitting behind the table, then she let her hair fall back against her face and released a breath as she righted her chair. "I wasn't sure I wanted to live anymore. I wasn't sure what going back home would do to my parents, to know I was alive but... like *this*."

"But you did go home."

Iris nodded.

"And how did your mother—"

"My father…" Iris grabbed her pack of Winstons and shook one free. "My dad killed himself because I had gone missing and he had given up hope I'd be found. Up and hung himself in the goddamn garage with an extension…" She cleared her throat, lit the cigarette, and took a drag.

"My mother had changed. She wasn't the same woman I knew. Hell, she had gone almost completely gray, and her eyes had this… her eyes looked dead inside." Iris took another puff on her cigarette and shook her head. "No, *not* dead… *desperate*. Like she wanted out of a situation in the worst way, you know? Like an abused wife at the end of her rope."

Iris flicked ash in the tray. "Mom called NCIC to tell them I had been found."

"They send someone out?"

"Not enough time or manpower. They gave a hearty congratulations over the phone, told her they would close the case, and moved onto the next thing. The *next* missing person. The next *daughter,* sister, aunt, whatever. Didn't even bother to ask about Nathan." She exhaled smoke and shook her head.

"So… I went back home. And every single day, I reminded her of Dad's suicide." Iris puffed on her Winston and leaned her head back, blowing smoke rings into the air. "Not that Mom would ever say it, but she didn't need to. I could see it there, could see how she looked at me."

"How was that?"

"Like I was a stranger. I wasn't the same daughter she knew. I had been…" Iris released a sharp humorless laugh. "Transformed."

CHAPER SIXTY-TWO
IRIS: then

Iris wasn't ignoring her mother. Not exactly.

But Mom's questions about what happened, where she had gone, how she had been *changed* had become akin to a scheduled event every afternoon since Iris had come back.

Changed.

It had been a full week at home and Mom still couldn't seem to bring herself to say the word burned *out loud, preferring to avert her eyes and use* changed *instead.*

She seemed unable to sit still very long, pacing or moving to other rooms, fussing with already clean dishes or wiping down the kitchen counter. Occasionally, she would pause and put a hand out against the wall, almost to steady herself for a moment.

Iris sat on the living room chair, staring at her cup of herbal tea, untouched and growing cold.

I can't tell her the truth. I can't. It would kill her. Kill what's left of her, at least.

As the days marched on, not answering her mother's questions became as damaging as what revealing the truth would have been. Her mother would speak softly, occasionally daubing at her eyes with a tissue, asking questions that went unanswered until the frustration got the better of her, and then she would stand and walk away to the kitchen or step outside. She would sit on the back porch and cry. Iris would watch her mother cradle her head in her thin-fingered hands, her entire body shaking with hurt.

A healing salve did not exist, nor words or actions to lessen the hurt.

Iris knew she was the cause of pain. For her mom. Her father. For everything. The numb feeling she had inside was changing, giving way to emotion again. It made Iris angry—*furious*—and the ache inside her felt like bits of glass grinding against one another.

Rage lived inside her now, but Iris couldn't answer her mother's questions. Her mother would *never* understand.

No one would, not ever.

To be able to sit inside a house, on furniture. To wear clean clothing. To get cool running water simply by turning on a faucet. To lie in a real bed without smelling the sweet, stinking fragrance of your own charred flesh.

Her mother would never understand waking up in the middle of the night, cupping a hand over your own gaping mouth, desperate to prevent your own noise. Your mouth remaining open in a scream captured on a silent film, while the dream-vision of a glowing red-hot iron moves toward your face. It had become so imbedded in you to keep quiet during pain, fear, anguish—become so absolutely *ingrained*—it was now part of who you were, awake or asleep.

Mom would never endure smelling her own body filth. Piss, shit, menstrual blood. To *wallow* in it like an animal. Mom would never live on dry dog food or drink warm, stale water from feeder bottles purchased at a pet store.

She would never understand.

Iris walked around the living room, looking at the knick-knacks on the shelves, the framed photos. Mom and Dad on their first real vacation together—palm trees in the Bahamas background, holding drinks with curly-cue straws and paper umbrellas.

Her high school graduation photo.

God, that seems so long ago. That girl's expression *even seems so long ago. Her smile, the hope in her eyes. I don't even look old enough to graduate high school.*

Iris picked up the photo and stared at it.

A different girl. A different life.

She put it back in place and lifted a photograph of her and Nathan during a Christmas visit. He wore a Santa hat, tilted to the side, and both of them held cups of spiked eggnog.

Iris smiled at the memory. It was their first holiday visit to her parents as a couple. Dad made a small fuss at the end of the day, grumbling to Mom in the kitchen where he thought no one could hear.

"He seems like a nice guy, sure. But they're not married and you expect me to be okay with him sleeping in the same bed as our daughter? My little girl? How do you—"

"Your memory might be piss poor, but don't think I've forgotten dating you before we got married, Mr. Handsy." Mom's voice, firm but with a slight prodding mischief only she could seem to completely get away with.

"Maybe so, but your father would have thrown me out in the street before letting me lay in the same bed with you."

"Times have changed, honey. Roll with it."

Dad coughed and returned to the living room, shaking his head. Mom followed, bringing the entire punchbowl of eggnog to rest on the coffee table.

Oh God, they had all laughed that night. Telling jokes and listening to stories. It had been amazing. An adult holiday. She had been with the man she loved.

When they shared the same bed that night, they made love slowly, tenderly, struggling to keep quiet. Iris remembered grabbing the pillow and putting it over her face at one point. She smiled at the memory, but the young woman in the photograph was as foreign to her as the girl in the graduation photo.

Mom walked into the living room, holding her purse in one hand and the car keys in the other. "Hey, you want to…"

Her mother's expression fell, descending from denial to realization.

"I'm going to the grocery store." Her mother inhaled a trembling breath as she turned and walked toward the door, adjusting the keys in her hand. "I'll be back in a little while."

Iris nodded at her mother's back as the woman closed the door on her way out. She returned her gaze to the photograph of her and Nathan and then she set the frame back in place.

The girl in that photograph is dead.

The pain and anger living inside Iris fully roused from its slumber.

CHAPTER SIXTY-THREE
IRIS: then

When the following morning crept past eight o'clock, Iris sat by herself in the quiet living room. She glanced at the ceiling in the direction of Mom's bedroom, tilted her head to listen and heard nothing from upstairs.

Iris waited, trying to quiet the thoughts in her own mind. At some point in the night, she had shuddered awake, gripped in a dream of glowing hot iron descending to her face. She sat there, clutching her blankets and biting back sobs, until she dragged them with her to the floor and lay there awake until early dawn shone through the bedroom window.

Outside, the neighborhood children played, riding bikes and jumping on a hopscotch grid chalked on the asphalt. Iris watched them from behind the curtains, brought her hand against the right side of her face. She ran her fingertips over the flesh, rippled and uneven beneath her touch.

She drifted on the sounds of the children's laughter until a delivery truck's diesel engine broke the moment and Iris sat down on the sofa again. Glancing at the clock, she realized she had been standing at the window for almost half an hour and her mother still wasn't awake.

Mom never slept with her bedroom door completely closed, so Iris crept upstairs, peered through the opening, and saw her in bed beneath the covers.

"Mom?" Iris whispered as she pushed the door open and walked inside.

There was no soft purr of breath from the bed, no rhythmic sound of peaceful sleep.

Iris stepped closer and sat down gently on the bed. "Mom?"

Beneath the covers, her mother's chest did not rise or fall.

The silence of the room rang in Iris's ears, and she sat there with her right hand resting against her mother's quilt-covered leg.

Nathan. Dad. Mom. I loved all of them and they're all dead, now. Gone.

I am completely alone.

She remained in the silent room for a few moments longer. Iris brushed her mother's hair away from her face. She stared at Mom's dead body, studying her with a half-blind stare, a brutal dichotomy of observation.

Finally, Iris rose from the bed and went downstairs to the maple hutch her parents used, as far back as Iris could remember, to store important papers. She began sifting through the file folders and business cards until she found what she was looking for, and then Iris sat on the living room couch next to the end table with the landline phone.

A swarm of frozen bees flowed through her veins, making her insides hum with current. Iris picked up the phone, and the torment and fury awakening inside her began to take on a form of its own.

CHAPTER SIXTY-FOUR
AUDREY: now

"I don't know how many gallons of bleach I used. Pouring it over the stall where she had been, splashing it on the cement floor and the stairs, the wooden planks. I'd do the entire space one day and then I'd think of something later on, maybe a spot I had missed, so I'd do it all over again. For about a month, I could smell bleach in my nostrils when I woke up."

Blevins steepled his fingers together and stared at Audrey. "What about the weapon, the cast iron he used? The blow torch?" The man shook his head in disgust.

Audrey reached for the bottle of water, took a sip, and then sat it back on the desk.

"I turned the valve open on the blowtorch until it ran empty. Kept it and the cast iron in the barn until Sarah started her fall semester. One day I drove north of the city along the Susquehanna River and parked. I taped the canister and the cast iron together with duct tape and threw them out in the water, as far as I could. Slung the chains in after them." She glanced down and then back at the detective's face, speaking in a lower voice. "If you need me to, I can show—"

"Mrs. Dugan..." The detective released a sigh, stood up from his chair, and walked away a few steps before turning around again. "You're a wealthy woman. You could have gone on living the rest of your life, without saying a word. There's no evidence, because you got rid of it all, so why—"

"Why am I telling you all of this?" Audrey nodded. The lines in her face seemed deeper, more defined. Her beauty was still apparent, but tarnished—the appearance of a former beauty pageant runner-up who had gone through a patch of addiction. "I'm tired, Detective. I'm just so... *tired.*"

"So, you got rid of everything and just... waited?"

"Yes. For something. Anything."

Blevins stuffed his hands in his pants pockets and leaned against the rear wall. He stared at the ceiling for a while and then let his focus return to her. When he spoke again, his voice was softer. "And something finally did happen. A couple of months ago."

Audrey closed her eyes and gave a slight nod.

CHAPTER SIXTY-FIVE
AUDREY: then

Cramps gripped the muscles in Audrey's thighs and she turned over and did the backstroke to the shallow end. She glided in the water until her hand touched the wall of the pool, and stopped. Her lungs burned with effort and she smelled chlorine.

She leaned her head back, closed her eyes, and felt the sunlight on her face. There wouldn't be many warm days left in the year, and she was already dreading the colder months ahead.

When Sarah had gone back to college, Audrey had driven her to Selinsgrove and helped her into the dorm with some groceries and two duffels of clean laundry. After a long hug, Audrey started the drive back home, and cried for the first ten miles, finally pulling off to the shoulder of the road to collect herself.

A week later, she joined a gym. It was a spontaneous decision—one she thought would be a good idea to get her out of the house and away from the quiet. But when she walked inside, the sound of people working out, the *clink* of weights against each other, reminded her of the chain the girl had been shackled with. The smell of sweat made her feel like her face was pressed against the girl's stained mattress pad.

She almost threw up on the elliptical machine as everything collided at once. Gathering her things, Audrey walked out and never went back. Instead, she returned to her pool, lap after lap, endlessly reaching forward and leaving a trail in the water behind her, swimming until her lungs ached, until she had nothing left.

The canvases in her upstairs art studio remained untouched, though she had picked up brushes several times, turned the polished wooden handles in her fingers before setting them down again. It was as if her creativity had gotten washed with gray, muting it through dirty glass.

Each day, Audrey glanced at the greenhouse outside, but each day it went unvisited. She used to enjoy it—the smell of fresh dirt and growing plants, but the thought of breathing in the earthy, wild scent turned her stomach.

The wind kicked up, rippling the pool water, and goosebumps covered Audrey's flesh. She held the stair railing, stepped free of the water, and then grabbed her towel and walked inside the house.

There were three short stacks of folded laundry on the living room coffee table, and Audrey pulled a shirt from one pile and a pair of beige shorts from another. The simple fact was there was no one around to judge her for doing it, so whenever she finished her laundry, Audrey separated and folded her clothes, and kept them on the coffee table. It had been weeks since she had slept in the bedroom, preferring to fall asleep on the couch with the TV on instead.

She peeled off her swimsuit, draped it on the arm of the sofa, and used the towel to finish drying the rest of her body. After getting dressed and throwing her damp suit and towel in the clothes dryer, Audrey went to the kitchen and opened the fridge. Behind her, on the kitchen counter, her phone buzzed, paused, and then buzzed again.

GLORIA was at the top of the phone screen, and Audrey pressed the green circle on the screen to accept the call.

"Hey hon. What's up?"

"Mrs. Dugan?" Gloria's voice sounded worried. Upset.

"Yeah, it's me. Honey, what's wrong?"

"Mrs. Dugan, is Sarah at home? Is she with you?"

CHAPTER SIXTY-SIX
IRIS: now

"How does one become a butterfly? You must want to fly so much you're willing to give up being a caterpillar." Iris whispered the words as she stared at the ceiling.

"What's that from?" Doctor Walker asked.

"Not sure, really." Her head still tilted back, Iris brought her cigarette to her lips and inhaled. "Used to have this professor, probably the smartest man I've ever known." She straightened and turned to the doctor.

"That kind of smart you just…you sort of understand about half of what he's trying to explain, right? But he was patient, too. He knew he was on another level, but wasn't conceited or arrogant about it. He really wanted to do whatever he could to bring you up to his level, to make sure you understood fully, what he was trying to explain."

"And the quote?"

Iris shrugged. "He used to quote things all the time. Dead philosophers and modern entrepreneurs, anything he could take lessons from, I guess. He was a good man."

"Is that how you view yourself? A butterfly?"

Iris exhaled a plume of smoke through a half-smile, pursing her lips so the stream blew downward. "Selinsgrove is a cute place, college town, you know? Main Street's nice. Has this section of painted Victorians in all these bright, Easter egg colors."

"Why didn't you move into one of those?" The doctor shrugged as he asked the question, urging her on.

"Naaah." Iris shook her head. "After Mom's life insurance check came through, between that and selling the house, I paid cash for a trailer a few miles north of town. Trailer was okay, nothing fancy, but the land backed up to the State Game Lands. Beautiful country up there. Acres and acres of woods and rivers."

She took a drag off her Winston. "I could stand in my back yard, bare ass naked, and scream and *screeeeeaaaam* and…" Iris shook her head slightly and smiled. "Not a single soul would hear. Not for miles."

"Is that what you were after, the isolation?"

"You know what they say, Doc... *location, location, location.* It's true, though. Sure sold me on this place. But the main selling point wasn't the remoteness or the kitchen or the bathroom." Iris slid forward onto the edge of her chair and leaned on the table.

"What really made my decision was this sort of... garage, I guess. This big concrete block building behind the trailer. No windows, all business. A working man's kind of building, you know?" She flicked ash in the tray. "Didn't have any overhead doors to the place so I'm guessing maybe it was used to grow weed or something. *Something* illegal. It just had that sort of *feel* to it."

Iris brought her cigarette between her lips and inhaled sharply. "It was the kind of building where you could... really get some things *done,* you know what I mean, Doc?"

CHAPTER SIXTY-SEVEN
IRIS: then

Iris watched the girl walk out of the Westminster Dorm.

Pretty, but not beautiful, as if her grandmother might have been a real dazzler but the genes had been diluted by the time the girl was born.

Another girl walked by her side, shorter, with dirty blond hair. The two of them laughed as they crossed the parking lot, walking toward the main building of campus. Iris tilted her head down to shield her face as she sat in the driver's seat and watched the two girls reach the sidewalk and continue into the building.

It's all about the planning. The studying and preparation. The discipline.

And time, Iris thought. *The patience of time itself.*

It had been surprisingly easy to find information about the girl. Social media was both a curse and a blessing for proud parents. So many photographs of college pride—smiling at football games, or lounging at her sorority house, or the Cinema Club she belonged to. So much information ripe for the picking.

The first time she saw Sarah Dugan in real life, Iris's body flooded with so much adrenaline it felt as if her heart was going to burst free of her chest. It made Iris want to touch the girl, run her fingertips over Sarah's skin to feel its smooth and unblemished texture. A blank canvas.

It made Iris want to transform her.

CHAPTER SIXTY-EIGHT
IRIS: then

The girl had the lean, graceful build of a swimmer, with long legs and the muscular arms of a body familiar with physical exertion. Her smooth skin was tan enough to give it a healthy glow, but not so dark to age it with wrinkles any time soon.

She wore a scoop neck blouse the deep pink color of freshly cut tuna and a pair of low-waisted cream-colored shorts. Her legs were slender and as beautiful as the rest of her, and she wore a pair of gray ankle-high sneakers.

Iris watched, from a distance, as the girl added a carton of orange juice to her shopping cart. Short but manicured nails on thin fingers befitting a piano player. The brunette walked onward, into the produce department, picking up and setting down several Honeycrisp apples before selecting two and putting them in a plastic bag.

Iris stood by the display of onions, two aisles over, mimicking the girl's actions, picking up onions and setting them down in another place again. She adjusted her hoodie to hide her face better.

It had taken several weeks before Iris had learned the brunette's habits and routines. By then, she knew quite a lot about the girl, even which evenings of the week she went grocery shopping, the sort of things she would buy, and that it was one of the few things she did by herself.

Iris knew how the brunette ordered her coffee, her schedule at the campus gym, and which of her connections on social media were *real* friends and who were only *acquaintances*.

The brunette walked toward the checkout registers.

Iris adjusted her hoodie and went outside to her van, right beside the brunette's silver Toyota RAV4.

Her heart raced. Her throat was dry and Iris felt her breath quicken.

She slid open the side door of the van and grabbed the bag of groceries she had bought earlier in the day. After tearing the brown paper bag, Iris spilled the contents on the parking lot to look like an accident, and then grabbed what she needed from the floorboard of the van.

It had taken time and patience. Planning, and research. But it was surprisingly easy to make chloroform at home. Iris knelt down, pretending to pick at the spilled groceries, and waited. She smiled to herself when she saw the shadow cast beside her on the asphalt, and heard the girl ask if she needed help.

Hello, Sarah.

CHAPTER SIXTY-NINE
AUDREY: now

"Hell would be a welcome thing compared to what it's like when your child goes missing." Audrey's eyes were red. She swallowed hard and wiped at her nose.

"After I filed the report, they started asking all these questions about Sarah. Was she dating anyone? How was she paying for college? Did she use drugs?"

"Part of the investigation." Blevins crossed his arms and leaned back in his chair.

"Oh, I know. I do. Guess they found out some girls at campus had sugar daddies. Few others were web cam girls on porn sites, working to pay for school. But the police just kept asking questions and I…" Audrey clenched her hands into fists. "I wanted to scream at them to find my daughter, to just stop asking questions and find her. But it's not like that, is it? Might as well scream at a person with cancer to get better. Can't rush anything, good or bad."

"Did it occur to you that the woman in your barn might have been the—"

"No." Audrey shook her head and tears spilled over her cheeks. "To think it might have been… her… that took my Sarah never crossed my mind. Why would it? That girl chained up in Paul's barn… she…"

"Wasn't real?"

"Detective." Audrey released a desperate sigh and put her hands against the edge of the desk. "She *wasn't* real. But she *was*, yes and I… No, it never occurred to me it might have been her. Not once."

"If it *had* crossed your mind, would you have told the police?"

Audrey stared at him, but didn't respond.

Blevins' phone went off again and he gritted his teeth as he withdrew it from his jacket and looked at the screen. "Excuse me," he whispered to Audrey and then stood and walked into the hallway.

Audrey couldn't understand the words Blevins said, but his tone was low and harsh, laced with frustration. The words he said right before his footsteps headed back toward the office were the only she could make out: *"I'm aware, you don't need to remind me."*

He sighed as he stepped into the room and took his chair, a tight expression on his face. "Mrs. Dugan, three months after your daughter was taken, she was found. The chances go down with every passing hour, and unless it's a domestics case or plain dumb luck, most abductees aren't found after the initial forty-eight-hour window. It's not much, and I know it offers no comfort, but at least you have answers. Most parents never do. The terrible, undeniable truth is that the world is full of plain white vans."

Audrey considered Blevins' words and gave a weak nod. "Having a child, raising them… watching them learn and grow into a young adult." She wiped at her eyes and inhaled sharply through her nose. "And they can be snatched away from you, just like that. It's nothing you can adequately describe to someone unless they've lived through it, too. Unless they've seen it with their own eyes."

Blevins tapped his fingertips against the desk. "I hear that's what they say about the Sistine Chapel."

CHAPTER SEVENTY
AUDREY: then

The only person to see anything was a teenaged bag boy at the grocery store Sarah shopped at, and the kid hadn't been fast enough to catch the license plate of the van before it sped away.

A plain white van, Audrey thought.

Parking lot security footage showed Sarah walking from the store to her car and stopping to help someone in a hoodie. The angle made it impossible to see what took place between the two vehicles, but the figure stood up, appeared to be struggling with something, and then slid the door of the van closed.

Audrey had watched the video footage over and over again, staring at the moment her child had been taken. It felt like a new wound each and every time.

I know it's her. I don't know how, but I know she fucking did this.

Her face crumpled on itself and Audrey bit down on her tongue, *hard*, to prevent herself from breaking into sobs. She checked her phone, for the tenth time in the last hour, to make sure it wasn't on mute. For the past three days, Audrey had barely slept, and when she did, it was short doses with her phone gripped in her hand.

The last call had been a useless one from the Selinsgrove Police Department to let her know there wasn't anything to update her about. They were searching for the white van, asking people in the area if they had seen anything. She could be anywhere by now.

Doing nothing was eating her alive inside, and the feeling of utter and absolute helplessness was making her want to crawl out of her skin. She stood from the couch and paced the living room. Her eyes were raw, swollen from constantly being on the verge of crying.

Audrey had considered calling Mr. Schmidt, getting him on the phone and letting him know one of his products was unpredictable and on the loose. She had run through the conversation in her head several times.

But then what? What if I tell him and he and his cronies get pissed?

I saw her chained up in my fucking barn and she got loose.

They'll blame me for that, there's no doubt in my mind. What will they do to me because of that?

She walked into the kitchen and glanced at the wine rack, considered tasting oblivion again, if only to numb the pain for a little while.

No. I need to be sober if they call.

She's your little girl, Audrey. They're going to find her.

Audrey screamed and slammed her fists onto the counter, rattling the dishes stacked by the sink. The voice in her head didn't sound convincing.

CHAPTER SEVENTY-ONE
IRIS: now

"The girl cried, *ohhhh,* she cried... part of me wanted to laugh, and another part of me wanted to scream in her face and tell her about her mother and what a *fucking cu—*"

Iris bit off her words, pulled back, and took a few slow breaths.

"When I got home, I dragged her from the van to the inside of the concrete block building. Set her up on an office chair I bought at the town thrift store, and taped her arms and legs to it. I waited there, watching. I felt her silky hair and ran my fingertips over the skin of her shoulders and down over her arms. Her eyes were closed for the longest time, but when she opened them, I got to see it there. The confusion. The absolute fear."

Doctor Walker's face was slack. His breathing was shallow. His attention moved between Iris and absently touching the folder on the table. When Iris didn't continue talking, he cleared his throat and stared at the iPad for a moment before he met her eyes.

"You knew what you were going to do. You... you had this thought out. Planned ahead of time?"

Iris nodded. "Of course, I did. Thought about it, planned it like it was going to be the most amazing surprise party ever." She smirked and pulled the dead cigarette butts from the tray, arranging them on the table one by one.

The doctor watched Iris smile. "You had her there, in the building, and then... how did everything else happen?"

"She woke up, started screaming and crying, pleading with me to let her go, asking me why I was doing this over and over." Iris nudged the cigarette butts into place until they spelled out FUCK YOU.

"I shut the lights off and locked the door behind me, left her there alone in the dark, screaming and crying." Iris smiled. "I've got to tell you, Doc, I slept better that night than I had in a long, *lonnng* time."

CHAPTER SEVENTY-TWO
IRIS: then

Iris watched as the girl worked her lips against the silicone bit strapped around her head and over her mouth. The rubber was slick with the girl's spit and a silver line dangled from her chin.

Her eyes were red and wide. Scared.

No, Iris thought, *not scared... terrified.*

Is that what I looked like at the beginning? Scared and weak?

Before Iris had put the rubber ball gag on her, the girl had been sobbing, babbling through tears. *"What do you want? My mother... my mother has money. She can pay you. Please let me go. Why are you doing this?"*

Over and over again, in a fast-moving train that ended in outright screams as the girl struggled against the tape restraining her arms and ankles to the chair.

And then it stopped as abruptly as it had begun, ended even before Iris had buckled the strap at the rear of Sarah's head.

The screams were the last of the girl's fight. Iris was disappointed the girl gave up so quickly, the utter *resignation* of it. But then, things were only getting started, so the girl might have more gas in her tank later. Iris could only hope.

A case of bottled water and a gallon jug of orange juice sat in the middle of a large oil stain on the cement floor. Iris had also bought a fifty-pound bag of *Alpo Prime Cuts* dry dog food because the grocery store didn't carry *Ol' Roy.* That had been another disappointment, but the Alpo would have to do.

SAVORY BEEF FLAVOR. EVERYTHING YOUR DOG NEEDS.

Iris tore off the threaded strip of paper at the top and set the opened bag aside. She dragged over a folding lawn chair in front of the girl and sat down.

Tears streamed from Sarah's eyes, but she was quiet except for a low whine coming from deep within. The line of spittle from her chin became a swinging pendulum, and Iris watched it for a moment, mesmerized by the teardrop of saliva at the end. The thread broke and dropped against the girl's bare hip.

"You know, I knew your father." Iris watched Sarah's eyes, watched the girl's mind at work behind them. "*Ohhh,* oh no. He wasn't *fucking* me... at least he hadn't." She scooted her chair closer to Sarah and leaned forward. "That would have been easy, but... distant. Unemotional."

Iris pulled a bottle of water from the package and opened it, stared at plastic cap in her hands for a moment, and then took a long drink. "What your father and I shared was something much more intimate than simply shoving a cock into any hole. What your father did took... *mental fortitude.*"

She capped the water, set it down on the cement, and then lifted a narrow yellow canister in front of her. A small hissing noise escaped as she adjusted the valve at the top of the tank. Iris withdrew a box of wooden matches from the pocket of her hoodie and held it in front of her. Diamond Strike Anywhere.

Sarah trembled in her chair and her whining noise changed pitch, became an animal's cries.

Iris scrubbed the head of a match down the side of her jeans and heard it flare. She held it in front of her, and then moved it toward the invisible stream coming from the torch canister. Immediately, a blue flame appeared from the tip and Iris waved the match, dropping it to the oil-stained concrete.

She reached behind the case of water and picked up a length of rebar, a little over two-feet long and mottled with rust. Iris had found it a week ago, one afternoon as she was walking some of the paths in the woods behind her trailer. Some hunter had cobbled together a deer stand from weathered two-by-fours and steel bars. The rebar had been there for quite some time if the rotting wood of the stand was any indication.

It seemed fortuitous, finding it out there in the woods like that, and she brought it home with her, studying it later that night, tracing her fingertips over the ridges of the steel bar, the spirals, so much like the ripples and whorls of scarred flesh.

Iris positioned the end of the rebar to be within the flame of the torch and whispered to Sarah. "You are *so* very special."

Mucus ran from the girl's nostrils, making parallel lines over the black straps of the gag. Iris studied it for a moment, and then moved south, marveling yet again at the girl's truly perfect skin.

While the girl had been unconscious, Iris used scissors to cut away her blouse and lacy pink bra. The shorts had come after, and Iris had paused for a moment to admire the girl's panties—cute and feminine, with a tiny bow at the top, a satiny fabric the same pale pink as her bra. Iris snipped the sides of the panties, pulled them free of the girl, and let them drop to the garage floor. Her gaze returned to the girl's body.

Golden Spring.

The phrase popped into Iris's mind—an ancient memory. After sifting through what seemed a thousand paint chips, she and Nathan had chosen a color for their living room—a hue of sun-kissed leaves in late fall, warm and cozy without being obnoxiously bright. It had been a toss-up between *Arizona Sun* and *Golden Spring.*

Golden Spring won.

It was the exact color of the girl's tanned skin.

Iris appraised the girl's bare body. Her breasts were perky with youth, small nipples with areola a fine blushing pink. Even slouched as she was in the chair, Sarah had a flat stomach that curved to the soft swell of her waist and hips. Long legs of a ballerina, spread wide as they were, revealing the core of her.

Iris had been wrong about her earlier judgment—the girl *was* beautiful.

Ridges along the steel bar had started to glow. The pattern of raised stripes had turned a blood red, and as Iris watched, their hue drifted to a bright Maraschino cherry.

She glanced up, watched the girl's fingers, the color bleaching from her knuckles as she gripped the armrests of the chair. A soft dripping sound caught Iris's attention and she saw urine pouring from the chair seat to the cement. Its sharp scent reached Iris and she nodded. "*Shhhhh,* it's okay. That happens sometimes."

The bar of steel matched the color of the raised ridges, and Iris saw it shift to a salmon color and past that, brightening to a muted orange and glowing lemon. It was beautiful to watch, the transformation.

Iris stood up from the folding chair and peered over the flame of the torch at the girl's face.

Iris smiled. "Let's begin."

CHAPTER SEVENTY-THREE
IRIS: then

By the end of the first week, Sarah's legs were tiger-striped with burns. Bits of flesh clung to the rebar like tufts of cotton on a harvester. Small flakes of rust speckled the charred skin along the girl's inner thighs and the fresh burns behind her knees.

Sarah had stopped begging by the end of the third day. Behind the gag, the girl had screamed hard enough for blood vessels to burst in both eyes, making them riddled with threads of crimson.

When Iris used the glowing rebar on the tops of the girl's feet, Sarah had screamed so hard she had thrown up, her nostrils the only open exit. It streamed out of her and she began to choke, making Iris frantically unbuckle the ball gag and yank it off her head.

Iris arrived at the conclusion it was why the Man had chosen to feed and slake her thirst only *after* sessions with the torch, so her belly wouldn't have anything to eject.

The girl's hair had become greasy and flat against her skull, and the golden color of her skin had faded enough to show crescent moons of shadows beneath her eyes. Sarah no longer cried when Iris sat down in front of her and set the rebar beneath the attention of the torch. The girl's eyes focused straight ahead, gazing somewhere or at something known only to her. Iris had the fleeting thought the girl had slipped into a catatonic state, but no. It was only during times of her *transformation.*

It had taken several days, but Sarah began eating the Alpo, crunching it slowly and deliberately between her perfect teeth, but also casually, as if she was at a coffee house having a biscotti.

When Iris walked inside the building, the girl sat there, still as a cement garden statue, and Iris wondered if Sarah's heart raced inside. Lifting the orange juice, Iris uncapped the gallon jug and held it at arm's length. She couldn't stand the smell, not anymore, but she held the opening to Sarah and angled it for her to drink several swallows. She took to the orange juice easily, slurping and swallowing at the open mouths of the tilted bottles, always thirsty for more. That, and the over-the-counter pain pills were welcome changes from the dog food, Iris remembered, almost like rewards.

Iris pulled the bottle away and sat it, uncapped, on the concrete, before she settled herself on the folding chair. She scanned over Sarah's body and Iris reminded herself she needed to purchase more ointment.

I need to get a garden hose too, maybe several, to reach into the garage and spray her down. My God, the stink of her.

Leaning back, Iris sighed and studied the girl's breasts like they were awaiting an artist's touch. Her gaze followed the soft swells and tender curves. It would take some time, yes, but Iris visualized a symmetrical pattern, rising up from the girl's hipbones, crossing over the girl's nipples, and meeting over the girl's sternum. She wet her lips and stared.

"In a former life, I was engaged." Iris spoke to the girl, but Sarah's eyes never acknowledged her words. "Almost engaged. I guess there's not a word for that, really. But I was almost engaged to this amazing man, this wonderful man."

Iris leaned forward, her knees on her elbows. "It's a shame you didn't have a boyfriend, actually. But this man, he uh… he used to love watching these weird documentaries about things he didn't know about."

She rose from the chair and reached behind Sarah's neck to grab the strap of the ball gag and slide it into place.

"We stayed up drinking rum and Cokes one night, watching this documentary about this guy, Lenny Bruce. I'd heard of him, thought he was some anti-establishment comedian, but no. No, I was wrong. He was…" Iris brushed down the back of Sarah's head, running her fingers through her tangled hair. "An observer, a commentator on human behavior. He was against any form of racism or segregation of any kind, for any reason."

Iris put the palm of her left hand on the girl's forehead and stretched the bit forward with her right hand, working it up higher until it fit against Sarah's mouth. "I remember this still shot from it, this black and white picture of his face and the words. *I'm not a comedian. And I'm not sick. The world is sick and I'm the doctor. I'm a surgeon with a scalpel for false values.*"

"There we go." Iris walked from behind Sarah and sat down again. She picked up the torch canister, and then turned toward the girl and paused. "Not exactly a scalpel, but we're gonna make you *soooo* pretty. I can't wait for your mommy to see."

If the girl heard Iris's words, she didn't so much as blink a response.

Iris lit the torch, held the rebar to the flame, and began again.

CHAPTER SEVENTY-FOUR
AUDREY: now

Detective Blevins reached forward, picked up the recorder and stared at it in his hand for a moment. He turned it off and his hand remained on the device a moment longer, before he sat it down on his desk.

Audrey met his gaze briefly and then returned her attention to her lap. "What now?"

"I find myself in unfamiliar waters, Mrs. Dugan." Blevins rested his elbows on the desk. "I'm sympathetic to what you've... considering what you've..." He stopped and cleared his throat. "In the broad scope of things, my advice, and I'm not supposed to be giving legal advice on the job, *ever,* is to go chase down that asshole attorney, or find a *different* asshole attorney, and put them on retainer as quickly as you can."

He spread his hands to emphasize his words. "What you did, leaving that girl..." He shook his head and turned away. "That's one thing entirely, but *Paul* was the person truly involved in all of this, not *you*. With the right defense attorney, you might not even see any jail time, especially if you give up any names of the other men Paul worked for."

"I don't care what happens anymore." There wasn't any self-pity, nor sadness, in Audrey's words, nothing but tired resignation. "I'll write down the names of the men for you, the ones I can remember."

"I figured you might." Blevins sighed and stared at her for a moment. "I have to ask... if nothing had happened to your daughter, would you have ever come forward?"

"No." Audrey drank from her bottle of water. "I don't think so. Probably not."

CHAPTER SEVENTY-FIVE
IRIS: now

"I wanted to make her mother feel the pain of seeing her like that. I wanted her to feel it in the core of her motherhood, right down to the marrow in her bones. I wanted that bitch to feel every single part of it. To experience what my mother went through." Iris leaned on the table. "The loss when her kid first went missing. The not knowing... the fear, the worry, the..." She motioned with her hands. "The entire agonizing event of it all. I wanted her to see her choices followed to resolution. To take care of her daughter for the rest of her life, knowing she was the one responsible, and it could have all been different, if she hadn't turned away from me."

Iris's chest heaved with effort as she breathed, and eased back into her chair. "You have to be able, as a person, to admit your weaknesses and accept your failures. Your... *shortcomings.* Mine was discipline. I thought I had it all thought out, but I was wrong. I hadn't planned on just how... *tenacious* the girl was."

"Tenacious?"

"Sarah was weak, *sooooo* weak, but she was strong enough, and smart enough, to *go after* her weakness, to pursue it until she reached her goal without ever letting go."

Iris smiled. "Like it was a little ball of tin foil."

CHAPTER SEVENTY-SIX
IRIS: then

Iris stepped into the building and left the door open behind her for a couple of reasons. The first was to drag in the triple length garden hose as far as she could to spray the girl down. She had bought lemon dish liquid to hopefully to dull the scent. The second reason was to let in some sunlight so the girl could see its warm rays from a distance and know what she was missing.

She walked toward the girl in the chair, unraveling the coil of hose behind her as she walked. "Rise and shine, Lovebug. *Biiiig* day ahead of us. Big day."

Iris dropped the spray nozzle of the hose against the cement and turned to face the girl. Sarah's head was slumped forward, hair hanging around her face in a shroud, but her mid-section was painted red with thin vertical ribbons. Iris stepped closer, grabbed a fistful of the girl's hair and lifted her head.

No. NoNoNoNoNoNoNoNOOOOOOOOOO!

Sarah's eyes had curdled to a pale blue-white. A thick coating of blood covered the girl's chin and had dripped sloppily down her neck and chest. Her cracked lips were parted, and Iris saw the source of all the blood inside her open mouth. The ragged stump of the girl's tongue, its pale outer layer housing a rose-colored interior, nested among thick clots of blood. Iris could see the shredded edge of the girl's tongue, chewed completely through.

Iris gripped the girl's chin and forced her mouth open wider. There, at the back of her throat like a swelled cork, was a mass of dull brown paste—a thick wad of chewed dog food—and Iris knew the remains of the girl's tongue lay beyond it, blocking the girl's airway.

She flung the girl's head away from her and it lolled backwards and remained.

"NONONONONOOOOOOO!"

"You *ruined* it!" Iris screamed and stepped backward. "You ruined *EVERYTHING!*"

CHAPTER SEVENTY-SEVEN
IRIS: now

"So, in your professional opinion, Doc, what do you think? Am I ready for the psych ward, or do you believe I'm of sound mind and…" Iris smiled and glanced down at the burn scars on her arms. "Well, I guess I really can't say the same for my body."

Doctor Walker had turned away from her as she spoke, resting his right hand on the table. He stared at the mirror, his eyes studying the room's reflection.

Iris drew a fresh Winston from her pack and the doctor looked at her and pointed at the cigarette she held. His voice was unsteady. "Do you mind if I uh…?"

She paused, smiled at him, and then put the cigarette in her mouth, lit it, and handed it over. The doctor took it from her, stared at the glowing end for a moment, and then put it between his lips and took a long, deep drag. He closed his eyes as he held the smoke in his lungs, and then exhaled toward the ceiling. His expression was bliss.

As Iris watched him, her smile turned into a grin. "How long has it been since you had a smoke?"

"A long, long while." Doctor Walker put it to his lips for a second drag. He opened his eyes to look at her as he breathed out, and his expression was the same guilty smile an alcoholic wore when they fell off the wagon after a decade-long dry spell.

"I have no one left, Doc. I am an orphan of fate. The bastard child of destiny." Iris raised her arms, almost as if she was giving a sermon. "If there ever was a God, he died long ago. I have no one left, and nothing you say in your little report will change that."

The doctor took another pull on the cigarette and took his time tapping the ember against the ashtray, carefully stubbing it out. He let out a long breath as he stared at the woman on the other side of the table. "You're right, nothing will change that. No one can change the past, we can only learn to live with what's happened."

Iris reached out, picked up his half-smoked cigarette, and turned it over in her fingers, staring at it. "For a while, I tried to push it away. I wanted to look through someone else's eyes, feel what someone else felt, breathe through another person's lungs. Then I began to accept it all. Embrace it and who I'd become. She put the cigarette butt to her lips, lit the end, and took a drag.

"The thing is, Doc... I can live with my choices." Iris exhaled a plume of smoke and leveled her gaze to meet the man's eyes. "Can she?"

CHAPTER SEVENTY-EIGHT
AUDREY: now

Detective Blevins straightened in his chair, tapped the desk, and then stood. "Someone will *definitely* be in touch."

"I don't understand." Audrey blinked at him several times. "You're not taking me into custody or—"

"If you have any of that special occasion wine left, I'd say tonight's the night to drink it, Mrs. Dugan." Blevins stepped around to the side of his desk. "If you were going to run, you would have already done so, and to be perfectly honest, I have no idea *what's next* in this fucking mess of a situation."

Audrey stood up from the chair and picked up her purse. She reached for the group of used tissues on the man's desk, but he waved her actions away.

"Don't worry about them. I'll take care of it." He stepped to the office door and opened it, holding his arm out for Audrey to leave. "For what it's worth, I'm sorry."

She nodded a *thank you*, walked into the hallway, and Blevins followed, closing the door behind them. They walked to the end of the hall and through the exit doors to the rear parking lot.

Audrey paused, met Blevins' eyes, and then watched him walk among the rows of parked cars. She leaned against the brick wall of the building and hugged her purse to her chest for a moment. She wished she felt lighter, as if unburdening the truth would have taken the leaden weight from her mind.

But the weight was still there, as crushing as ever.

She fished her car keys from her purse and walked to her car. She didn't want to go home, didn't want to walk inside the empty house full of shadows and still see the patches of carpet that used to be spattered with blood. Didn't want to walk from the driveway to the house imagining the clinking of thick steel chain against the cement floor of the barn.

Audrey pressed the fob on her keyring and heard her car doors unlock with a chirping sound. She reached forward and gripped the handle of the car when an arm reached from behind her and a hand clamped over her mouth. A thick arm wrapped around her body and pinned her arms tightly to her sides.

She tried to scream but the sound was muffled. Audrey's purse fell to the asphalt as she fought and tried to kick out, but the grip was too strong and her body was wrenched sideways and she was thrown off balance. The lamplights overhead were bright against her eyes and she winced as she felt herself being dragged backwards. The hand across her mouth stank of smoke and alcohol, and then another hand was brought up to cover her nose, holding a sweet-smelling cloth.

Several cars away in the lot, Audrey saw Detective Blevins, standing there motionlessly.

Watching.

The voice behind her was low and gruff—an angry hiss. "All you had to do was enjoy the money and keep your fucking mouth shut. That's all you had to fucking do."

Her world was a river of onyx.

Author Notes:

I wrote the first draft of Burner in June of 2019. I was finishing up a few large projects and had already turned my attention to the second most asked question of a writer (second only to "Where do you get your ideas?"), which is "What's next?"

It was a beautiful Memorial Day, and I grabbed a blank notebook and a cold beer, and went to sit outside and think for a spell. I'd had some peripheral ideas in the back of my head I figured all had a chance at becoming my next writing project, and figured it was time to form some sort of a plan.

I took my time, enjoying the sunshine and my beer, and jotted down two novel concepts and three novella ideas. After shuffling them around in my head for a while, I decided on tackling a novella first, two novels right after, and then back to the novellas. Satisfied with having a solid plan of attack that would tie me up for the next six months of the year, I sat back, satisfied, and finished the last swallow of my beer.

And on the way back inside to grab a second tasty beverage, something happened. That little voice in the back of my head whispered, the shy but smart one that rarely raises its hand because it doesn't want the attention — not really, not unless it has something really important to say.

That voice spoke up and asked me about a newspaper article I'd saved a year ago. It reminded me I'd also written a few paragraphs as notes.

I came back outside and started scribbling, remembering this weird newspaper article about a housewife in Japan, who realized much too late, she had no idea who her dying husband really was.

The notes I scribbled down grew until I had roughly twenty handwritten pages of concept notes. I put the pen down and stared at the notebook. Part of me felt like I'd just finished some sort of marathon after furiously jotting everything down.

Little did I know what was in store for me.

The next day, I began writing what would be the first draft of the novel you now hold in your hands. To say I was driven would be an understatement. I was a man possessed. I woke up in the mornings, grabbed a cup of coffee and got to it. I'd write all damned day, angry at myself for having to leave the laptop for almost any reason.

The voices of the two main characters did not *ask* to be heard—they *demanded* it.

I rarely, if ever, outline anymore, and though I had a vague, overall idea of the arc the characters would take in the novel, there were many moments I was surprised at the dialogue I was writing, or some of the actions they would pursue.

I know writers who scoff at this idea… they'll say things like "You're the creator! You control what your characters do and don't do!"

Yes. You're absolutely correct, except for the times you're not. And when that happens, *it truly does feel like magic*.

After I finished the first draft, I felt as if I had expelled something from me, and that sensation was more than bothersome. I put the manuscript aside, took a week off, and moved onto other projects as it aged and waited for me to work on it again with fresh eyes.

In August of 2020, during the year of insanity, I dug back into the manuscript with a renewed fervor, pushing ahead, fighting through, and I felt the same sort of urgency as I did when I'd first written it.

This is a brutal book, and a book that has come from some of my deepest fears in life. I'd like to say those fears have lessened as my children have grown older and become more capable of defending themselves, but that would be a lie.

It's terrifying to think these things can happen in your state, your town, your neighborhood, but they do.

The world is not always a good place. There are terrible people who do terrible things. Some will be discovered. Many others won't. But the truth is, those things happen more than anyone likes to believe.

And the world we live in is full of plain white vans.

Robert Ford, October 2020

Additional Information:

In 2019, the United States had 11,500 human trafficking cases reported. The most common type of trafficking was sex trafficking (8,248 reports), with the most common venues being illicit massage/spa businesses and pornography.

States with the Highest Human Trafficking Numbers

California consistently has the highest human trafficking rates in the United States with 1,507 cases reported in 2019. 1,118 of these cases were sex trafficking cases, 158 were labor trafficking, and 69 were both sex and labor. The remaining cases were not specified. Most of the sex trafficking cases reported in California were illicit massage and spa businesses and hotel or motel based. Of the cases reported, 1,290 were female, 149 were male, and 10 were gender minorities.

This is followed by Texas with 1,080 cases, Florida with 896 cases, and New York with 454 cases. These four states with the highest human trafficking rates have the highest populations in the U.S., which can explain why their numbers of cases are significantly higher than other states, as well as very high immigrant populations. This combined with certain industries such as agriculture creates prime environments for forced labor.

Here are the 10 states with the highest rates of human trafficking:
Nevada (7.61 per 100k)
Mississippi (4.95 per 100k)
Florida (4.07 per 100k)
Georgia (3.88 per 100k)
Delaware (3.87 per 100k)
Ohio (3.83 per 100k)
Missouri (3.78 per 100k)
California (3.77 per 100k)
Texas (3.66 per 100k)
Michigan (3.62 per 100k)

The Human Trafficking Hotline serves victims and survivors of human trafficking across the United States. The Hotline is available 24/7, 365 days a year, and in more than 200 languages. The confidential Hotline helps any person of any age, religion, race, language, gender identity, sexual orientation, or disability.

To contact the Hotline to report a tip, seek services, or ask for help, dial 1-888-373-7888. Hearing and speech-impaired individuals should dial 711. You can also send an SMS text to 233-733 or start a live chat on their website at https://humantraffickinghotline.org

Robert Ford has written the novels *The Compound*, and *No Lipstick in Avalon*, the novella *Samson and Denial*, *Inner Demons*, a collection of novellas, and *The God Beneath my Garden,* his collected short fiction.

He has co-authored the novella *Rattlesnake Kisses*, and *Cattywampus* with John Boden.

He can confirm the grass actually is greener on the other side, but it's only because of the bodies buried there.

You can find out more about what he's up to by visiting robertfordauthor.com

Additional titles by Robert Ford

The Compound

Inner Demons

Samson and Denial

Rattlesnake Kisses (with John Boden)

Cattywampus (with John Boden)

Printed in Great Britain
by Amazon